To my parents, who taught me to taste the world, and to Craig and Bessie, my favorite people to taste it with. — G.L.

To Edy Tavares, who showed me love through Cape Verdean food. —T.G.

Phaidon Press Inc.
111 Broadway
New York, NY 10006

phaidon.com

First published 2024
© 2024 Phaidon Press Limited
Text © Gabrielle Langholtz 2024
Illustrations © Tânia García 2024

Artwork created digitally

ISBN 978 1 83866 914 0 (US edition)
004-0724

A CIP catalog record for this book is available from the Library of Congress.

Printed in China

Edited by: Alice-May Bermingham
Production by: Rebecca Price
Design by: Laura Hambleton

A WORLD OF FLAVOR

A CELEBRATION OF FOOD
AND RECIPES FROM
AROUND THE GLOBE

Gabrielle Langholtz

Illustrated by **Tània García**

TABLE OF CONTENTS

TASTE THE WORLD

Working on this book reminded me that two opposite ideas are both true: one is that all around the world, we're different. The other is that all around the world, we're the same! I'll explain.

These pages celebrate the many wonderful ways that cultures and cuisines are unique. Depending on where you live, you might catch fish or milk goats, cook over coals or in well-seasoned woks, prefer potatoes, pasta, or plantains, breakfast on rice congee or mandazi doughnuts, snack on empanadas or injera, shop streetside carts or floating riverboat markets, eat with forks or fingers, from skewers or chopsticks, smoke salmon or salt cod, pick papayas or pomegranates, offer guests yerba mate or lemonade, feast on camel or go vegetarian, keep jars of togarashi or za'atar, sip sharbat or soursop smoothies, slather toast with Marmite™ or marmalade, ferment cream into yogurt or cabbage into kraut, crown ice cream with dulce de leche or corn kernels, warm up with hot chai or cool down with the juice of a machete-whacked coconut, or top your dinner with shaved parmesan, spicy mayo, crushed peanuts, fresh lime, smoky salt, or fermented fish sauce.

But the more I learn about the different foods we eat, the more I see how much we all have in common. We savor fresh fruit and preserve summer's bounty. We welcome guests with sweet treats, refreshing drinks, and handmade hospitality. We celebrate births, weddings, holy days, and holidays with feasts rich in memory and meaning. We boil grains, slurp noodles, bake flatbreads, stuff dumplings, simmer soups, and sop up the juices. From little villages to big cities, we gather to give thanks for bountiful harvests.

While some cultures make traditional foods that go back millennia — so you might have to travel to Tibet to taste yak-butter tea — many immigrants have now brought beloved recipes to new lands. Today, you can enjoy Indian chapati in Kenya, Brazilian black beans in Canada, Japanese ramen in Peru, Nigerian jollof rice in England, pad thai in Australia, and Taiwanese boba in the United States. And as people mix and mingle, our foods do too. Parisians savor North African merguez sausage in baguettes, while Californians top their tacos with Korean kimchi. You might say the world gets a little more delicious every day.

I was lucky to work on this book with super smart people from around the globe. Of course, we couldn't fit all the world's foods into one book, so we focused on the most populous countries on each continent, with shoutouts to many more cultures along the way.

Some people say kids are picky eaters, but I hope this book will help you prove them wrong. Children everywhere love all kinds of foods, including fishy fish, blood sausage, spicy broth, stinky cheese, and all sorts of fresh vegetables, and help in the kitchen from the time they're little. Maybe you already like pita, baba ganoush, fresh ceviche, steaming pho, minty tabbouleh, and steak with chimichurri sauce — these pages include recipes to make them all yourself, along with many other world favorites from Afghan plov and Australian pavlova to Moroccan harira and mohinga from Myanmar. And the truth is, you don't need to cook to enjoy this book. I hope just reading it will open your mind and your mouth, inspiring you to seek out global flavors, wherever you are. Food is a wonderful way to learn about how we're different, and how much we have in common, no matter what we like for lunch.

Gabrielle Langholtz

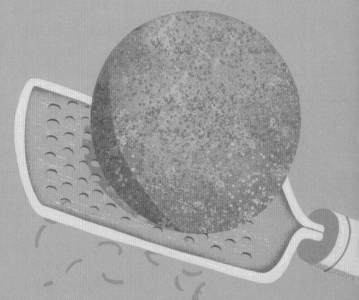

With every recipe, you'll see a series of circles indicating how challenging it is to cook. Many have only one circle, indicating they are easier than average; most have two circles, and are of average difficulty; and a handful of recipes have three circles, meaning that they are harder than average (and the most challenging in this book). Consider these ratings alongside your own experience level when deciding what to cook.

LEVEL OF DIFFICULTY
●

LEVEL OF DIFFICULTY
● ●

LEVEL OF DIFFICULTY
● ● ●

COOKING TIPS

Check in with a grown-up before you start cooking.

Make sure that there's someone close by who can help with any cooking or chopping, or in case you have questions.

Pay attention to the times given with each recipe to make sure you have enough time to see it through.

In most cases, there is no real way to speed things up, and if you're new to cooking, it may take longer than noted.

Always read a recipe all the way through before you begin.

This way, you'll know which ingredients and equipment you need, and there won't be any surprises once you've already started cooking.

Measure carefully and accurately.

This makes a big difference, especially when you are learning to cook.

Clean your work surface as you go.

Wash your hands and tools well, especially after touching raw fish or meat; move dirty things to the sink or dishwasher, and wipe down the work surface as you move from one step to the next to avoid one big mess at the end.

Avoid throwing away good food.

You can often save bits of unused ingredients for other recipes.

Mind the heat!

Use heatproof mitts when handling food in and around the oven, and follow what the recipe says about heat levels.

Learn to use your senses.

Sometimes you may be able tell that something is done cooking by the way it looks, smells, sounds, feels, and, of course, tastes. Recipes give you things to watch out for, but if you think that something is done before the time in the recipe, trust your instincts. Just make sure your meat, fish, and eggs are fully cooked.

Have fun!

The goal is not to make something that looks picture-perfect but to be proud of your process and, hopefully, to cook something delicious! Like most skills worth learning, cooking is all about practice. The more you cook, the more you will improve, and the more good things you will have to eat and share!

COOKING TERMS

BOILING

You'll know a liquid is boiling when you see large bubbles bursting rapidly on its surface.

SIMMERING

This happens just before boiling, when small bubbles just start to rise up to the surface of the cooking liquid. Often a recipe will ask you to bring something to a boil and then turn it down to a simmer. In that case, lower the heat until you just see bubbles breaking on the surface.

STEAMING

This is one way to cook vegetables with moist, gentle heat. Usually it involves using a steamer basket over simmering water in a pot with a tight-fitting lid.

GRILLING

Cooking over a live fire. This is almost always over metal grates, with charcoal or gas flames.

ROASTING

This uses dry heat in the oven to make tender meats and vegetables.

BRAISING

This can happen on the stovetop or in the oven. When foods are braised, they are partially submerged in liquid and slowly cooked over low heat until deliciously tender.

BROILING

Cooking directly under high heat in the oven. It's one way to get meats and vegetables to taste almost as good as those cooked outside on a backyard grill.

BAKING

When something bakes, the dry heat of the oven is cooking it. This is usually how breads, cakes, pies, cookies, and biscuits are made.

PAN-FRYING

Foods such as chicken, meat, or fish are cooked in a large skillet in a small amount of oil or butter until they are cooked through but still crisp.

STOCKING AN INTERNATIONAL PANTRY

Getting to know global cuisines will be easier — and more fun! — if you stock your pantry with global ingredients. Fill your kitchen with staples like these, and you'll always be ready to cook your way around the world.

Grains. Get to know basmati rice from India, jasmine rice from Thailand, quinoa from Bolivia, farro from Italy, wild rice from North America, and buckwheat groats from Russia.

Noodles. Stock up on soba from Japan, ramen from China, rice noodles from Thailand, little bitty couscous from North Africa, and pasta from Italy.

Vinegars. Add acid to everything from salads to soups, with balsamic, apple cider vinegar, rice wine vinegar, coconut vinegar, and red wine vinegar. Some are sweeter; some are sharper.

Oils. Try olive oil from the Mediterranean, palm oil from Africa, peanut oil from Asia, sunflower oil from Europe, avocado oil from Central America, and coconut oil from Southeast Asia. Plus ghee from India!

Peanut butter. This savory groundnut paste is a base for everything from Indonesian gado gado to Sudanese salata tomatim bel daqua. (Find recipes for each in this book!)

Spices. Whole or ground, individual or blended, you'll find that a well-stocked cabinet of these treasures is the spice of life. Try saffron from Iran, garam masala from India, berbere from Ethiopia, nutmeg from Indonesia, and five-spice powder from China.

Dried beans. These protein-packed powerhouses could keep for years, but you'll want to cook them long before then. With dried beans on hand you'll be ready to make chickpeas into hummus from the Middle East, black beans into feijoada soup from Brazil, lentils into dal from India, kidney beans into frijoles from Mexico, and fava beans into ful from North Africa.

Hot stuff. Cultures across continents capture chili heat in spice pastes and bold bottles. Try sriracha from Thailand, sambal from Indonesia, Tabasco™ from the United States, piri piri from Mozambique, harissa from Tunisia, and tongue-numbing Sichuan peppercorns from China.

Sweet stuff. Experiment with cane sugar, date sugar, palm sugar, panela, muscovado, and jaggery — plus honey, molasses, agave, and maple syrup.

Condiments. Whether Dijon mustard from France to ponzu from Japan to gochujang from Korea, everything is better with flavor-packed sauces.

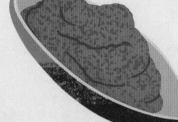

KITCHEN TOOLS

Great cooks around the world may have kitchens full of gadgets or just a knife, a pot, and an open fire. You don't need a tricked-out kitchen to start cooking, but here are a few of our favorite tools:

Knives and cutting boards. One good, sharp 8-inch knife may be the most important tool in your kitchen. Ask an adult to help you learn to hold it correctly and to use it safely for mincing, dicing, chopping, and slicing.

Skillet or frying pan. Look for a heavy 8- or 10-inch skillet with a sturdy, metal handle that's safe to put into a hot oven (cast iron is a good choice). You'll use skillets for everything from scrambled eggs to sautés to stir fries to shakshuka.

Saucepan. Essential for everything from boiling potatoes to simmering soup. A tight-fitting lid is useful for steaming, or anytime you want to keep in the heat.

Sheet pan or rimmed baking sheet. You'll use it for everything from roasting vegetables to baking cookies. Don't forget to use oven mitts when handling them hot!

Graters. You'll use them for parmesan, ginger, and many other hard ingredients. Graters are great! Watch your fingers.

Peeler. Handy for peeling skins off vegetables like potatoes and parsnips, also for shaving hard cheese and making curls of chocolate.

Tongs. For tossing, transferring, grabbing, grilling, and serving.

Wooden spoons. For mixing, stirring, spooning, and serving.

Instant-read thermometer. Experienced cooks can tell when meat is done just by the look, smell, or even sound. For the rest of us, instant-read thermometers are a huge help.

Skewers. For skewering everything from kebabs from Israel and chicken satay from Indonesia to s'mores from the United States. Who doesn't love food cooked on sticks over flames?

Mortar and pestle. An essential since the Stone Age, this tool is used for pounding pesto from Italy, curry paste from Thailand, salsas from Mexico, fufu from Ghana, and so much more. These days, many cooks whir things in a food processor instead, but there's nothing like hand-pounding your food to smooth perfection with a piece of rock!

Wok. Originally from China, this deep pan with sloping sides isn't just for stir-frying, though it's world-famous for that technique. Woks can also be used for deep frying, steaming, and even boiling. Some chefs say not to wash woks with soap, which would strip the metal of its seasoning.

Rice cooker. Okay, you don't really need this plug-in appliance. After all, people have made perfect rice in plain pots for ages. But . . . these electric tools do make perfect rice every time, keep it warm, and even turn themselves off. Millions of families use theirs daily!

Bamboo steamer basket. These pretty, round baskets stack right into your wok or wide skillet. Simply set them over boiling liquid to steam vegetables, fish, chicken, or dumplings.

Tagine. Every kitchen in North Africa is home to these clay pots with domed lids. From Morocco to Algeria, they're used for slow-cooking stews and tagines, and they're often hand-painted with gorgeous designs.

Mandolin. Beloved from Japan to France, these slicing tools allow for perfectly precise, paper-thin slices of anything from potatoes to pears. Be careful not to slice your fingers!

Pasta roller. Yes, you could just roll out dough and slice it into ribbons — or buy dried pasta at the store — but few things are as much fun as feeding dough into one end and seeing noodle shapes come out the other. Manual pasta-makers require turning a crank by hand, while stand-mixer attachments are as fast as magic. Both make delicious fresh pasta for everything from lasagna to fettuccini.

Sushi rolling mats. Have you ever tried making your own sushi? These bamboo tools, known as makisu, are essential for shaping each delicate roll. Pro tip: don't overstuff them!

CONTRIBUTORS

TÀNIA GARCÍA

Born in Barcelona, Spain, Tània has always been inspired by travel for her illustrations. This time her passion for learning new cultures, gastronomy, and art come together. She loves her native Mediterranean cuisine, but she also really enjoys Moroccan or Thai food. When she is not drawing, you can find her preparing some delicious pancakes for breakfast, her favorite meal of the day.

GABRIELLE LANGHOLTZ

Writer Gabrielle loves learning about the world through food. She's worked at *Fortune* magazine, on organic farms, and at Princeton University, and has been fortunate to visit such places as Argentina, Austria, Belgium, Brazil, Canada, Italy, Jamaica, Paraguay, Scotland, Spain, and every state in the U.S. After working on this book, she really wants to go to Morocco next.

MAYA GARTNER

Born in the U.S. to a Japanese mother and a British father, Associate Publisher Maya grew up in the U.S., Japan, France, and the United Kingdom, and has been eating food from around the world since she was a baby. She can't live without eating Japanese rice, American cookies, French cheese, or drinking British tea at least once a week!

ALICE-MAY BERMINGHAM

Originally from Staffordshire, United Kingdom, and now living in London, editor Alice-May's favorite food is anything comforting. Her top food experiences include a bike tour of the taco stands of Mexico City and ordering every pierogi on the menu while sheltering from the snow in Krakow, Poland.

LAURA HAMBLETON

The designer of this book, Laura, is an art director, illustrator, and author who has been working in children's books for many years. Laura loves pasta and anything chocolatey and enjoys cooking tasty meals (like those in this book!) with her two children.

LOUISA SHAFIA

Louisa is a chef and author of the cookbook *The New Persian Kitchen*. She has lectured and written widely about the foods of Iran.

MARY ROSE MADDEN

Journalist Mary Rose writes about the intersection of health and sociology, ethics and culture for podcasts, radio, and print. Some of her favorite worldwide eating experiences have included a reporting fellowship in East Africa and an anchovy-catching visit to the Basque region of Spain. She loves to cook with her children and share meals and stories with family and friends.

RACHEL NUWER

Rachel is an award-winning writer who has written for the *New York Times*, *National Geographic*, and many other publications, and has eaten in seventy-nine countries. Her favorite foods from around the world are Vietnamese pho, French butter, El Salvadoran pupusas, and Japanese takoyaki. If she had to eat only one thing for the rest of her life, it would probably be cheese.

AHMED KHATER

Growing up in Egypt, Ahmed visited diverse landscapes, from Alexandria's beaches to the vibrant Nile Delta and the historic deserts of Sinai. Now a Fulbright scholar, his favorite foods include Egypt's national dish, koshary. He says nothing compares to the simple joy of a ful and falafel breakfast with fresh pita and olive oil.

MÔNICA VALLIN

Born to a Bolivian mother and Mexican father, Mônica spent her formative years in Colombia and Bolivia. Her father instilled in her a love of tacos and spicy food, and encouraged gastronomic adventuring. Growing up with her maternal grandmother, who hailed from Peru, Mônica developed a fondness for desserts, particularly suspiro limeño. She holds a PhD in Spanish and Cultural Studies from Georgetown University. Her literature, history, and food interests inspired her dissertation, which explores identity in Colonial Latin America.

RACHEL WHARTON

Rachel is an award-winning journalist and cookbook author with a master's degree in food studies from New York University. She remains forever fascinated by the history and the ingredients that connect cuisines across the continents.

MARIE VILJOEN

South African-born food writer and forager Marie grew up in Bloemfontein and in Cape Town, where she learned to grow and gather edible plants and to cook over coals under the Milky Way. She writes books, leads wild-food walks, grows yuzu, and transforms persimmons into hoshigaki.

NORTH
AMERICA

SOUTH
AMERICA

**SIX INHABITED CONTINENTS
EIGHT BILLION PEOPLE
NEARLY 200 NATIONS
ONE PLANET
ONE HUMANITY
ONE WORLD OF
INNUMERABLE TASTES**

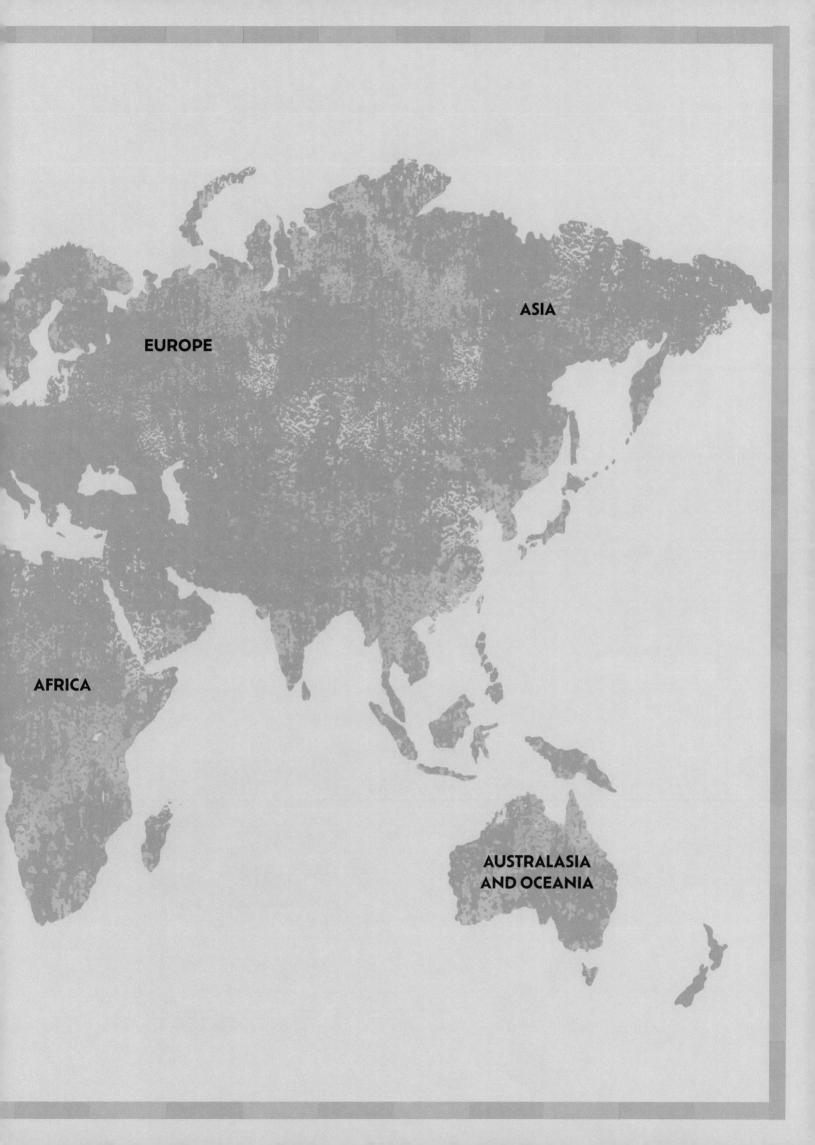

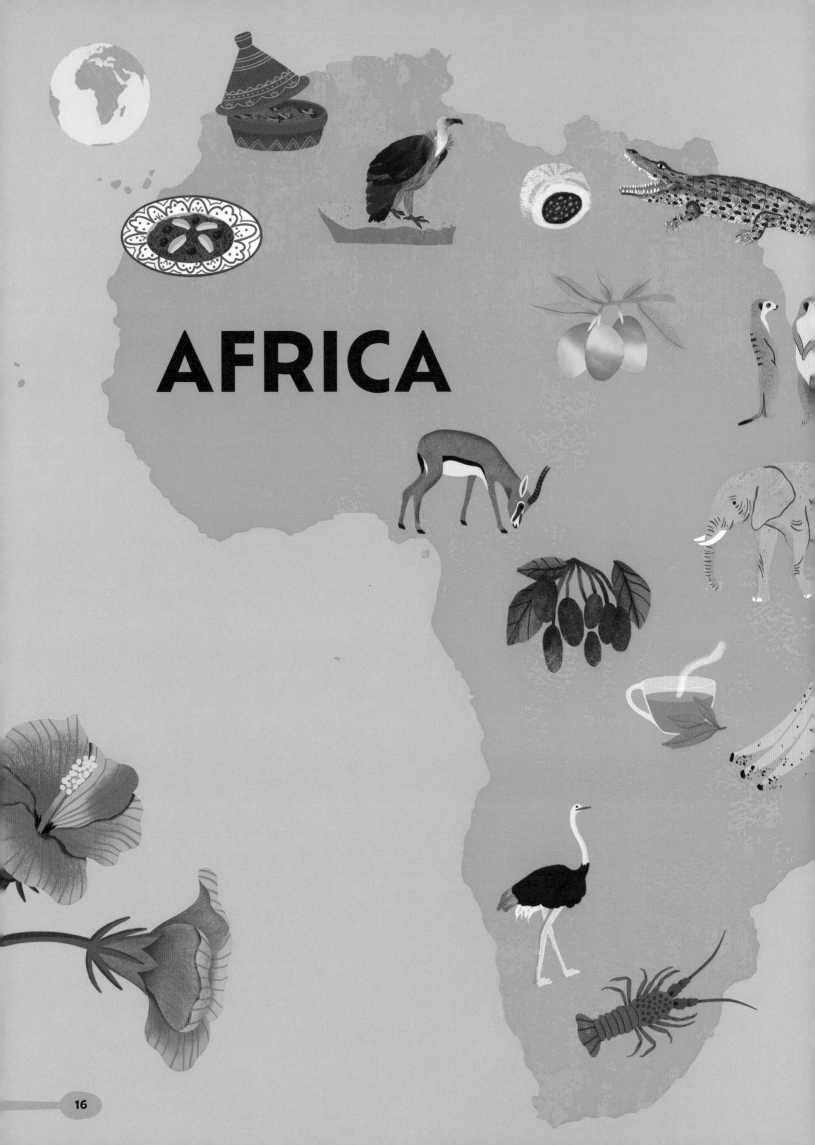

AFRICA

This massive continent is home to fifty-four countries and stunningly rich landscapes: lush rainforests, vast deserts, dramatic waterfalls, towering jungles, deep rivers, majestic mountains, iconic grasslands, and beautiful beaches. Africa is famous for lions, elephants, and giraffes, and as the birthplace of another species: humans! Ancient civilizations here developed advanced farming, intricate trade networks, iconic architecture, and elaborate foods. Today, you'll find a modern mosaic of cultures, languages, and traditions. Despite the devastating legacies of colonization and enslavement, this diverse continent is now home to forward-thinking, indigenous-led farming practices focusing on sustainability as well as vibrant and world-leading film, technology, and design industries.

From Algeria to Zimbabwe, the flavors are unforgettable. People feast on white yams, great greens, and black-eyed peas. They prepare peanut sauces and slippery okra soups, and snack on plantain chips and fried egusi-seed patties. Palm nut oil— made for millennia from trees in the Congo River Valley—gives its signature flavor and pretty red color to West African recipes. People mash yams, taro, plantains, or cassava into fufu—also known as ugali, sadza, nsima, or posho—a smooth paste rolled into bite-sized balls to dip in savory sauces.

ALGERIA

Algeria is big—the size of western Europe—but almost everyone lives in the north, along the coast of the beautiful Mediterranean Sea. If you go south, across the Atlas Mountains, you'll reach the vast Sahara Desert. France occupied Algeria for over one hundred years, and cafés still serve French-inspired mussels and steak frites, but local food stars delicious North African ingredients such as couscous, olives, lamb, citrus, dates, eggplant, artichokes, and spices—all sold in lively, colorful outdoor markets called souks.

COUSCOUS

Algerians enjoy this tiny semolina pasta so much that it is called ta'am, or "food," in Arabic. Couscous is served at family dinners, weddings, funerals—and just about every other meal too. Every Algerian kitchen includes a couscoussier, a big pot with an insert for steaming the pearl-shaped pasta over stew.

LAMB

Algerians love lamb, from kebabs and sausages to stew, and mechoui may be their single favorite dish. To make it, a whole lamb is slow roasted on a spit and basted with clarified butter or olive oil for moist meat and crispy skin.

HARISSA

This legendary red paste of hot and sweet peppers—pounded with garlic, salt, olive oil, and spices like cumin, coriander, and caraway—is found in kitchens across North Africa and has become beloved throughout the world, on everything from cauliflower to kebabs.

SHAKSHUKA

This Ottoman-influenced breakfast features eggs poached in a skillet over a spicy stew of tomatoes, peppers, and onions, often served with pita for sopping up the savory sauce. The origin of this North African dish is much debated between Algeria and neighboring Morocco and Tunisia!

RAS EL HANOUT

This complex spice blend, which means "head of the shop" in Arabic, brings flavor to many Algerian dishes. The blend can include up to thirty spices, including cumin, paprika, turmeric, coriander, cinnamon, fennel, anise seeds, cardamom, and nigella seeds—even rosebuds.

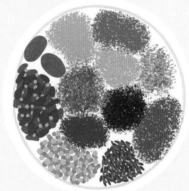

MERGUEZ

This little lamb sausage has big flavor, thanks to harissa, which gives it a red color and deliciously spicy kick. Usually enjoyed grilled, merguez has found its way across the globe, as Algerians and Moroccans take it wherever they go—including to France, where the delicious sausages are a popular street food.

TAGINE

Algerians and their Moroccan neighbors use this clay cooking vessel to make the classic North African stew that goes by the same name. Its dome-shaped lid allows long slow cooking, traditionally cooked over coals by the Amazigh people in the Atlas Mountains.

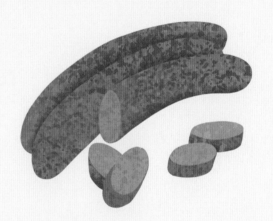

CITRUS

Citrus groves thrive in Algeria, and their fruits are an essential ingredient in local dishes. Lemons preserved in salt keep for months and go into many stews and sauces, rind and all, adding a bright tartness. Clementines, which were first bred in Algeria by a French monk, are a common dessert—sometimes served with honey-soaked semolina cake.

DATES

During Ramadan, many people break their daily fast by eating a date. The pits are often removed and replaced with delicious walnut or almond or pistachio paste. Algeria's amazingly soft, sticky, super sweet deglet nour—"the queen of all dates"—is exported around the world.

STREET FOOD

In the evenings, Algerian town squares transform into intoxicatingly aromatic bazaars where you can find everything from paella to pastilla (a sweet and savory chicken pie made with almonds). Or try a sandwich aux merguez, a baguette stuffed with French fries and spicy lamb sausage.

SANDWICH AUX MERGUEZ

SPICY LAMB SAUSAGES IN TOASTED BAGUETTE

PREPARATION TIME	COOKING TIME	LEVEL OF DIFFICULTY	SERVES
5 mins	35 mins	●	4

Across North Africa you'll find merguez: spicy lamb sausages that come in skinny little links. The sausages cook quickly in an oven, frying pan, or, as here, on a hot grill, which gives their casings a delightful snap. Many people enjoy merguez served over one of North Africa's favorite starches, the quick-cooking tiny pasta called couscous. Others stuff the delicious links into baguettes with caramelized onions, mayo, and extra harissa. Easy to make at home, this sandwich is also popular in Algeria's famous markets, where some people crown their sandwich aux merguez with French fries!

INGREDIENTS

2 tablespoons unsalted butter
2 large red onions, halved, peeled,
    and very thinly sliced
salt
1 long baguette
olive oil, for greasing
8 merguez sausages
mayonnaise, for spreading (optional)
harissa, for spreading (optional)

1. In a deep skillet, melt the butter over medium-high heat. Add the onions and cook, stirring, until you start to see some browning on the bottom of the pan, about 6 minutes. Splash a little water into the pan and cook, scraping up any browned bits from the bottom of the pan. Continue cooking the onions, stirring, and each time you see more browned bits forming on the bottom of the pan, add a few tablespoons of water and scrape it up. Cook until the onions are nicely browned, 15 to 20 minutes. Season the onions with salt and let cool until they are warm.

2. Cut the baguette into four pieces, then slice each piece so you can fill it.

3. Light a grill over medium-high heat or preheat a grill pan. Oil the grill grates. Grill the merguez sausages, turning frequently, until cooked through, about 8 minutes.

4. During the last minute of cooking, toast the split side of the baguettes on the grill for 30 seconds.

5. Spread the baguettes with mayonnaise and harissa, if desired. Stuff with the sausages and top with the onions. Serve warm.

DEMOCRATIC REPUBLIC OF THE CONGO

Known as the DRC for short, this country is named for the Congo, one of Earth's mightiest rivers, which snakes through the country. The DRC contains Africa's biggest tropical rainforest, home to gorillas, chimpanzees, and forest elephants. At different times Portugal, France, and Belgium colonized the DRC; today its cuisine combines Central African traditions with European and New World flavors.

CASSAVA

Cassava is a root vegetable from Mesoamerica that has been a staple in the DRC—and much of Africa—for almost 500 years. Congolese cooks fry, mash, ferment, purée, boil, and ground cassava, but there's one way they never eat it: raw. Raw cassava contains a poison called cyanide, but the tuber becomes harmless (and delicious) when cooked.

MIKATE DOUGHNUTS

While the most popular desserts here are fresh tropical fruits, doughnuts are the second-favorite sweet. Similar fluffy, fried-dough treats are called togbei or bofrot in Ghana or puff-puff in Nigeria. Here in the DRC they're called mikate, which means "fried dough bread" in the local Lingala language. You'll find vendors frying them up fresh on the street corners of Kinshasa, where people buy them for breakfast with coffee.

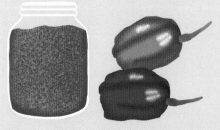

PILI PILI

Pili Pili means "pepper pepper" in one of the Swahili languages and refers to a type of super spicy chili about twenty-two times hotter than a jalapeño called the African bird pepper—it also refers to the sauce made when you combine it with garlic and vinegar or lemon. For delicious heat and creamy relief, people slather a combination of pili pili sauce and mayonnaise onto meat, fish, and fried plantains.

FUFU

To make fufu, cassava, plantain, or maize is peeled, soaked for days, dried, pounded into a fine flour, and shaped into balls to be served with dishes like fish stew or bean soup. Fufu can take time to make, so families and friends gather to prepare and enjoy it together.

KWANGA

A popular accompaniment to daily dishes like meats and stews, kwanga is a traditional cassava flour cake. A bit like Mexican tamales, the dough is wrapped in leaves and then steamed. Since some foods here can be very spicy with pili pili sauce, bites of neutral kwanga can give your tongue a contrast to the hot-pepper heat.

INSECTS

Insects like grasshoppers and caterpillars are popular in the DRC. Their flavor can vary depending on what they themselves ate, but some have a deliciously nutty flavor! They are also a great source of protein and rich in amino acids, with a long history in local diets and culture in the DRC.

FRESH FISH

As the DRC only has a tiny ocean coastline, much of the country's delicious seafood is caught wild here in the beautiful Congo River. While in markets, you can buy fresh fish to take home and cook yourself. The local catch is also widely available—alive or fried, steamed, smoked, or cooked whole, wrapped in banana leaves, and ready to eat.

SAFOU

The DRC's climate is perfect for growing tropical fruits. One favorite is safou, also called the African butter pear. It is a nutritious tree fruit that is cultivated but also grows wild in the DRC's tropical forests. Safou look like little eggplants and have a buttery texture. Its taste? It may be a fruit, but it's not sweet! More like a savory avocado, with a little sourness like green olives. Safou is great as a jam, and is even used to make ice cream.

GAME

Hunting wild game is still one of the main ways of acquiring meat, from the crocodiles in the Congo River to the antelopes in the forests. One popular way to eat crocodile is to cure it with sugar and salt for a few hours, then smoke the meat in wood chips.

POULET MOAMBE

CHICKEN WITH ONIONS, TOMATOES, PEANUT BUTTER, AND PALM OIL

PREPARATION TIME	COOKING TIME	LEVEL OF DIFFICULTY	SERVES
20 mins	1 hr 15 mins	●●	6

This traditional stewed chicken dish gets its distinctive taste from its rich, flavorful sauce. Palm oil, made from the African palm fruit, gives the dish a red color. Often served with sides like fufu, plantains, or rice, Moambe chicken is widely popular in Central and West Africa. It is considered the national dish of both the Republic of Congo and the Democratic Republic of the Congo, as well as Angola and Gabon, and has become a dinner staple in Belgium too.

INGREDIENTS

3 pounds bone-in chicken thighs or drumsticks
salt
6 tablespoons red palm oil, peanut oil, or ghee
2 medium yellow onions, diced
3 cloves garlic, minced
1-inch ginger root, peeled and grated
1 6-ounce can tomato paste
1 14.5-ounce can diced tomatoes
3 scallions, thinly sliced
½ teaspoon cayenne pepper
¼ teaspoon ground nutmeg
½ cup creamy unsalted peanut butter
steamed rice, for serving
fried plantains, for serving

1. Pat the chicken dry with paper towels and season with salt.

2. In a large, heavy Dutch oven, heat 2 tablespoons of the oil over medium-high heat until shimmering. Working in batches, add the chicken, skin side down in a single layer, and cook until golden brown, 5 to 8 minutes. Flip and cook the chicken on the other side until golden brown, about 5 minutes longer. Transfer to a plate and repeat with the remaining chicken.

3. Add the remaining 4 tablespoons of oil, the onions, and a large pinch of salt, and cook over medium-low heat until softened, about 10 minutes. Add the garlic and ginger and cook until fragrant, about 2 minutes. Add the tomato paste and cook, stirring occasionally, until the paste darkens, 3 to 5 minutes.

4. Add the diced tomatoes, scallions, cayenne, nutmeg, and 1 cup water and bring to a boil over high heat. Reduce the heat to medium-low, cover, and simmer for 20 minutes.

5. Scoop out about 1 cup of the sauce and transfer to a heatproof bowl. Add the peanut butter and whisk until smooth. Scrape the peanut sauce into the pot, stir in the chicken, and simmer everything together uncovered until the chicken is cooked through and the sauce is thick and coats the chicken, about 10 minutes. Taste the sauce and season with salt, if desired.

6. Serve with rice or fried plantains.

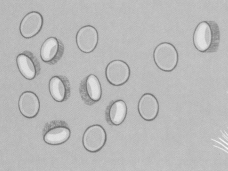

EGYPT

Egypt is mostly covered in vast deserts, but people have built thriving civilizations here for thousands of years, thanks to the Nile River and its famously fertile floodplain. This watery lifeline nourished one of the most sophisticated societies in history, a series of kingdoms that we refer to today as ancient Egypt. Ancient Egyptians grew leeks, cucumbers, lettuce, arugula, watercress, carrots, herbs, peas, okra, and green beans. Pigeon and quail have been grilled and stuffed since the pharaoh days. Tourists who come from around the world to feast their eyes on ancient Egypt's famous pyramids can afterward feast on falafel, kebabs, rotisserie-style roasted meat called shawarma, and filled puff pastry known as fateer.

COFFEE

Egypt has had a thriving coffee culture since the sixteenth century, long before it was widespread in Europe. Today, Egyptians make espresso with cardamom in stovetop pots called *kanaka*, or hang out in coffee shops called *ahwa*—the Egypt-dialect Arab word for coffee.

DESERT FRUIT

Egyptians long ago mastered the skill of growing fruit in the desert—including dates, figs, and melons, all of which are still popular here today. Grape, tamarind, pomegranate, and strawberry juices are simmered into sweet syrups to make drinks and flavorful fruity pastries.

KHAN EL KAHLILI

Khan El Kahlili is one of Egypt's oldest surviving bazaars, held in the heart of Cairo, the capital city. Locals still frequent the market for daily needs, while visitors come to soak up the bustling atmosphere and friendly bargaining. There are also countless cafés to stop at for a refreshing cup of Egyptian mint tea.

FOOD FOR ETERNITY

Ancient Egyptians were famous for mummifying leaders and placing them in elaborate tombs with items to use in the afterlife—King Tut's tomb held seventeen boxes of food, including grapes, figs, pomegranates, jujubes, a jar of honey, and meat preserved in resin from pistachio trees.

KAHK

This sweet, crumbly cookie dates back to the times of pharaohs. Sometimes stuffed with gold coins and given to the poor, today they're often sprinkled with powdered sugar and stuffed with nuts or dates and decorated with elaborate swirls of icing. They are also given as gifts at Egyptian weddings and during religious holidays such as Eid al-Fitr and Easter.

KOSHARY

Lentils have been popular here for thousands of years and today Egyptians still simmer red, brown, and black lentils, into savory stews. Koshary—a street food staple and Egypt's national dish—features lentils, rice, chickpeas, and small pasta, with cumin-scented tomato sauce and crispy fried onions.

MOLOKHIA

This thick, green soup is named for the type of leaf that gives it its bright color. Molokhia leaves may be chopped then boiled with garlic and coriander. Some cooks throw in shredded chicken too. Served over rice, or sometimes with bread, a warming bowl of molokhia turns into a full meal.

LATE EATERS

No wonder Egyptians love a nutritious, filling breakfast like ful medames—lunchtime is between 1:00 p.m. and 4:00 p.m. Dinner typically starts from 8:00 p.m. and can last until midnight! Some people skip dinner and instead have a light late meal of leftovers from lunch.

NUTS FOR NUTS!

At late-night movie-watching parties and sporting events, Egyptians snack on peanuts, cashews, walnuts, and pistachios, while watermelon seeds, sunflower seeds, and spiced, roasted chickpeas are favorite street-vendor snacks.

FUL MEDAMES

This native variety of fava bean was one of the first crops ever cultivated in human history. The name also refers to a breakfast favorite, a savory stew made from the softly cooked ful, simmered with olive oil, cumin, chopped parsley, garlic, onion, lemon juice, and chili peppers.

EGGS
AROUND THE WORLD

People have been eating eggs throughout history, since long before we domesticated poultry. Eggs are a cheap protein source with endless uses in cooking. While duck, goose, and chicken eggs are the most common eggs to eat, local specialties from other bird species are important in some cultures. And chicken eggs alone are cooked into thousands of recipes around the world, from scrambled eggs at breakfast to custardy desserts.

PRESERVED EGGS

Fresh eggs can spoil quickly, so before refrigeration, people around the world found ways to preserve them. Throughout Southeast Asia, eggs have long been preserved with salt. A traditional Chinese recipe called "century eggs" uses ash, clay, salt, and quicklime. The process doesn't really take a hundred years; after a few months, the eggs are black, salty, and creamy—a delicacy!

EGG HOPPERS

Sri Lankan egg hoppers are a popular breakfast street food. A crispy rice and coconut milk pancake is baked into a deep, lacy cup shape to nest the cooked egg. Egg hoppers might be served with spicy sambal sauce and soft lentil dal.

SCRAMBLED EGGS

This quick breakfast starts the day around the globe. In Mexico, migas are eggs scrambled with fried tortilla chips and crumbs. In Malta, balbuljata includes onions, tomatoes, and parsley.

FRIED EGGS

Fried eggs are a staple in cuisines worldwide. In Egypt, egg aagwa is a dish of eggs fried with dates. Often served with a fried egg, nasi goreng is a smoky, chili-infused fried rice known throughout Indonesia and Malaysia, also popular in South America's Suriname and in the Netherlands in Europe.

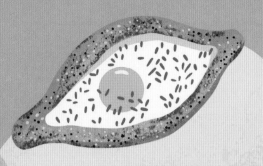

KHACHAPURI

This beautiful boat-shaped cheese bread is a centuries-old national dish from the country of Georgia. An egg is cracked onto the bread's cheesy center, then it's popped into the oven to bake. Tear off the crust to dip into the hot runny center!

MERINGUE

Meringues are like magic, created with sugar and egg whites beaten with a whisk until fluffy with air, then baked into sweet pillows of cloudlike dessert. Costa Rican suspiros cookies ("tiny sighs") are miniature meringues flavored with lime juice.

EGG SOUP

In many cuisines, eggs make soups richer. Colombian changua is an eggy breakfast soup with scallions and cilantro. In Azerbaijan, dovga is a chilled yogurt soup with chickpeas, eggs, and fresh herbs like mint, parsley, and cilantro. In Greece, avgolemono is a smooth, golden, thick soup made with eggs and lemons that often includes chicken and rice.

EGG BRICK

If you see brik à l'oeuf or "egg brick" on the menu in Tunisia, the name is actually referring to the "brick" dough, a light, flaky, paper-thin semolina dough fried so quickly that when you cut into this treat, the barely cooked egg yolk within will drip right out!

LEITE DE CREME

This sweet, rich, eggy custard, popular in Portugal, is flavored with lemon peel and cinnamon. Chefs sprinkle sugar on top and brown it with a torch, giving it a crisp caramelized top over the smooth, warm confection within.

TOPPED WITH AN EGG

Many Asian soups bob with poached or boiled eggs. South Korean jang-jorim is a savory side of soy-sauce-braised beef, often studded with spicy peppers and jammy, golden-yolked hard-boiled eggs.

SHAKSHUKA

POACHED EGGS IN TOMATO AND PEPPER SAUCE

PREPARATION TIME	COOKING TIME	LEVEL OF DIFFICULTY	SERVES
15 mins	40 mins	●●	4 to 6

This dish of eggs poached in a sweet-spicy pepper-tomato sauce is now beloved around the world. Named for the Arabic word for "mixture," it's all simmered in a single skillet. First you make a simple savory sauce of tomatoes, onion, garlic, and red peppers, spiced with cumin, coriander, and sweet or smoked paprika, then you gently crack the eggs into the sauce, where they cook to a jammy perfection in just a few minutes. This version calls for sweet bell peppers, but some cooks also add fiery hot chilies—other variations include cured olives, salty white cheese, artichoke hearts, or spicy sausage.

INGREDIENTS

3 tablespoons olive oil
1 medium yellow onion, finely chopped
3 to 4 fat garlic cloves, thinly sliced
1 red or green bell pepper, seeded and diced
salt and pepper
1 tablespoon sweet paprika
2 teaspoons ground cumin
2 teaspoons ground coriander
1 28-ounce can diced tomatoes
4 to 6 large eggs
chopped parsley or mint, and crusty bread, for serving (optional)

1. In a large, deep skillet with a lid, heat the olive oil over medium heat. Add the onion, garlic, and bell pepper, and season with ½ teaspoon salt and a few grinds of pepper. Cook, stirring, until softened, 5 to 6 minutes. Add the paprika, cumin, and coriander and cook until fragrant, about 30 seconds. Add the tomatoes and bring to a simmer. Reduce the heat to medium-low, cover, and simmer the sauce for 15 minutes. Uncover and cook until the sauce is thickened, about 5 more minutes.

2. Using your spoon, make 4 to 6 indentations in the sauce, depending on the number of eggs you're using. Carefully crack the eggs into the wells, then cover the skillet, and cook until the egg whites are set but the yolks are bright and jammy, about 6 minutes. (If you prefer hard cooked eggs, let them cook to desired doneness.)

3. Spoon the shakshuka into bowls, sprinkle with the parsley or mint, and serve with crusty bread.

Bread makes the perfect "scoop" for the delicious sauce!

Shakshuka is traditional to have at breakfast, brunch, or lunch, but it's just as delicious at dinner.

ETHIOPIA

One of the oldest countries in the world, Ethiopia is called "the cradle of humanity" because archaeologists have found so many early human fossils here. It's also one of only two countries in Africa never to have been colonized. Maybe that's why the food in this rugged country on the Horn of Africa—the continent's easternmost peninsula—is unique in all the world. Here you'll find the wonderfully spongy injera bread, flavorful butters, succulent meats spiced with berbere, and the world's first coffee.

COFFEE'S BIRTHPLACE

Legend has it that a ninth-century Ethiopian goatherd discovered coffee when he noticed certain berries gave the goats more energy. Today, most Ethiopians enjoy a daily coffee ceremony: raw beans are roasted, then pounded in a mortar (*mukecha*) with a pestle (*zenesena*), and boiled in a pot called a *jebana*. Even young kids drink coffee here!

INJERA

This national dish of Ethiopia also serves as plate and utensil! Injera is a spongy, slightly sour flatbread made from teff—a tiny supergrain native to Ethiopia. Stews, meats, and vegetables are each placed in mounds on a big circle of injera, which may be up to 20 inches across. To eat, you tear off a small piece of injera and use it as a scoop to pick up each delicious bite.

BERBERE

This key Ethiopian spice blend usually includes chili peppers, garlic, ginger, black pepper, fenugreek, allspice, and cloves. It can be used dry or mixed with oil to form a paste. Berbere packs a spicy punch, so have some soothing injera on hand!

ENSET

The enset looks so much like a banana tree, people call it the "false banana." Ethiopians mash parts of the plant with yeast, bury it underground for as long as two years, then make the fermented paste into a dense, breadlike staple called kocho.

DORO WAT

This chicken stew is often served at celebrations, especially weddings, and can take days to make. First you simmer onions in water with berbere; then you add nit'ir qibe (a spiced, clarified butter), aromatics, marinated chicken, and hard-boiled eggs. It's served with a ricottalike cheese called alibi and, of course, injera.

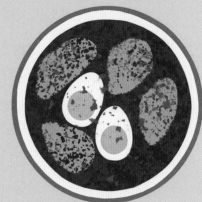

SPICES

Spices are extremely important to Ethiopian cuisine. These include cayenne peppers, cone peppers, amharic cabbage seeds, black mustard, cardamom, coriander, basil, black pepper, ginger, black cumin, fenugreek, and garlic.

VEGETARIAN FOOD

Members of the Ethiopian Orthodox Christian Church are vegetarian for much of the year. They feast on meals like yetsom beyaynetu: injera topped with heaps of veggie-based curries and stews in a kaleidoscope of colors.

GURSHA

Ethiopians are widely known for their hospitality. One way guests are shown respect is through the very old tradition called *gursha*, the Amharic word for "mouthful." When people perform *gursha*, they each pick up a portion of food with a piece of injera by hand and graciously feed each other.

KITFO AND OTHER MEATS

Many Ethiopians love meat . . . especially when it's raw! Kitfo is minced raw beef marinated in a spice blend and nit'ir qibe; gored consists of raw beef cubes with chili sauce and lemon; and tere siga (literally "raw meat") is a long strip of meat cut straight from the hanging carcass.

TIBS

A cross between a stir fry and a stew, tibs is often the first dish prepared on holidays. The meat—cubes of beef, lamb, or goat—is usually sautéed in a rich sauce of nit'ir qibe, vegetables, aromatics, and berbere.

NIT'IR QIBE

CLARIFIED BUTTER WITH GARLIC, GINGER, AND SPICES

PREPARATION TIME
15 mins

COOKING TIME
1 hr 15 mins

LEVEL OF DIFFICULTY
● ●

MAKES
About 1 cup

This clarified butter, infused with onion, garlic, ginger, and spices, is essential in many Ethiopian recipes—and is delicious on its own. Clarifying the butter is when you slowly heat it and remove the solids, like making the world-famous ghee of India! The result is a butter that keeps longer and can cook at higher temperatures. Ethiopian cooks use nit'ir qibe in a raw beef dish called kitfo and when cooking doro wat, their beloved, slow-cooked, deeply spiced chicken dish.

INGREDIENTS

1 pound unsalted butter, cut into
 small pieces
1 teaspoon ground turmeric
⅛ teaspoon nutmeg,
 freshly grated
½ teaspoon ground cardamom
1 whole clove
1 cinnamon stick
½ an onion, coarsely chopped
3 cloves garlic, minced
1-inch piece of fresh ginger,
 peeled and grated
1 teaspoon fenugreek seeds
½ teaspoon cumin seeds

1. In a medium saucepan over medium-low heat, slowly melt the butter but do not let it brown.

2. Meanwhile, in a dry, heavy skillet over medium-low heat, toast the turmeric, nutmeg, cardamom, clove, and cinnamon for 4 to 5 minutes, until fragrant. Be careful not to let them burn.

3. Once the butter is fully melted, add the toasted spices, onion, garlic, and ginger. Raise the heat and bring to a boil. Lower to a simmer and cook gently for 1 hour. Let it cool until warm.

4. Strain the nit'ir qibe through two layers of cheesecloth draped over a sieve or use a coffee filter. Stir in the fenugreek and cumin. Store in a glass jar in the refrigerator for up to three months.

Drizzle over meats and stews, add a tasty spoonful to beans or lentils, or use when cooking eggs or for seasoning boiled vegetables.

It's also pretty
great on popcorn!

KENYA

Kenya is famous for its wildlife, its stunning Indian Ocean coastline, and its vibrant mix of traditional and modern cultures, foods, and architecture. Lions, leopards, elephants, rhinos, and Cape buffalo roam Kenya's fifty national parks and reserves. The East African nation's capital city of Nairobi is home to skyscrapers, international corporations, and a hip music scene, along with amazing street food. Its more rural areas feature a rich history and variety of traditional cultures and tribes, each with their own distinct foods and recipes.

CHAI

Visit a Kenyan family and you'll likely receive a hot cup of chai, made by boiling tea leaves in a large pot with milk, lots of sugar, and spices like cardamom, cinnamon, and black pepper. In rural areas, chai is made over a wood fire, with milk carried fresh from the cow—or goat—to the pot!

INDIAN INFLUENCE

Kenya, like India, is a former British colony. In the late 1800s, the British brought more than 30,000 Indian laborers to Africa to build the Kenya–Uganda railway. It was a brutal job: some workers were even eaten by lions. But many survived and stayed, and today Indian recipes for samosas, chapatis, curry, and biryani are beloved across Kenya.

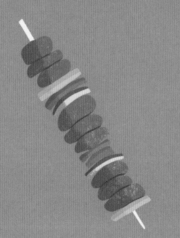

STREET FOOD

Kenyan cities are bursting with street food. Try makai—grilled corn seasoned with chili powder, lime, and salt. Or sink your teeth into mshikaki, a marinated, grilled kebab. Don't forget mandazi doughnuts—for a local experience, grab another for tomorrow's breakfast!

UGALI

This East African staple is made by boiling cornmeal until it is almost like an edible spoon. At mealtime, Kenyans roll a lump of ugali into a little ball, press a dimple with one thumb, and scoop up other foods—sauce, cooked greens, or meat—so each delicious bite includes the corny ugali base. To be polite, only use your fingertips!

NYAMA CHOMA

In Swahili, nyama choma—often simply roasted goat meat with salt and pepper—means "burned meat." Originating from the nomadic Maasai people, it may be Kenya's most popular dish, served everywhere from roadside shacks to Nairobi's finest restaurants, often with ugali.

GITHERI

A traditional food of the Kikuyu tribe of central Kenya, githeri is a nutritious stew of corn and beans that often includes greens, onions, potatoes, meat, and curry powder. It's popular across Kenya—in fact, many locals ate it in school cafeterias when they were children!

MURSIK

Kenya's world-champion marathoners are perhaps helped by training at high altitudes and eating nutritious foods like this fermented milk. To make mursik, the cook brushes the inside of a dried gourd, or calabash, with soot from a particular type of tree. Cow or goat's milk is poured in and sealed for up to a month. The soot blocks harmful bacteria and gives the milk a smoky flavor.

SUKUMA WIKI

Sukuma wiki is a green vegetable (a cousin of kale), chopped and braised with tomatoes and onions. Its name means "stretch the week" because its energy can help fuel you for days! Most Kenyans eat it nearly every day of the year.

FRUIT

Kenya's warm climate is perfect for growing tropical fruits. Mangoes, guava, pineapples, papaya, bananas, limes, watermelon, coconut, and pawpaws are often sliced and served for breakfast. Coconut is cooked with a variety of fresh fruits to make a mousselike dessert. People enjoy amazing fresh juices, from passionfruit to sugarcane.

TEA

AROUND THE WORLD

The practice of drinking tea originated in southwestern China during the Bronze Age, when the leaves were mixed with herbs in a medicinal drink. A tea tree in the region's Yunnan province is said to be the oldest in the world—3,200 years old! Portuguese traders wrote about tea-drinking during their travels in the 1500s, but it was not until the early seventeenth century that tea arrived in Europe, on a Dutch East India Company ship. By the mid-1600s, people everywhere in Europe were drinking tea, and it quickly spread to European colonies in Africa, India, and the Americas.

THAI ICED TEA

Thailand's sweet drink is caffeinated and cold, so it cools you down and wakes you up! It features strong brewed black tea, and its creamy orange color comes from tamarind and creamy sweetened condensed milk. Sometimes steeped with anise or cardamom, Thai iced tea will cool down your tongue between bites of spicy Thai dishes like kua kling and pad prik king.

BUBBLE TEA

In Taiwan, bubble tea can now be found in flavors from brown sugar to strawberry, but it's often made with just brewed tea, milk, sugar, and big, black, chewy tapioca balls called boba or pearls. People drink the tea and suck up the boba through special giant straws.

AMERICAN ICED TEA

In the U.S.'s southern states, tea is served ice cold and enjoyed on sweltering summer days. Hosts will ask if you like "sweet or unsweet," and you'll find it everywhere: poured from crystal pitchers on grand porches and sipped from red plastic cups next to paper plates of barbecue. Sometimes it's even steeped in the sun!

YERBA MATE

Made from the leaves of a plant in the holly family, yerba mate is served hot or cold in traditional cups made to resemble gourds. This herbal drink is served with special metal straws that strain as you sip and originated with the indigenous people of present-day Paraguay. It is now drunk in many South American countries.

ROOIBOS TEA

South African rooibos "tea" is named for the Afrikaans word for "red bush," after the local native plants used for the tea. Its leaves are steeped for their naturally earthy, slightly sweet flavor. Rooibos is enjoyed hot or iced, and people may add milk, lemon, sugar, or honey.

TEA CEREMONIES

Many East Asian countries have elaborate tea ceremonies, with special objects and rituals for brewing and serving tea, many of which reflect the influence of Buddhism. The Japanese tea ceremony *sado/chado* ("the way of tea") is a preparation and presentation of matcha (powdered green tea) using a special procedure called *otemae*, which can be a formal (*chaji*) or informal (*chakai*) tea gatherinxg.

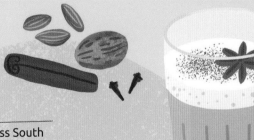

MINT TEA

In North African countries like Morocco, many people sip tea, made with fresh mint leaves and lots of sugar, all day. Often poured from ornate silver teapots and served in clear glasses, this Maghrebi mint drink is sometimes brewed with green tea, too, for a caffeine kick.

CHAI

Born in India and beloved across South Asia, chai is made by boiling black tea in milk. Masala chai is spiced with ginger, cardamom, cinnamon, cloves, and black pepper, and served sweet. Immigrants from India brought chai to East Africa, where it's still popular today.

BISSAP

ICED HIBISCUS TEA

PREPARATION TIME	COOKING TIME	LEVEL OF DIFFICULTY	SERVES
5 mins, plus 2 hrs cooling	15 mins	●	4

This beautiful ruby-colored tea, the national drink of Senegal, is an iced tea brewed from a species of hibiscus flower native to West Africa. People have brought the flower—and the drink—around the world, and it now goes by many names: sorrel in the Caribbean, sobolo in Ghana, agua de Jamaica in Central and South America, zobo in Nigeria, and karkade in Egypt and northern Sudan, where glasses of it are raised in wedding toasts. In Senegal, it's known as bissap.

Tart when first brewed, bissap is sweetened with sugar and sometimes also spiced with ginger, cloves, allspice, or cinnamon.

INGREDIENTS

½ cup dried hibiscus flowers
1 small bunch fresh mint
   (optional)
2 cinnamon sticks (optional)
4 tablespoons sugar, plus more
   to taste

1. In a small pot, bring 4 cups of water to a boil. Add the hibiscus flowers, reduce the heat to medium, and simmer for 2 minutes.

2. Add the mint and cinnamon sticks and remove the pot from the heat. Let the tea steep for 10 minutes. Stir in the sugar and taste. Add more sugar, if you prefer.

3. Refrigerate for at least 2 hours, then serve over ice.

MOROCCO

Mountainous Morocco is the only country in Africa that borders both the Mediterranean Sea and the Atlantic Ocean. Foods here reflect the influences of its neighbors: France, Portugal, and Spain, as well as the other North African nations of the Maghreb and the indigenous Amazigh cultures. In Morocco's famous mazelike marketplaces, people sell everything from spices to silk scarves to citrus. As you might expect in a country with so much coastline, lots of people here make their living catching and selling fish—which also features in the gorgeous cuisine here—served with couscous, fresh olives, pickled lemons, and warm bread.

FISH

In Morocco, which boasts more than 1,500 miles of coastline, fish virtually leap onto your plate. Sea bream, sardines, anchovies, and tuna are all major catches, and Moroccans feast on them poached, marinated, braised, grilled, simmered, and fried. Fish also play a starring role in couscous dishes or tagines, and fresh fish is often served alongside a selection of Moroccan salads.

COUSCOUS

This tiny traditional pasta has been eaten daily in North Africa and many other parts of the world for centuries, and while it's now easy to buy in stores, many cooks still make it from scratch. First, they will sprinkle salted water into a bowl of semolina flour, then move their fingers in a circle so small granules form. They then sort each granule by size for drying. After steaming, it's time to eat.

TAGINE

This stew is of the best-known dishes in Morocco and much of North Africa. It is named for the vessel in which it's made: a clay pot with a cone-shaped lid. Tagines vary, but a chicken tagine might be made with onions, garlic, parsley, olive oil, cooked until the meat is tender, then served with paprika, almonds, ginger, and more olive oil!

LAMB

Lamb has been a favorite meat here for centuries, and some preparations date back to the Middle Ages. Steamed sheep's head, often served with couscous, is traditional at Eid al-Adha, a major Muslim holiday commemorating Abraham's willingness to sacrifice his son (fortunately he sacrificed a lamb instead!)

DAIRY

Moroccans make magic with milk. Sheep, goat, or cow's milk may be made into jben (cheese), or into rayeb, a sweetened custardlike preparation, made by curdling milk with wild artichoke.

PASTILLA

This giant pie—also a specialty in neighboring Algeria—may be the grandest of Moroccan dishes. Pastilla is traditionally filled with stewed pigeons (although now chicken is often used), with toasted almonds, eggs, saffron, and cinnamon. The layers of flaky pastry are so thin they're called warqa, a word that means "leaf" in Arabic, as in leaf of paper.

LEMONS

In Morocco, round, sweet lemon varieties called doqq and boussera are pickled in salty brine and then used as a condiment in salads or stews. Moroccans call preserved lemons lim mraqqed, which translates to "lemons put to sleep"!

ARGAN OIL

The tree argan oil comes from is famously thorny and bears fruit just once a year. Each nut's oily kernels are toasted, ground, and pressed by hand. But all this work is worth it for the rich oil. You can dip bread in the nutty-flavored oil or drizzle it over pasta.

SMEN

Known as smen, preserved butter makes many Moroccan dishes even more delicious. Made from clarified butter, salt, and sometimes herbs, smen is fermented for months or even years. The flavor is intense, something like aged cheese. Smen is used as a spread, added to stews, and even sometimes enjoyed in coffee.

KISRA

Many Moroccans knead and shape this semolina flatbread at home, then bring the dough to a local bakery to pop in the oven. The round dense loaves are flavored with anise, nigella, fennel, or sesame seeds, and are often served with tagine.

HARIRA

SPICED VEGETABLE SOUP

PREPARATION TIME	COOKING TIME	LEVEL OF DIFFICULTY	SERVES
20 mins	1 hr 10 mins	●●	6

This flavorful savory Moroccan soup is lush with vegetables and perfumed with spices. During Ramadan, a holy month for Muslims, so many Muslims break their daily fast with this soup that you can smell it cooking every afternoon. There are many regional variations, including some with vermicelli or rice and meat versions.

INGREDIENTS

4 tablespoons olive oil
2 onions, diced
2 cloves garlic, minced
5 stalks celery, including leaves, chopped
3 to 4 carrots, sliced into moons or half-moons
½ teaspoon ground turmeric
½ teaspoon ground ginger
½ teaspoon ground cumin
½ teaspoon harissa
1 cinnamon stick
1 29-ounce can tomatoes, crushed or diced
1 teaspoon salt
1 bunch cilantro, chopped
7 cups vegetable stock or water
1 cup dried green lentils
1 15-ounce can chickpeas
salt and black pepper
juice of 1 lemon

1. In a large, heavy-bottomed pot over medium heat, warm the olive oil and sauté the onion, garlic, celery, and carrots for 10 minutes, stirring occasionally.

2. Add the spices, tomatoes, salt, half of the cilantro, and the stock or water, and bring to a boil.

3. Reduce the heat to medium-low and simmer for 20 minutes, then add the lentils and chickpeas and simmer for 30 minutes. Test a lentil to be sure it's cooked through.

4. Season with salt and pepper to taste, and finish with the remaining cilantro and the lemon juice.

Lamb is also delicious in harira. If you'd like to include a pound of cubed lamb-stew meat, first lightly brown it in oil for a few minutes on all sides, then add to the pot in the first step.

NIGERIA

Nigeria is home to plains and plateaus, tall mountains, a long coastline on the Gulf of Guinea, and the Niger River, for which the country is named. This varied tropical landscape is rich in natural resources, including excellent farmland that produces deliciously diverse flavors. The city of Lagos is one of the biggest metropolitan areas in the world, home to over 20 million people, including many millionaires and billionaires. Nigerian culinary traditions have influenced food as far away as Brazil, Cuba, and the United States.

YAMS

Yams are an edible tuber grown in enormous quantities in Nigeria. Here, yams are a daily staple, prepared in many ways: they are boiled, fried, and pounded into a paste; made into flour; sliced into chips; and cooked into porridge. To quote a Nigerian saying, "Yam is food and food is yam."

EGUSI SOUP

Egusi soup gets its rich umami flavor from a special ingredient: the edible seeds of an inedible watermelonlike gourd. The seeds are ground to a fine powder and mixed into a silky soup with spices, onions, tomatoes, leafy greens, and sometimes chicken, or dried crayfish.

GARRI

Garri, a staple across Nigeria, is made from freshly harvested cassava. The roots—poisonous raw—are carefully peeled and cooked, grated into granules, and dried. Once reconstituted, garri can be eaten hot or cold, sweet or savory, and as eba, a "swallow." The Yoruba, one of Nigeria's largest ethnic groups, often enjoy garri as a doughy accompaniment to okra stew or egusi soup.

SWALLOWS

Several Nigerian meals consist of a soup and "a swallow." the term for any starchy paste that you don't need to chew—simply swallow! Nigeria is a land of many swallows. Examples include eba (made from garri), pounded yam, amala (a paste made from the yam's skin), and fufu (made from fermented and ground cassava).

RED PALM OIL

Extracted from the pulp of the oil palm fruit, unrefined palm oil is a deep orange-red with a nutty flavor. It has been a staple of the West African diet for a long, long time. Archaeological evidence found that people in the region were cultivating and eating it 5,000 years ago!

KOLA NUTS

Kola created that world-famous "cola" flavor, but in Nigeria, the nuts, which grow in West Africa's tropical rain forests, are also known as a typical snack, and sometimes form part of sacred Igbo ceremonies, where they can symbolize hospitality, respect, and ancestors. Kola nuts contain caffeine and some believe they can taste bitter at first, but they become sweeter as you chew.

MOIN MOIN

This savory bean pudding is made by grinding black-eyed peas into a paste, adding palm oil and seasonings, and, once they are wrapped in banana leaves or a heatproof container, placed in a pot to cook. Some cooks add meat, shrimp, and hard-boiled eggs. If you add enough extra ingredients, you end up with moin-moin elemi meje, meaning "seven lives."

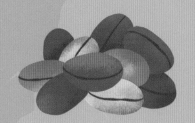

KULI KULI

These salty, spicy, crunchy snacks are often sold at roadside stands in Nigeria, Cameroon, Benin, and Ghana. Vendors roast groundnuts (peanuts), grind them into a paste, and mix in spices and sometimes sugar. The paste is then shaped into balls, skinny squiggles, flat squares, or rings, and deep-fried until crisp.

MEMORIES OF OKPA

Chimamanda Ngozi Adichie, the world-famous Nigerian writer, reminisced in *The New Yorker* about her childhood memories of "warm okpa, which remains my favorite food: a simple, orange-colored, steamed pie of white beans and palm oil that tastes best cooked in banana leaves."

JOLLOF RICE

RICE WITH TOMATO PURÉE AND SPICES

PREPARATION TIME	COOKING TIME	LEVEL OF DIFFICULTY	SERVES
20 mins	45 mins	●●	6 to 8

This wonderfully flavorful and often a little spicy rice recipe is beloved across West Africa and south of the Sahara. While every family has their own recipe—some add curry powder, cloves, or mint—most include puréed tomatoes, making the finished dish a beautiful red. You might taste versions with chicken, ham, seafood, pumpkin, or peas, and in some French-speaking parts of West Africa, cooks might add carrots, eggplant, or cabbage. While most cooks make their own tomato purée, this recipe simply asks for canned tomato purée. The whole chili gives the dish a lovely citrusy flavor and heat.

INGREDIENTS

2 cups long-grain white rice, such as basmati
4 tablespoons olive oil
1 medium red onion, thinly sliced
3 garlic cloves, thinly sliced
1-inch piece of fresh ginger, peeled and finely chopped
1 cup tomato purée
1 teaspoon smoked paprika
1 Scotch bonnet or habanero chili, stemmed but kept whole
1 teaspoon garlic powder
1 tablespoon onion powder
1½ teaspoons salt
2¼ cups chicken stock, vegetable stock, or water

1. Preheat the oven to 350°F.

2. In a bowl, cover the rice with water and stir a bit to rinse it. Drain. Cover the rice again and let soak for 30 minutes. Drain and shake dry.

3. In a large, heavy saucepan or Dutch oven, heat the olive oil over medium heat. Add the onion, season generously with salt, and cook, stirring, until softened, about 8 minutes. Add the garlic and ginger and cook until softened, about 3 minutes. Add the tomato purée, smoked paprika, and whole chili. Reduce the heat to low, and cook, stirring frequently, until the tomato purée loses some of its acidic bite, about 10 minutes.

4. Add the garlic powder and onion powder and 1½ teaspoons of salt.

5. Add the rice and stir to coat with the seasonings. Add the stock or water.

6. Increase the heat to high to bring to a simmer, then turn off the heat and put the lid on. Transfer the dish to the oven and cook for 20 minutes, or until all the liquid is absorbed and the rice is tender. Remove the pot from the oven and let stand for 10 minutes, then fluff the rice. Remove the whole chili and taste the rice. Season with more salt, if desired, then serve.

The African diaspora brought versions of this rice recipe around the world, where it evolved into dishes like the flavorful jambalaya in the American city of New Orleans.

A popular main dish at festivals and special occasions, it's often made in giant batches to serve a crowd and served with braised goat and fried plantains.

SOUTH AFRICA

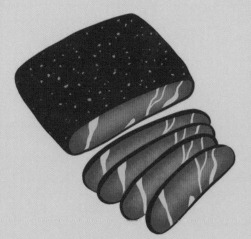

At the southern tip of Africa between the Indian and Atlantic oceans sits sunny South Africa. The foods here are influenced by diverse cultures and by native plants and animals. With deserts and grasslands, forests and fynbos, magnificent mountains and coastline, South Africa's regions are extremely varied. In 1652, the Dutch East India Company created a settlement at the Cape of Good Hope (now Cape Town) to provide fresh food to their ships traveling between Europe and Indonesia on the spice trade route. Enslaved people and political prisoners exiled to Cape Town from Southeast Asia brought with them local culinary traditions and spices that still influence recipes here today.

BILTONG

These strips of air-dried beef, venison, or ostrich are flavored with dried coriander. Biltong is salty, nutritious, and—according to South Africans—much, much better than beef jerky!

BRAAI

This beloved, communal tradition of open-fire cooking uses charcoal or wood to traditionally braai meat, from lamb chops to sheep's intestines. Boerewors—lamb sausage spiced with coriander seeds and malt vinegar and coiled like a snake—are beloved at a braai. The sausages even hiss while braaing.

LAMB AND MUTTON

South Africans love to eat lamb! The arid Karoo region grows the best-tasting sheep because of the aromatic wild plants they graze on. An affordable alternative to lamb chops is a smiley: a sheep's head, boiled and braaied, or barbecued. Another beloved lamb dish, bobotie, features curried lamb baked with savory custard and lemon leaves.

BREDIE

This one-pot family meal is a lamb or chicken stew, with vegetables like spinach or tomatoes, all spiced with ginger, cinnamon, or chilies. Waterblommetjie bredie is made with the flowers and tender seed pods of a juicy, crunchy, fragrant aquatic plant, gathered from ponds in winter and spring. The sour stems of cape sorrel are added instead of lemon juice.

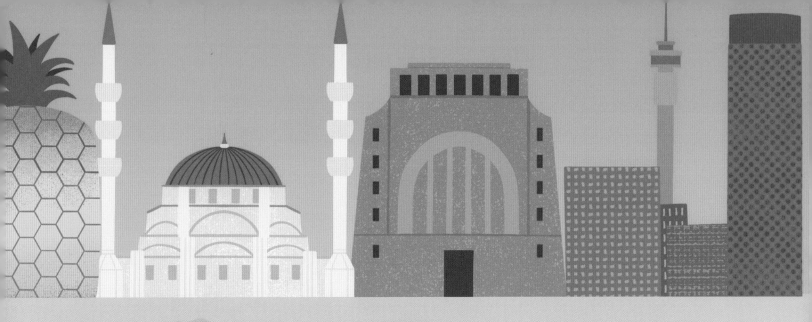

RUSKS

Rusks are slightly sweet cookies or biscuits that start off soft but are sliced open while hot and allowed to air dry. They become wonderfully crunchy and can be dunked into hot tea or coffee for breakfast or a snack.

BUNNY CHOW

This traditional dish is a hollowed-out white bread stuffed with steaming-hot meat or vegetable curry, made with a local curry powder blend. It evolved in Durban, a city in KwaZulu-Natal province that's home to a large Indian community, many of whom are descendants of indentured laborers brought here in the late nineteenth century.

NELSON MANDELA

Nelson Mandela was an activist who fought the white-supremacist system of apartheid and was imprisoned for twenty-seven years before becoming South Africa's first Black president in 1994. Supporters smuggled chicken curry to him in prison. The day he was released, he celebrated with a curry and rum-raisin ice cream with Bishop Desmond Tutu, his days of hunger strikes long behind him.

AMAGWINYA

These deep-fried, yeasted dough balls—a bit like doughnuts without the hole—are eaten as a snack, as breakfast with syrup, or lunch with a curried or saucy topping.

AMASI

Creamy and tangy, amasi (or suurmelk—"sour milk") is a cultured drink similar to buttermilk. It probably evolved as a way of using milk that had turned sour before refrigerators were invented. Amasi is sold in supermarkets alongside milk and is also easy to make at home.

SEAFOOD

The coast here is nearly endless, so people feast on seafood like mussels, oysters, abalone, and kreef (spiny rock lobster). Barracudalike snoek is braaied. Bokkoms (a herring) are salted and dried. Fish and chips are eaten everywhere, served with slapchips (floppy fries) soused with malt vinegar.

POTELE

SIMMERED CORNMEAL WITH WILD GREENS, BROTH, AND BUTTER

PREPARATION TIME	COOKING TIME	LEVEL OF DIFFICULTY	SERVES
5 mins	20 mins	●●	4

Potele is the Sotho name for a dish of mealie meal—mealie is the South African word for corn or maize—cooked with edible wild greens. It is an inexpensive and nourishing meal and a beloved traditional comfort food for many Black South Africans. Potele is often made with umsobo (black nightshade leaves), but any wild edible green—or so-called weed—can be used, such as amaranth (also known as pigweed), lamb's quarters, nettles, quickweed, or sow thistle.

INGREDIENTS

FOR THE GREENS
4 packed cups washed cooking
    greens, such as kale, Swiss
    chard, collards, or spinach
1 cup scallion greens, chopped

FOR THE MEALIE MEAL
½ cup mealie meal (cornmeal)
¼ teaspoon salt
2 tablespoons butter

TO MAKE THE GREENS

1. In a pot, bring 1½ cups water or broth to a boil and add the greens and the scallions. Cook, stirring, for a few minutes until the greens are tender but still bright green. Turn off the heat and transfer the greens and their broth to a bowl. Return the pot to the stove.

TO MAKE THE MEALIE MEAL

2. In a bowl, mix the mealie meal with one cup of the water to form a loose slurry and stir until no lumps remain.

3. Pour this into your (now empty) pot, add the salt, and cook over medium heat, stirring continuously. Add the rest of the water gradually as the mixture stiffens. Cook until the mealie meal is done, about 8 to 10 minutes.

4. Stir in the blanched greens and their broth and the butter. Cook for another 3 minutes to gently heat the greens, then serve warm, with a spoon.

Fresh corn cobs are delicious roasted on the braai or boiled and munched hot. The kernels are often added to steamed mealie bread, eaten hot with butter and golden syrup.

CORN

AROUND THE WORLD

Corn, now a global crop, was first grown in what is now southern Mexico over 9,000 years ago, when the people of ancient Mesoamerica cultivated and cherished a wild grassy plant called teosinte until it bore delicious kernels. Over time, people developed diverse varieties, from the sweet tender kernels eaten right off the cob to the broad, starchy dent corn eaten in the Andes paired with salty fresh cheese or cooked into a tortilla.

POPCORN

Some types of corn, once dried, can be heated until the moisture within causes the kernel to POP. This was likely discovered by accident when kernels fell too close to a fire. Today, it's topped with everything from melted butter to lime and Salsa Valentina™.

CORN TORTILLAS AND TORTILLA CHIPS

Tortillas—made from corn masa dough, cooked on a hot griddle—become tacos when wrapped around delicious fillings or quesadillas when layered with cheese. Fry leftover tortillas into crispy tortilla chips to dip into guacamole and salsas, or make chilaquiles for breakfast!

TAMALES

This traditional Mexican dish isn't just made of delicious corn dough. Since pre-Hispanic times, they've also been cooked in yellow corn husks. The ribbed husks naturally leave tiny beautiful stripes imprinted in the cooked tamale.

SUB-SAHARAN AFRICAN CORN PORRIDGE

Corn was brought to Africa by Portuguese merchants in the sixteenth century. From there, it quickly became a favorite ingredient for porridge, for example, used in the stiff, thick ugali served in Kenya or for the softer pap served in South African stews.

CHICHA AND TEJUINO

Special corn drinks date back to pre-Hispanic times. Chicha is originally from the Andes, where sprouted corn kernels are mashed and fermented until sour and bubbly. In Mexico, people make tejuino by mixing corn masa with boiling water. Once cooled, it's served over shaved ice with lime and a dash of chili powder.

CORNBREAD

Originating from Native American recipes, people in the United States today bake cornmeal into golden cornbread, often cooked and served in a cast-iron skillet. People like to argue about whether to add sugar—only in the north, never in the south!—but many people add buttermilk, bacon, chili peppers, or fresh corn kernels.

ITALIAN POLENTA

Corn was sailed back to Europe and is enjoyed in Italy as a ground grain simmered into a golden yellow porridge called polenta. Often cooked with flavorful stock or parmesan, polenta can be served in place of pasta or cooled until firm, cut into slices, and fried or grilled.

SUCCOTASH

A traditional Native American dish of North America, succotash combines sweet yellow corn and lima beans. Meaning "broken corn" in the Narragansett language, the recipe was adopted by English colonists and is still enjoyed from coast to coast today.

ESQUITES

In Mexico, boiled corn kernels are served warm in a cup, topped with your choice of lime juice, mayonnaise, chili powder, or butter and salt! The sweet-salty-spicy snack can be served as a side or bought on the go.

BABY CORN

A favorite in Chinese cuisine, baby corn is exactly what its name describes. Harvested very young, tiny, inch-long immature corn is treasured for its sweetness, soft cob, and complete munchability. It's tossed into stir fries and eaten whole.

SUDAN

Sudan is a vast country in northeastern Africa, bordered by seven other countries and the Red Sea. Two strands of the Nile River converge in Sudan's capital, Khartoum, and while Sudan is famous for its deserts, it is also home to mountains, savannas, and woodlands. At the crossroads of Africa and the Middle East, it's a cultural melting pot of Arab, Nubian, Egyptian, Turkish, and Levantine influences. More than one hundred tribes live here, speaking one hundred languages, and many of the foods enjoyed by Sudan's 45 million citizens have roots going back for centuries!

GUHWAH COFFEE

Coffee first grew wild in East Africa, and people here in Sudan and in neighboring Ethiopia have been enjoying it for centuries. The traditional Sudanese coffee ritual starts with grinding roasted beans in a mortar and pestle, and simmering the grounds in a clay pot or jar, often with spices like cardamom, ginger, and black pepper.

KAJAIK

Sudan is country rich with rivers, lakes, and swamps, and people who live near these waters feast on lots of freshwater fish. Kajaik is a classic fish stew that originated in South Sudan. It's made with dried fish, tomatoes, and vegetables like onions, carrots, bell peppers, and potatoes. The ingredients are cooked together in coconut water, and some cooks add curry powder for extra flavor.

ESSENTIAL MANGOES

Mangoes have thrived in Sudan for generations and are highly prized. Today, dozens of different varieties of the juicy-sweet fruits grow all across the country.

MEAT LOVERS

In much of Sudan, meat makes the meal. Lamb, mutton, goat, beef, chicken, fish, and camel are popular. Some chefs like to flavor their meat with ground-up roasted peanuts, cumin, and salt before threading it onto skewers and grilling.

SWEET TREATS

Desserts here showcase the influence of Arabic flavors. Many people enjoy dried dates or apricots, as well as treats like assidatal-boubar (a pumpkin-based dessert), basbousa (a semolina cake soaked in sugar syrup), and mukhbaza (a pudding made of breadcrumbs blended with mashed banana and honey).

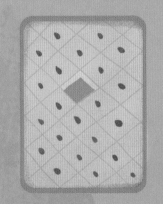

STREET FOOD CITY

Some of the capital city Khartoum's most delicious food can be found at street stalls. Some vendors specialize in grilled meats cooked with a technique called salat, which uses a bed of hot rocks for searing. Kisra, a type of super thin pancake made of fermented sorghum flour, is a popular street snack often served alongside savory stew.

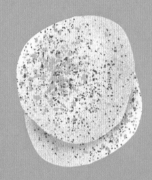

MOULLAH (OR MULLAH)

This classic, savory Sudanese stew is often studded with lamb or fish, and can also contain robe—the Arabic word for "yogurt." Garlic, onions, red peppers, and aromatic spices give the stew big flavors, while okra or peanut butter can make it nice and thick.

FUL MEDAMES

The single most beloved dish here might be ful medames—a delicious blend of fava beans mixed with garlic, lemon juice, tomatoes, chili pepper, and spices, which is enjoyed across North Africa and the Middle East. Ful medames can be eaten for any meal, but it's beloved at breakfast—when it's served with eggs and bread.

ASEEDA (OR ASIDA)

This staple Sudanese starch is made by stirring wheat flour, sorghum, or millet into boiling water. The resulting oatmeallike porridge can be topped with salt and melted butter or honey and is a favorite for breakfast. In the afternoon or evening, it often accompanies moullah or other savory stews.

DATES

Behhah, or Sudanese dates, are prized for their large size and great flavor. Farmers cultivate date palms along the banks of the Nile and anywhere else that groundwater can support the tall trees. Sudanese farmers pollinate the fruits by hand, which can require expertly climbing quite high up the narrow trunks!

SALATA TOMATIM BEL DAQUA

PEANUT-PASTE SALAD

PREPARATION TIME	COOKING TIME	LEVEL OF DIFFICULTY	SERVES
30 mins	0 mins	●	2 to 4

Peanuts, also known as groundnuts, are a Sudanese favorite. Farmers grow them for both eating and to export, and people across the region enjoy them in their daily diet. Street vendors offer roasted peanuts everywhere, and Sudanese cooks add peanut-paste to meat dishes, stews, and more. Peanut-paste is also the base of the sweet-tart dressing in this refreshing salad, which is commonly served alongside Sudanese favorites like spiced goat and the cracker-thin bread called kisra.

INGREDIENTS

⅓ cup peanuts, freshly ground
    (or 3 tablespoons peanut
    butter)
2 tablespoons sesame oil
    (or peanut or olive oil)
1 lime, juiced
1 teaspoon salt
1 teaspoon sugar
pinch ground cloves
pinch ground curry leaves
¼ teaspoon ground coriander
1 clove garlic, minced
4 to 5 medium tomatoes, diced
1 medium cucumber, diced
a small red onion, diced, or
    4 scallions, minced
1 sweet pepper, seeded and
    diced
small handful cilantro, chopped

1. In a medium bowl, combine the ground peanuts or peanut butter, oil, lime juice, salt, sugar, spices, and garlic. Add ¼ cup of water and whisk gently into a smooth paste. If the paste is too thick to dress a salad, add more water, 1 tablespoon at a time, until thin enough. Taste and adjust seasonings.

2. Add the chopped vegetables to the bowl and toss gently to dress. Serve the salad garnished with the fresh cilantro.

If you enjoy a little heat, try adding a small minced chili pepper to the dressing.

TANZANIA

This East African country is home to Africa's tallest mountain (Kilimanjaro), the world's second-largest freshwater lake (Lake Victoria) as well as the world's second-deepest freshwater lake (Lake Tanganyika). Tanzania is also home to the fertile island of Zanzibar, where the tropical climate and rich soil are perfect for growing prized spices! Combining African, Arab, Indian, and European traditions, and drawing upon a spectacular selection of fresh seafood, Tanzanian menus offer a tantalizing range of seafood-coconut stews, grilled goat, flavorful chutneys, healthful greens, sweet doughnuts, and dizzyingly diverse bananas.

MEAT OF THE MATTER

Meat here is highly prized. Beef, chicken, and pork (except in Muslim areas) are on the menu, but goat is the favorite. Meats may be cooked over charcoal fires and served with chapati (Indian flatbread). Barbecued nyama choma, typically made with goat, is roasted slowly over hot coals and served in restaurants or sold on the street.

THE SPICE TRADE

The Island of Zanzibar here grows nearly every spice you can think of, like nutmeg, cinnamon, cardamom, turmeric, ginger root, vanilla pods, licorice, ylang-ylang, lemongrass, and a rainbow of brilliantly colored (and flavored) peppers. Many people from India settled in East Africa, and today Tanzanian recipes incorporate Indian spices too—few home kitchens here are without mchuzi (curry powder).

THE MAASAI

The Maasai people raise cattle and goats, roaming where the flock can find good grazing land. Maasai enjoy a diet of goat meat, milk, and the blood of the cattle they raise.

FLUSH WITH FISH

With its amazing coastline and huge lakes, Tanzania sparkles with fresh fish. Open-air stalls sell shrimp, squid, tilapia, catfish, and octopus that has been grilled whole or skewered into kebabs. Many fish dishes here are rich with coconut milk—thanks both to the Asian influence and to the many coconut trees!

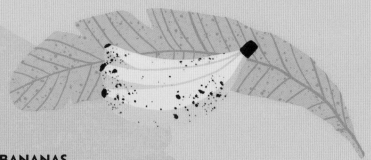

BANANAS

Tanzanian farmers grow over twenty varieties of bananas. The little ndizi kisukari is so sweet, it's named for the Swahili word for "sugar." The nkonjwa variety with its thick peel and bigger fruits is often roasted over a low flame. And the mbire banana is used to make banana beer! Bananas also feature in many traditional dishes, including supu viazi.

CAMEL HUMP

Ever wonder why camels have humps? Mostly fat, a camel hump is sort of a fuel tank that helps the animal sustain itself for up to two weeks by using up this stored fat as energy. Young camel hump meat is also considered a delicacy in Tanzania, especially on the island of Zanzibar.

CLOVES

Tanzania clove—karafuu in Swahili—comes from the plant's flowers. The spice isn't just an ingredient—Tanzanians also have a tradition of offering cloves to dinner guests and chewing cloves before a meal to aid digestion.

BAOBAB

The beautiful, fat-trunked baobab tree, which is found in Tarangire National Park, is known as the tree of life. Tanzanians enjoy the tree's papaya-shaped, coconut-sized fruits, which are called monkey bread, as well as the leaves, which can taste similar to spinach.

SUPU VIAZI

This traditional Tanzanian coconut-potato soup starts with a base of peppers, onions, and tomatoes, an essential flavor trio across the region. Next, cooks add potatoes, coconuts, and green banana, yielding a lusciously thick and velvety soup. And to make it even creamier, locals top it with sliced avocado.

NDIZI KANGA

FRIED PLANTAINS

PREPARATION TIME	COOKING TIME	LEVEL OF DIFFICULTY	SERVES
10 mins	15 mins	●	4

People across Africa have been growing and eating bananas for many centuries. Some varieties, like plantain, are best cooked. Eating it raw would be similar to trying to eat a raw potato! Here in Tanzania, plantains are so popular that people enjoy millions of tons of them each year. They're simmered into stews, cooked in coconut, braised with beef, fried into crisp cakes, or even brewed into beer. But perhaps they're most famous as this simple snack. If you haven't cooked plantains before, here's a great way to try them. Use plantains that are yellow but firm.

INGREDIENTS

2 yellow plantains
4 tablespoons unsalted butter
salt

1. Peel the plantains and cut them into slices that are about ½ inch thick.

2. Line a plate with paper towels.

3. In a large nonstick skillet, melt the butter over medium heat. Add the plantains in a single layer (you might need to do this in batches) and cook until nicely golden on the bottom, about 3 minutes. Flip each slice over and cook until golden on the bottom, 2 to 3 minutes longer.

4. Transfer the cooked plantains to the paper-towel-lined plate to drain, and season with salt to taste. Enjoy warm.

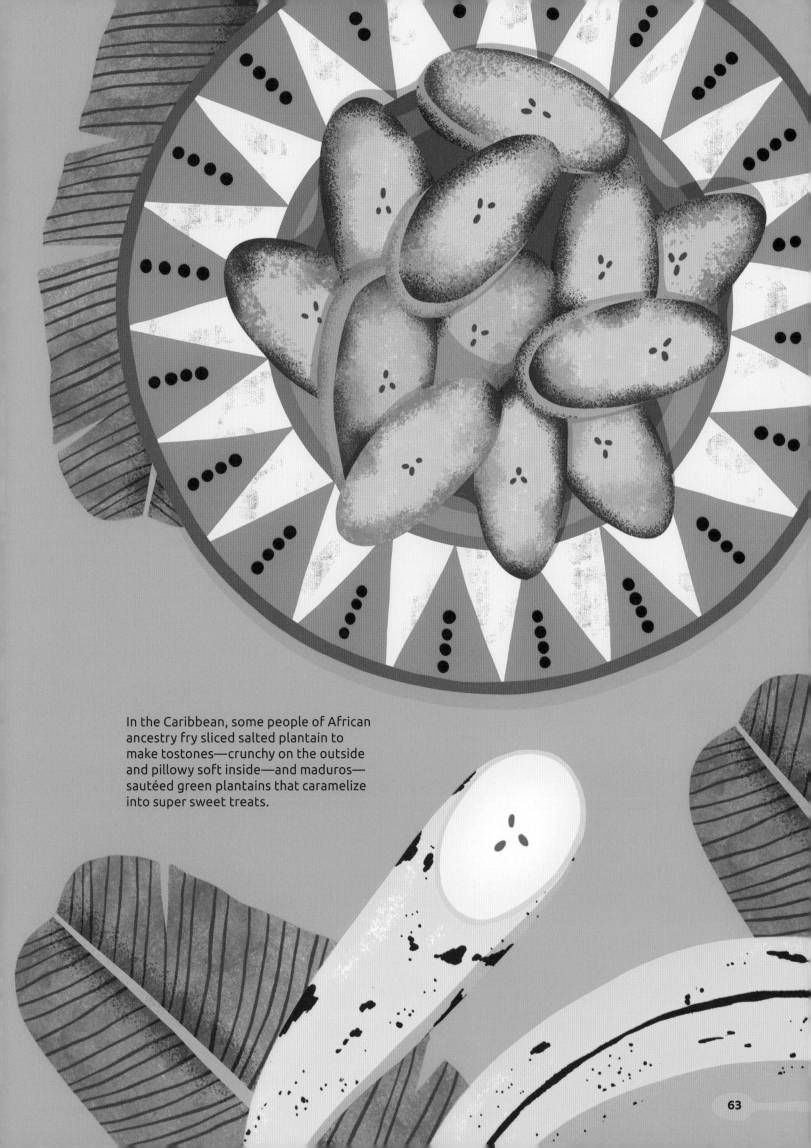

In the Caribbean, some people of African ancestry fry sliced salted plantain to make tostones—crunchy on the outside and pillowy soft inside—and maduros—sautéed green plantains that caramelize into super sweet treats.

FRUIT
AROUND THE WORLD

Fruit has beckoned us since our days as hunter-gatherers. Ancient civilizations in such places as Egypt and India tended orchards of luscious fruits like dates, figs, and pomegranates, celebrated by sacred ceremonies and heartfelt poems. Even today, when we can choose from endless processed and packaged sweets, there's still nothing as magical as spring's first strawberries, a perfectly juicy summer mango, or the ripe crunch of apples in fall.

PAPAYA

The fruit of a giant herb native to Central America, papaya has soft, sweet, orange flesh when ripe, with glistening black seeds at its center. Eat it fresh with a spoon or pick it green and shred it into Thailand's famous som tum salad, dressed with chilies, peanuts, fish sauce, and lime juice!

COCONUT

Native to Oceania, coconuts have ridden waves to distant shores, planting themselves as palm trees on tropical beaches worldwide, from the Philippines to Tanzania, Mozambique, and the Caribbean. Hack one open and you can drink its sweet juice, eat its gelatinous flesh with a spoon, or make coconut cream, oil, sugar, or vinegar. People even serve food in the shells!

PASSIONFRUIT

The passionfruit plant bears beautiful purple flowers and egg-sized fruit that wrinkles when ripe. The soft orange pulp is delicious straight or when made into jelly, juice, or ice cream. Brazilians make passionfruit mousse and cocktails, while Australians put passionfruit icing on cakes.

BANANA

Growing wild in Southeast Asia for a million years, bananas are now farmed in warm climates worldwide and beloved everywhere. There are countless varieties of sweet bananas, eaten raw or added to smoothies and muffins, while plantains are pounded into African fufu and fried into Caribbean tostones. In India, giant banana leaves are used as beautiful green platters.

PINEAPPLE

The pineapple is native to Brazil, where many types grow wild. Christopher Columbus was wowed by pineapple in Guadalupe, so he brought cuttings with him to Spain, and soon the fruit was growing in Asia, Africa, and beyond. Today, it's farmed from Hawaii to Malaysia, and while much ends up in cans, some people grill it, put it on pizza, or bake it into pineapple upside-down cake.

MANGO

Mangoes first grew wild in India and have been cultivated there for over 4,000 years. The "king of fruits" is now farmed as far away as Mexico, but India still grows the most mangoes in the world. Try mango in spicy mango chutney, sour mango pickles, sweet yogurt drinks called lassis, or simply enjoy its sweet flesh raw, sprinkled with lime and chili pepper.

POMEGRANATE

Native to Iran and Afghanistan, where they still grow wild, pomegranates were so beloved by ancient Egyptians and Greeks that they appear in their classic mythology. Pomegranates are eaten fresh, sprinkled over salads, pressed into juice, made into jelly, and simmered into a sweet grenadine syrup that's stirred into pink drinks.

FIGS

Each little fig is actually over a thousand tiny fruits, historically pollinated by a tiny insect called the fig wasp. First farmed in Egypt 6,000 years ago, figs were beloved by ancient Romans and today Italians still enjoy them in salads and on cheese plates. Fig skins may be yellow-green or blue-black with soft, sweet, pink-purple flesh.

LYCHEE

Native to China, lychees were so prized by imperial courts that they were transported from the south by special fast horses. During the Ming Dynasty, people met in temples and gardens to eat hundreds at a time; once you taste its aromatic white flesh, you'll see why. Now many markets carry them canned in sweet syrup, no fast horses needed.

GRAPES

Grapes have been celebrated since ancient times, appearing in Egyptian tomb paintings and the Bible. They are eaten fresh, dried into raisins, turned into wine, and made into what many in the U.S. would consider peanut butter's best friend, grape jelly!

SOURSOP

Native to the West Indies and South America, this tropical fruit with spiny, prickly skin grows on flowering evergreen trees. The soft, sweet pineapple-y pulp is refreshing in juice, ice cream, custards, and candies.

UGANDA

Uganda is a lush, landlocked East African country stretching from the shores of Lake Victoria, which is home to crocodiles and hippos, to the slopes of the Rwenzori Mountains, where gorillas famously roam. It is also home to over 47 million people. The land is extremely fertile and more than 70% of Ugandans work in farming. The most important crops are coffee, tea, and sugarcane.

MATOOKE

Matooke, a popular starch in Uganda, is made from green bananas that are peeled, tied into packages made of banana leaves, and steamed. The whole bundle is then squeezed and mashed until the contents are smooth. Matooke, sometimes cooked over a charcoal fire, is often served with a peanut sauce and may be paired with smoked fish or mushrooms.

FOOT STEW

Kigere, also known as mulokoni, is a stew made of cows' or pigs' hooves. When slow cooked, the hooves become gelatinous and release their marrow into the thickening broth. Recipes vary, but kigere commonly includes onions, garlic, peppers, carrots, tomatoes, potatoes, and coriander.

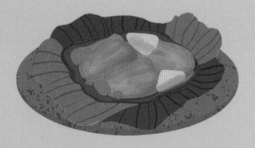

MEAT LOVERS

Ugandans enjoy a meaty diet with lots of beef, chicken, goat, and pork. Arguably the country's most famous dish is luwombo, said to have been created in 1887 by the personal chef of King Kabaka Mwanga. It's made with diced meat that's sautéed with onions, tomatoes, peanuts, and mushrooms, then wrapped in a banana leaf and steamed.

BANANA BONANZA

Ugandans have literally hundreds of ways to prepare bananas, including frying, stewing, roasting, broiling, and steaming. Green bananas are usually served as an accompaniment or ingredient in savory main dishes, whereas sweeter, ripe yellow ones are reserved for desserts. Gonja, or sweet plantains, are also very popular and are eaten ripe or unripe.

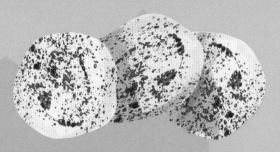

CHAPATI

Chapati—pan-fried, unleavened flatbreads—were introduced to the region by Indian laborers who came to East Africa to build a railroad from Kenya into Uganda. Although many Indian Ugandans were forced to leave during the 1970s, their influences on the country's food culture remain today.

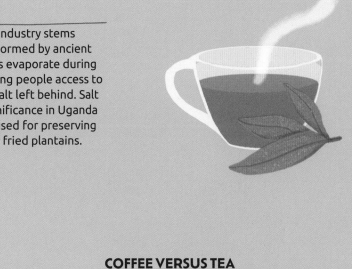

ROLEX

If someone in Uganda says they want a rolex they probably aren't referring to a watch but to a favorite food sold by roadside vendors around the country. Rolex is slang for "rolled egg," and these savory treats consist of a vegetable omelette rolled up in a chapati—creating a perfect on-the-go street breakfast, lunch, or snack.

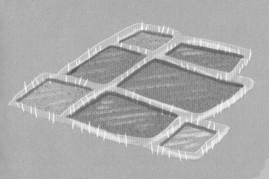

SALT MINING

Uganda's salt mining industry stems from its many lakes. Formed by ancient volcanoes, these lakes evaporate during the dry season, allowing people access to the delicious, crusty salt left behind. Salt has a rich cultural significance in Uganda and is added to rice, used for preserving fish, or sprinkled over fried plantains.

FRIED GRASSHOPPERS

Nsenene, or fried grasshoppers, are a popular rainy season snack. To prepare the grasshoppers, their feet and wings are pulled off before they're fried. According to some Ugandans, it tastes like crispy chicken skin. Some cooks add them to rolexes for extra crunch and flavor, or make them into burgers.

COFFEE VERSUS TEA

Uganda produces millions of bags of coffee for export each year, representing up to 19% of the country's foreign exchange. Yet Ugandans usually prefer tea—a legacy of British colonialism. Commercial tea cultivation began in the 1920s, and Uganda is now the second-largest tea producer in Africa, after Kenya. Ugandans take their tea "cooked and spiced," short for adding milk, sugar, and ginger.

MANDAZI

BAKED DOUGHNUTS WITH CARDAMOM AND POWDERED SUGAR

PREPARATION TIME
45 mins

COOKING TIME
20 mins

LEVEL OF DIFFICULTY
● ●

MAKES
About 16
doughnuts

These not-too-sweet doughnuts are beloved across East Africa, especially in Uganda, Tanzania, and Kenya. They can be enjoyed with a cup of spicy-sweet chai at breakfast, as a snack at teatime, or served with dinner to sop up the savory sauce of pigeon peas simmered in coconut milk. While mandazi dough is often yeasted and deep-fried, in this super simple version it's leavened with baking powder and then simply baked in the oven, rather than boiled in oil. For extra sweetness, dust the finished mandazi with powdered sugar.

INGREDIENTS

3 cups all-purpose flour
½ cup sugar
1 teaspoon baking powder
1 teaspoon ground cardamom
½ teaspoon salt
½ cup whole milk or coconut milk
4 tablespoons unsalted butter,
    melted and cooled
2 large eggs
¼ cup powdered sugar, for
    dusting (optional)

1. In a large mixing bowl, whisk together the flour, sugar, baking powder, cardamom, and salt.

2. In a separate bowl, whisk together the milk, melted butter, and eggs.

3. Gradually pour the wet ingredients into the dry ingredients, stirring until a sticky dough forms. Turn the dough out onto a floured surface and knead until it becomes smooth and elastic, about 5 minutes. Cover with a tea towel and let it rest for 30 minutes.

4. Preheat your oven to 350°F and line two baking sheets with parchment paper.

5. Roll out the dough into a rectangle so it's about ¼-inch thick and, using a sharp knife or pizza cutter, slice it into eight rectangles, then cut each rectangle in half on the diagonal to form triangles.

6. Transfer the triangles to the prepared baking sheets and bake for 18 to 20 minutes, or until the mandazi are lightly golden and cooked through.

7. Let the mandazi cool for a few minutes, then dust them with powdered sugar, if using.

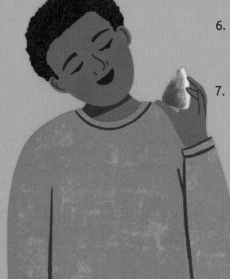

Don't skip the cardamom, which perfumes mandazi with its unmistakable aroma.

ASIA

Asia is the largest, most populous continent, stretching from the Mediterranean Sea to the Pacific Ocean and from snowy Siberia to Indonesia's tropical islands. Asia boasts the world's largest freshwater lake (the Caspian Sea) and the world's highest mountain (Mount Everest). Forests shelter Siberian tigers, Indian elephants, and Sumatran orangutans, while sea turtles swim in Malaysian coral reefs. Asia includes the two most populous countries—India and China. Here you'll find past and future; cities like Tokyo and Beijing are home to both ancient temples and modern skyscrapers.

While Asia's 4.5 billion residents enjoy diverse cuisines, some ingredients cross cultures. Tea goes back thousands of years, and today you can sip Thai iced tea or Indian spiced chai, attend a Japanese tea ceremony, and eat a Burmese tea-leaf salad. Noodles were invented here, and now include ramen, udon, soba, jap chae, laska, and lo mein just to name a few. Asian chefs have perfected dumplings, like Chinese wontons, Nepalese momo, Japanese gyoza, Korean mandu, and Filipino siomai. And rice is a nearly universal staple, often paired with soy that's been transformed into tofu, soy sauce, miso, or simply steamed into edamame.

AFGHANISTAN

This ancient land includes high mountains, vast deserts, great fertile green valleys and plains, and lots of winter snow. This diverse terrain grows diverse ingredients, from grapes and mulberries to sour oranges. Along a major crossroads on the ancient Silk Road (a network of trade routes that linked countries across Europe and Asia), Afghanistan was a place for the exchange of ideas, ingredients, and recipes. Despite conflicts that have led to hardship, many families here still prepare traditional elaborate nightly dinners, with home-baked bread, rich cheese, unctuous lamb, steaming tea, and sweet cakes.

LAMB

Afghans love to eat lamb, often from special sheep with extra-fat tails! The flavorful tail fat is made into roghan-e-dumbah, used for traditional Afghan cooking.

RICE

This essential daily staple is often cooked with meat and stock into a delicious dish called pulao. For weddings and other special feasts, Afghans make special kabuli pulao—rice studded with lamb, carrots, raisins, and almonds.

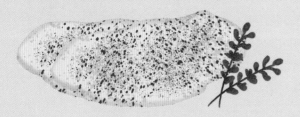

NAAN

This flatbread is often used to scoop up food or soak up yummy juices. Many Afghans bake theirs in a clay tandoor built into the ground at home—or you can take your homemade dough to be baked in a tandoor at a local bakery. For breakfast, naan is often topped with butter, yogurt, honey, or jam.

KORMAS

These traditional Afghan curries are made of braised meats or vegetables in a flavorful base of fried onions, tomatoes, and turmeric. Kormas are served with rice and bread, and with mast—a homemade yogurt sauce with lemon, salt, and mint, or salata—a refreshing salad of diced tomatoes, cucumbers, onions, lemon juice, and mint.

TEA

Friends and family love to visit for teatime, when hosts steep loose green or black tea with flavorful cardamom pods. Afghans also love to meet for tea at cafés called samovar or chikhana, some of which serve a dish called teapot soup, made of lamb, onions, split peas, and fresh cilantro, simmered in a teapot!

MANTU

These traditional dumplings require lots of handwork—cooking the onions and beef, sealing the filling into little pieces of dough, and then steaming—so they are best made by groups of people to share the work. The results are an Afghan favorite.

DAIRY

Afghanistan is home to diverse dairy, especially in the mountains, where herders enjoy milk from cows, water buffalo, sheep, and goats, and make it into maska (butter), panir (cheese), and mast (yogurt). Afghans rarely drink milk but do enjoy dogh, a refreshing drink of yogurt with water and mint.

SAMANAK

Nowruz, the Persian New Year, celebrates the start of spring, with festivals, picnics, and a special treat called samanak. To make it, people carefully sprout wheat, grind the young green shoots with water and walnuts, and cook it over an outdoor fire into a sweet pudding!

ROSE WATER

Roses grow all over Afghanistan, and many people make the fragrant flowers into aromatic rose water, used to perfume Afghan desserts.

SWEETS

Favorite desserts, especially to end Ramadan fasting, include jalebi, a sweet-syrupy-crunchy cake served in swirls; faluda, thin noodles, with ice, custard, rose water, and pistachios; roht, a cardamom-kissed yeasted cake; and gosh-e-feel, crisp pastries, whose name means "elephant ears"—which they resemble!

PLOV

SAVORY RICE PULAO WITH LAMB AND SPICES

PREPARATION TIME
20 mins

COOKING TIME
45 mins

LEVEL OF DIFFICULTY
● ●

SERVES
4 to 6

Descriptions of this delicious dish go back to tenth-century Arabic cookbooks written in Baghdad and Syria. Today, plov—and its cousins pilaf and pulao—are enjoyed in endless combinations of rice simmered in aromatic liquid with meats, spices, vegetables, and often fruits and nuts. Persian pilafs may include sour cherries or pomegranate, while Turkish cooks may add almonds and currants. In Central Asia, plov is cooked in a cauldronlike pot called a qazan, slow-simmered until fluffy and flavorful. In Afghanistan, where plov is the beloved national dish, it's often served outside in summer with sour pickles and platters of cabbage, carrot, eggplant, and beet salads.

INGREDIENTS

1½ cups basmati or other long-
grain white rice
4 tablespoons canola or
vegetable oil
2½ teaspoons salt
1½ pounds boneless leg of lamb
meat (or substitute an equal
weight of goat or chicken
meat), cut into bite-sized
pieces
1 small or ½ large onion,
chopped
3 medium carrots, grated
1 tablespoon ground cumin
2 teaspoons ground coriander
pepper, to season
2 cups chicken stock or water
1 head garlic, halved through the
middle crosswise
3 bay leaves

1. Put the rice in a fine mesh sieve and rinse it well while moving it around with your hands until the water goes from chalky looking to a bit more clear. Tip the rice into a bowl, cover with water, and let soak for 30 minutes.

2. When you're ready to start cooking, drain the rice in the sieve and shake it dry.

3. In a large Dutch oven or other heavy saucepan with a tight-fitting lid, heat 2 tablespoons of the oil over medium-high heat. Season the lamb with 1 teaspoon salt. Add the lamb pieces in a single layer, taking care not to crowd the pan (you might need to do this in batches) and cook until nicely browned on the bottom, 3 to 4 minutes. Flip the meat and cook until browned on the other side, 3 to 4 minutes longer. Transfer the lamb to a plate.

4. Add the remaining 2 tablespoons of oil to the empty saucepan, then add the onion and carrots, and cook over medium heat until very soft and starting to brown, about 12 minutes. Add the cumin, coriander, ½ teaspoon salt, and a few grinds of pepper, and cook until fragrant, about 1 minute. Add the rice and stir to combine. Add the stock or water and the two halves of the head of garlic and the bay leaves and bring to a boil over medium-high heat.

5. Reduce the heat to medium-low, stir in the lamb with the rice, and cover with the lid. Cook until the rice is tender and absorbs the liquid, about 20 minutes. Turn off the heat and let stand for 5 minutes.

6. Uncover and fluff the rice. Season with more salt and pepper if necessary and serve hot.

People say that when President Nixon visited Uzbekistan in 1966, where this dish is also popular, he loved plov so much that he requested the recipe.

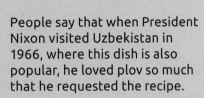

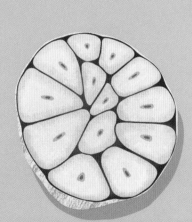

BANGLADESH

This lush country of mangroves and rivers is often described as a food-lover's paradise. It's also the eighth most populous nation in the world. The cuisine here stars abundant rice, luscious fruit, tangy dairy, rich nuts, and fresh fish from the rivers, canals, floodplains, ponds, and lakes, as well as the Bay of Bengal. Aromatic spices are essential, and some recipes still show a centuries-old love of cream, cardamom, cloves, and cinnamon.

RICE AND FISH

The rivers here produce abundant fish and rice, two foundations of the daily diet. Rice is served alongside all sorts of fish and meat curries, dahl (soupy lentils), bhorta (mashed veggies), and bhaji (sautéed vegetables). Bangladesh's favorite fish is a deliciously oily, bony type called hilsa.

DAILY DAIRY

Bangladesh diets are rich with dairy. Many rural women raise goats, whose milk is made into ever-popular goat yogurt and churned into goat butter. Cow's milk, on the other hand, is usually reserved for making sweets.

FANTASTIC FRUIT

The Bangladeshi climate is perfect for farming tropical fruits like mangoes, jackfruit, pineapple, lychees, guava, papaya, coconuts, tamarind, and palmyras, a coconut cousin whose fruits are harvested when they're young and gelatinous. Many other delicious fruits grow wild in the jungle, including latkan, durian, rattan, and the wild date palm.

BREAKFAST

Bangladeshi breakfast is often a bowl of cheera: flattened rice, sweetened with sugar, and served with fruits and yogurt. Rural people often start the day with panta bhat, boiled rice soaked overnight so it starts to ferment, which is then mixed with salt and chilies.

GRILLED CHICKEN

As sunset approaches in Bangladesh, across the country the street vendors come out, selling savory pastries, kebabs, and salty snacks. But don't miss the chicken, which is marinated in spices and then grilled, creating a tasty evening snack that has a spicy crunch on the outside and super moist on the inside.

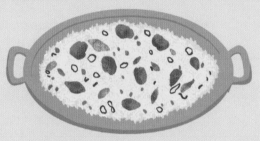

BIRYANI

Biryani is a popular dish usually consisting of rice mixed with meat, vegetables, and spices. One type, kachchi biryani, is strongly connected to Bangladeshi festive occasions and family gatherings. A version of this dish sees raw meat and vegetables layered with the rice, then the dish is sealed with dough, forming an edible lid that traps steam, tenderizing the meat and vegetables inside while cooking.

THE NATIONAL COMFORT DISH

Patla khichuri is a soupy mix of rice, lentils, vegetables, and potatoes flavored with green and red chili, ginger, garlic paste, turmeric, cumin, garam masala, mustard oil, and sugar. It's a cozy comfort food during the rainy monsoon season.

FUCHKA

These crunchy-yet-soupy snacks are the most popular street food in Bangladesh. Mashed potatoes are mixed with spices and lime juice, then the mixture is spooned into thin, hollowed-out shells of puffed rice. Fuchka is finished with a tangy tamarind sauce and a sprinkle of grated eggs.

BANGLADESHI DESSERTS

Sweets are one of the glories of Bangladeshi cuisine, and they're often given as gifts. A thick, sugary yogurt called mishti doi is a treat after lunch or dinner, sometimes mixed with rice, bananas, and other fruit to create doi chira. A richer after-dinner option is rasmalai: soft cheese balls simmered in cardamom-flavored milk.

POTATOES

Here potatoes may be mashed with mustard oil and fried chilies or roasted with spices like cumin, turmeric, mustard seed, and ginger. Spiced mashed potatoes are wrapped around a hard-boiled egg and deep-fried into aloo chops, potato croquettes served at teatime.

SHONDESH

SWEET PRESSED CURD WITH ROSE WATER AND CARDAMOM

PREPARATION TIME
1 hr 30 mins

COOKING TIME
20 mins

LEVEL OF DIFFICULTY
● ● ●

MAKES
About 12

This confection—sweetened, pressed curd cooked into a wonderfully plush, fudgelike consistency—is one of the finest sweets in India and Bangladesh. There are countless types, flavored with everything from almond extract and saffron to mango, topped with pistachios (as here), almonds, or dried fruit. This version calls for rose water, which was first made by the ancient Egyptians, Greeks, and Romans. The aromatic elixir is still beloved across the Indian subcontinent and Middle East, perfuming recipes from halva and baklava to lassi and Turkish delight.

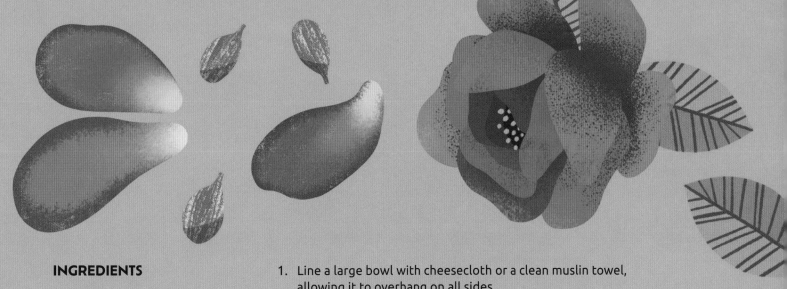

INGREDIENTS

4 cups whole milk
2 tablespoons lemon juice or
    white vinegar
½ cup confectioner's sugar
½ teaspoon cardamom
½ teaspoon rose water
shelled pistachios, for topping

You can also make this dish with premade paneer, but it's fun to make your own from scratch. If you prefer to use premade paneers, start at step 4.

1. Line a large bowl with cheesecloth or a clean muslin towel, allowing it to overhang on all sides.

2. In a medium pot over medium-high heat, bring the milk just to a simmer. Reduce the heat to medium-low and add the lemon juice or white vinegar and stir. After a few minutes, when the milk looks curdled, carefully pour it into the bowl with the cheesecloth. Let cool.

3. When it's cool enough to handle, gather the cheesecloth or muslin and twist it from the top so you can strain out the whey (liquid) from the curds (called the chenna). Squeeze to release as much liquid as you can. While holding the curds in the cloth, run them under cold water to remove any flavor from the lemon or vinegar, then squeeze out any excess moisture again. Set the wrapped chenna in a colander in the sink and place an unopened can of beans or something similarly heavy on top to weigh it down. Let drain for 30 minutes.

4. Unwrap and transfer the chenna to a clean bowl and lightly knead it for several minutes until it becomes smooth, like dough. Add the sugar, cardamom, and rose water, and knead them in until evenly incorporated. (If you have a stand mixer, you can knead in its bowl, fitted with a dough hook.)

5. Heat a nonstick cast-iron skillet over medium-low heat. Add the chenna and cook, stirring occasionally, until it looks soft and cohesive, but no longer liquid, 8 to 10 minutes. Remove from the heat, and let the mixture cool to room temperature.

6. Form the mixture into slightly flattened balls that are about the size of your palm and transfer to a plate. Press a pistachio in the center of each sandesh. Serve right away or cover and refrigerate for up to 3 days.

Shondesh can also be made in a tray and cut into squares. Some confectioners press it into wooden molds to create pretty shapes.

CHINA

China's civilization formed over 4,000 years ago, making it one of the oldest cultures in the world. The world's oldest known cookbook, *The Yinshan Zhengyao*, was written there in the tenth century. Today, China is home to more than 1.4 billion people, more than 90% of whom identify as Han—the world's largest ethnic group—while the rest are divided among about fifty-five other ethnic groups. China's landscapes include mountain ranges, rivers, deserts, forests, and seas. China's size has resulted in cultural diversity, with at least eight unique culinary styles, including Sichuan, Cantonese, and Hunan cuisine.

TEA

Around 2737 BCE, Shen Nong, the first emperor of China, discovered that he preferred the taste of water when herbs or leaves were added. Today, it is a daily drink for just about everyone, day and night.

RICE

People have been farming rice here for more than 10,000 years. Today, China is both the world's largest consumer and producer of the grain—a daily staple for two-thirds of the population—which is used to make everything from rice noodles to rice wine. Rice is so fundamental that when greeting someone, instead of asking how they're doing, you ask, "Have you eaten your rice today?"

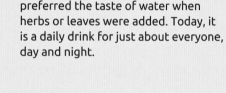

CHOPSTICKS

Invented in China over 2,000 years ago, chopsticks are still used for everything from dipping dumplings to slurping noodles. (Just please don't point your chopsticks at anyone—that is considered rude!)

PEKING DUCK

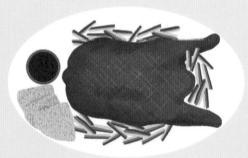

This elegant dish originated in Beijing's Imperial court over 500 years ago and has changed little since then. The duck is roasted for hours and served tableside, along with the crackly-crispy glazed skin.

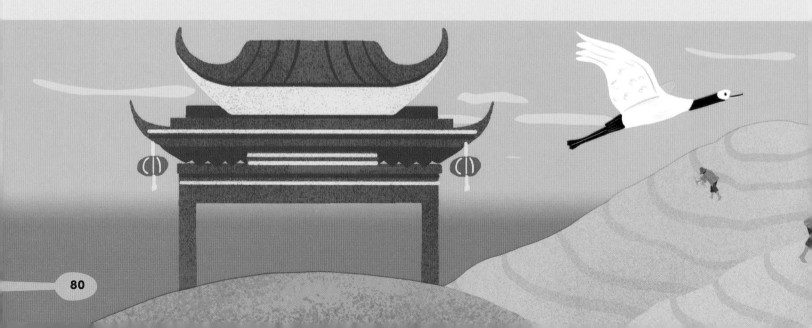

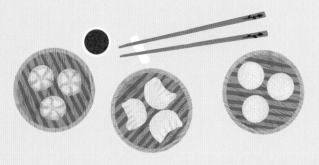

YUM CHA AND DIM SUM

The Cantonese brunch tradition of *yum cha*—"drink tea"—is closely linked to *dim sum*, or "touch the heart" foods. Dim sum includes delicious bite-sized snacks that number in the thousands. Diners order from servers who wheel carts laden with stacks of bamboo baskets from table to table.

HOT POT

This tradition is just what it sounds like! A flavorful stock simmers at the table in a large metal pot, and diners add helpings of meat, fish, shellfish, vegetables, noodles, sauces, herbs, and other aromatics to the bubbling broth. The hot pot is now popular in Japan, South Korea, and Vietnam.

SNACKS GALORE

Chinese cuisine includes a famous snacking culture and lots of nibbling between meals. Street-food stalls called *xiaochi*, sometimes also known as *xiaoye*, or "midnight snack," are open day and night and usually specialize in just a few or even one food.

LUNAR NEW YEAR

An important holiday in many parts of Asia and in China especially, Lunar New Year is a springtime celebration that marks the beginning of a new year on the lunar-solar calendar. Throughout the sixteen-day festival, people feast on traditional foods with symbolic importance. Fish represents prosperity; dumplings and spring rolls signify wealth; sweet rice is thought to bring family harmony; and longevity noodles embody a wish for long life.

SICHUAN PEPPER

Have you ever eaten a Chinese dish that made your entire mouth tingle? That sensation was likely thanks to Sichuan pepper, a spice that, despite its name, is more closely related to citrus than it is to chili peppers or black pepper. Chinese people refer to the special tingly-mouth feeling it produces as *mala*, or "numb-spiciness."

DUMPLINGS

PORK AND CHIVE DUMPLINGS

PREPARATION TIME	COOKING TIME	LEVEL OF DIFFICULTY	MAKES
1 hr	10 mins	●●●	35 to 50 dumplings

These adorable dumplings are sometimes filled with both shrimp and pork, but this delicious version is pure pork. To encase the pork, there are two main types of dumpling wrappers: Shanghai style, which are thin and white, and Hong Kong style, which are even thinner and yellow because of the use of eggs. Shanghai wrappers are more common, but you can use either style here. This recipe includes two methods—you can either steam the dumplings in batches in a bamboo steamer or boil them in a pot all at once. Try both ways and see which you like best!

INGREDIENTS

8 ounces fatty ground pork

4 ounces Chinese chives or
    scallions, thinly sliced

2 inches ginger, peeled and finely
    grated

2 garlic cloves, minced

1 tablespoon toasted sesame oil

1 tablespoon soy sauce

1 tablespoon Shaoxing wine

2 teaspoons sugar

½ teaspoon salt

½ teaspoon vegetable oil

1 package dumpling wrappers

1. In a chilled metal bowl, combine the ground pork, chives, ginger, garlic, sesame oil, soy sauce, Shaoxing wine, sugar, and salt. Use a sturdy spoon to vigorously mix until it forms a paste.

2. It's best to cook a small amount so that you can test a mouthful of the filling and adjust the flavors as needed. To do this, heat ½ teaspoon of oil in a skillet over medium-high heat. Add a small spoonful and cook, turning, until cooked through. Taste the cooked filling and add more salt or seasonings to the raw filling, if necessary.

3. Remove one dumpling wrapper from the package. Keep the rest covered with a wet paper towel until you're ready to use. Have a small bowl of water nearby and line a baking sheet with parchment paper.

4. Dip your finger in the water and moisten the edges of the wrapper. Put 1 teaspoon filling in the center of the wrapper. Fold the wrapper in half over the filling to form a rectangle and press the edges to seal. Bring the lower corners of the rectangle (the side with the filling) together and pinch to make the traditional curved dumpling shape. Use a little water if you need to help them stick. Arrange the dumplings on the prepared baking sheet.

5. To steam the dumplings: fill a wok or deep skillet with an inch or so of water. Line a bamboo steamer with a liner or round of parchment paper. Bring the water to a boil over high heat. When you see steam coming from under the basket, use tongs to place the dumplings in a single layer in the basket. (You will need to do this in batches.) Cover and steam until cooked through, about 7 minutes. Use tongs to transfer the cooked dumplings to a plate and cook the remaining dumplings.

6. Alternatively, you can boil the dumplings: bring a large pot of water to a boil. Add the dumplings and stir once or twice to help prevent them from sticking. When the dumplings float to the surface, cook them for 1 minute longer. Use a slotted spoon to transfer them to a plate.

To serve, you can float your dumplings in good-quality chicken broth or toss them with a little chili oil or chili crisp.

DUMPLINGS

AROUND THE WORLD

What's better than eating pasta or bread with a delicious topping? Eating pasta or bread with a delicious filling! Cooks love to enclose yummy bite-sized morsels inside little pieces of dough. Whatever you call them, these filled dumplings are usually simmered or steamed, sometimes served in soups. People love to bite into them and find a sweet or savory surprise inside! Some historians say the first dumplings were made in China at least 1,800 years ago, during the Han Dynasty, while Italians have been stuffing ravioli for nearly a millennium. Today, there are hundreds of types of dumplings worldwide, but they're especially popular across Asia and Europe, where just about every country has its own favorite dumpling, especially in colder climates.

SOUSKLUITJIES

Meaning "sauce dumplings" in Afrikaans, these South African sticky dessert dumplings have a light and fluffy texture and are served soaked in custard or sweet cinnamon syrup.

SAMOSAS

These hand-held savory Indian pastries often have a pyramid shape and a crisp crust. They may be filled with anything from green peas and spiced potatoes to cheese and minced meat. A popular snack, they're often sold from street vendors and served with sweet-tart chutneys.

MANTOU

This diverse family of dumplings are found from Turkey to China. Variations in some parts of Asia are called manti and stuffed with ground lamb, spiced with sumac, red pepper, and dried mint, and served slathered with yogurt, garlic, or melted butter. In Central Asia, manti may be stuffed with meat, onions, diced winter squash, mashed potato, mung beans, radish, sugar, and sheep fat—served with yogurt and vinegar.

RAVIOLI

The earliest record of Italy's famous filled pastas is found way back in the fourteenth century, when people wrote letters describing them as stuffed with pork, eggs, cheese, and parsley. Today, they're popular around the world, and may be stuffed with seafood, wild boar, chanterelle mushrooms—or those same great fillings from the 1300s!

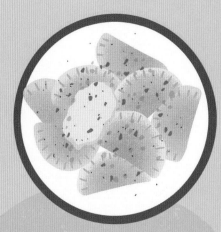

MANDU

Korean mandu are little beef-filled dumplings served floating in a soup—this recipe, called mandu-guk, is one of the most popular in all of Korean cuisine.

PIEROGIES

Polish and Ukrainian pierogies are doughy half-moons often filled with potato, cheese, or ground meat, served with a pat of butter and fried onions or a dollop of sour cream. These dumplings are so beloved, many Polish families serve them at Christmas Eve dinner.

MOMO

Tibetan momo are meat-filled dumplings, related to mantou and often served at formal meals and celebrations. To tell someone to be quiet, Tibetans say "*Kha momo nangshin dhe*," which means "keep your mouth like a momo"—because momo dumplings are sealed shut!

ONDE ONDE

This Indonesian sweet dumpling (also known as klepon) is a sticky, bite-sized cake made from glutinous rice flour, filled with palm sugar, boiled until the filling melts, then rolled in grated coconut. It's popular in Java and often served on banana leaves!

EMPANADAS

With a name that literally means "wrapped in bread," empanadas are crisp, folded pastries stuffed with fillings from beef to fruit. Descended from a Spanish recipe for pepper, onion, and meat pie, brought west by sailing conquistadors, the dish took root and is now popular across Latin America, from Mexico to Argentina.

KNÖDEL

Knödel are a family of dumplings made across East and Central Europe, including Austria, Hungary, Romania, Bosnia, Croatia, Slovenia, and the Czechia. Sometimes filled with meat or potatoes, they're also often popular filled with fruit. Some variations, like the German Zwetschgenknödel dumplings, may each contain a whole plum or apricot.

INDIA

India's landscapes include deserts, lush forests, tropical beaches, and the soaring Himalaya mountains. The seventh largest country by area, it is also home to a huge population and has recently overtaken China as the world's most populous country. Its more than 1.4 billion people speak over one hundred different major languages and belong to more than 700 ethnic groups. Not surprisingly, all this natural and cultural variety has resulted in some of the world's most famous cuisines.

SPICES

Indian cuisine boasts spectacular spices, including coriander, cumin, pepper, fenugreek, cardamom, cinnamon, and turmeric. Traditionally, Indian cooks freshly prepare their spices for cooking by roasting the whole seeds, bark, or roots and then grinding them into a powder. Spices add flavor to everything from rice dishes, roast meats, and sauces to drinks and desserts.

VEGETARIANISM

India is one of the best places in the world to be vegetarian or vegan. This is thanks in part to the ancient philosophy of ahimsa, or nonviolence, which means causing no harm to other living beings, including animals. Today, up to 39% of India's population is vegetarian, and the country is home to several distinctive vegetable-based cuisines.

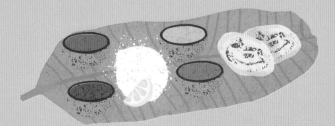

CEREAL STAPLES

Cereals star in most Indian meals. Indians use wheat to make breads such as naan, which is pillowy like a pita, and roti, which is flat like a tortilla. For serving, rice or bread is often placed at the center of a platter or large banana leaf. This arrangement of small containers is often called a *thali*.

KARI VERSUS CURRY

Kari is a Tamil word that means "spiced sauce." When the Portuguese and British colonized India, they misunderstood this word to be "curry." They also began wrongly referring to all kinds of Indian dishes—from saucy ones to dry-spiced ones—as curries. Today, the giant, generic label "curry" is applied to dishes with spiced sauces all over the world.

PANEER

Paneer is India's favorite cheese. It's made from fresh buffalo or cow's milk that's been curdled into a soft block, usually by adding lemon juice. Mild and very versatile, it can be paired with spinach or potatoes in different karis, rubbed with spices and grilled, or just eaten on its own.

CHATNI

Chatni are tangy, spicy, flavorful relishes served as side dishes to brighten up milder foods like rice, dal, or crispy papadums (a waferlike flatbread). These relishes may feature a paste of anything from mango to tomato and be seasoned with lots of ground spices and herbs like ginger, mint, and coriander leaves, plus flavor boosters like tamarind, garlic, or coconut.

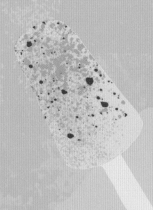

SWEETS

India has dazzlingly distinctive desserts, and people here love to give sweets as a sign of hospitality. Milk often serves as the basis of sweet treats here, including a special type of dense, creamy ice cream called kulfi that is traditionally flavored with rose, saffron, or pistachio. India also has lots of deep-fried desserts, including gulab jamun—little doughy dumplings soaked in sugar syrup.

DAL

In India, dal can refer to two things. It can be an ingredient, specifically a split pulse like beans, peas, lentils, or chickpeas, and it can also be one of about sixty different dishes made from those pulses. Dal dishes are a delicious daily staple, ranging in color from golden yellow or bright orange to deep green or black. Many are simmered to a soupy consistency, while others are thick and hearty.

YOGURT

India's traditional yogurt, dahi, is made from cow, buffalo, or goat's milk. It is thought people started making yogurt in India as long ago as 6000 BCE, and for millennia, this was the only way to keep milk from quickly going bad. Lots of Indians continue to make their own yogurt today, and it's a key ingredient in many dals, karis, and smoothielike lassis that are seasoned with anything from mango or banana to salt.

MASOOR DAL

RED LENTIL STEW

PREPARATION TIME	COOKING TIME	LEVEL OF DIFFICULTY	SERVES
30 mins	25 mins	●	2 to 4

India is wonderfully, wildly diverse with many cultures and cuisines, but nearly everyone across the vast subcontinent enjoys this lentil dish—sometimes at every meal. Dal is often served with rice and roti, sometimes alone, and at feasts with dozens of other delicious dishes.

Millions of people in India cook dal daily, so there are countless versions. Some cooks add vegetables, from sweet potatoes to spinach to cauliflower, and spices may vary from kitchen to kitchen, ranging from curry leaves to black onion seeds. This version calls for red lentils, which cook in a snap, and it's aromatic with ginger, turmeric, lemon, and cilantro.

To draw out their full flavor, you can heat spices in oil. This is called "blooming."

INGREDIENTS

1 cup red lentils
1 teaspoon salt
1 small onion, roughly chopped
3 fat cloves garlic, peeled
2 inches of ginger, peeled and
    coarsely chopped
1 chili pepper, stem removed
    (optional)
2 tablespoons ghee or canola oil
1 teaspoon cumin seeds
1 tablespoon tomato paste
½ teaspoon turmeric
½ cup finely chopped cilantro
    or mint leaves, plus more for
    garnish
1 tablespoon lemon juice
cilantro, for garnish (optional)

1. In a sieve, rinse the lentils very well and run your fingers over them to make sure there are no little stones in the mix.

2. In a pan, combine the lentils with 4 cups water and ½ teaspoon salt and bring to a boil over high heat. Reduce the heat to medium-low and simmer until the lentils are tender, about 20 minutes.

3. While the lentils simmer, combine the onion, garlic, ginger, and chili pepper in a food processor and pulse until the ingredients are finely chopped. (If you don't have a food processor, you can also mince these ingredients with a knife or pound them into a paste in a mortar and pestle.)

4. In a small skillet, melt the ghee. Add the cumin seeds and bloom until they just start to darken, about 10 seconds, then add the onion mixture and ½ teaspoon salt. Cook, stirring frequently, until just starting to brown, about 4 minutes.

5. Add the tomato paste and turmeric to the onion mixture and cook until the tomato paste just starts to darken, about 1 minute. Stir in the cilantro.

6. Scrape the onion mixture into the lentils and continue to simmer, about 5 minutes. Stir in the lemon juice.

7. Ladle the dal into bowls and garnish with more cilantro, if desired.

INDONESIA

Bridging Southeast Asia and Oceania, Indonesia is the world's largest archipelagic nation (meaning it's made up of islands—over 17,500 in Indonesia's case)! Indonesia's more than 275 million citizens, spread over 6,000 of these islands, speak hundreds of languages and belong to over 1,100 ethnic groups. The wildlife is unique: over a third of local birds and mammals live nowhere else on Earth, and Indonesians enjoy 6,000 different spices! No wonder the country's motto is "Unity in Diversity"!

SACRED RICE

Indonesians eat rice with practically every meal. More than just a food, it's also a sacred symbol of prosperity and fertility. Special celebrations like weddings are usually held in rice-harvesting season and often include nasi tumpeng—a mountain of rice colored golden with turmeric. The most important person at the celebration has the honor of cutting off the top of the rice cone.

THE SPICE ISLANDS

Renaissance-era Europeans craved flavor but grew few spices. Around 1520, Portuguese traders began sailing to Indonesia to buy boatloads of prized spices that grew nowhere else on Earth: cloves, nutmeg, and mace. Soon the Portuguese, Spanish, and Dutch were fighting over control of the flavorful, valuable trade.

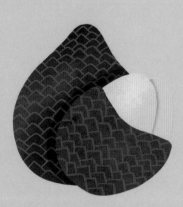

SALAK

This golf-ball-sized fruit is covered in shiny brown scales that look so reptilian, its nickname is "snakefruit." The scales peel off to reveal spongy flesh inside, which tastes a bit like a pineapple blended with lemony soap. The flavor can be surprisingly tart the first time you taste it.

SAMBAL

Indonesian dishes are often served with a side of sambal, a spicy condiment made from crushed chili peppers mixed with aromatic ingredients like shrimp paste, garlic, ginger, lime juice, or palm sugar. Other countries have adopted it, too, including Thailand, Sri Lanka, Brunei, Singapore, Suriname, and the Netherlands, creating their own versions.

COFFEE

Indonesia is so famous for its coffee that people around the world nickname the drink "Java," after one of Indonesia's largest islands. Kopi luwak is a local delicacy: coffee beans that have been eaten and then pooped out by an Asian civet cat. These beans have a smooth, less-bitter taste and sell for hundreds of dollars per pound!

RENDANG

One of Indonesia's most beloved national recipes, rendang is a creamy, complex, caramelized curry of beef that's slow-cooked in aromatics like lemongrass, galangal, ginger, coconut, and chilies, until the meat is tender. A dried, jerkeylike version can keep for months.

DURIAN

Known here as the "king of fruits," the durian's giant spikes hold famously smelly flesh. The fruit's perfume is sometimes compared to the aroma of sweaty gym clothes. For this reason, some airlines ban people from taking the fruit in carry-on luggage! But many Indonesians love it, and compare the fruit's taste to cheese, caramelized onions, or butterscotch pudding.

BANANA TREATS

Banana fritters called pisang goreng are a popular snack across Indonesia. People eat fried bananas for breakfast, sometimes with boiled rice and grated coconut, soursop juice, or avocado-chocolate smoothies.

CRISPY KRUPUK

Much of Indonesian cuisine combines salty and sweet with a crispy crunch. The most famous example is krupuk, a wafer that may be nibbled between bites of rice, dipped in gravy, or eaten straight. Krupuk's name is likely derived from the crunch when you eat it!

SPECTACULAR SEAFOOD

With so many islands and so much coastline, it's no surprise Indonesians enjoy spectacular seafood. On August 17, people celebrate Indonesian Independence Day with feasts of spicy salads, salt fish, and contests for who can eat the most shrimp chips.

GADO GADO

SAVORY SALAD WITH PEANUT DRESSING

PREPARATION TIME	**COOKING TIME**	**LEVEL OF DIFFICULTY**	**SERVES**
20 mins	45 mins	●●	4 to 6

Peanuts appear in many Indonesian dishes but the best-loved is gado gado. Literally "mix-mix," the term is often used to describe situations that are all mixed up—the big city Jakarta, for instance, is a gado-gado city. This dish is an Indonesian favorite and is essentially a vegetable salad bathed in the country's classic peanut sauce, with its sweet, nutty, slightly spicy flavors. Everyone here has their own version. Some stick to raw vegetables like cucumbers, carrots, or tomatoes; others add cooked tofu or tempeh, boiled potatoes, hard-boiled eggs, or pressed rice cakes.

Some season the sauce with lime leaves, shrimp paste, chili peppers, tamarind paste, or the sweet Indonesian soy sauce called kecap manis.

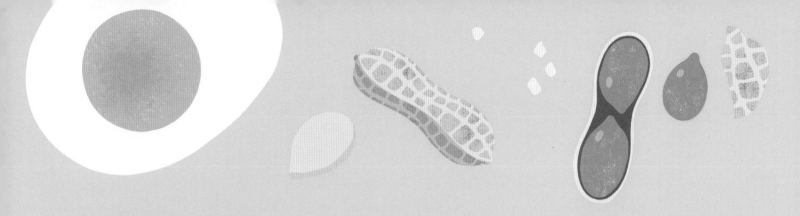

INGREDIENTS

FOR THE SAUCE

1 tablespoon sunflower or
    peanut oil
3 shallots, peeled and sliced
1 clove garlic, minced
¾ cup peanut butter
2 tablespoons Indonesian palm
    sugar (or coconut sugar or
    brown sugar)
3 tablespoons soy sauce
1 teaspoon chili-garlic sauce or
    sambal oelek (optional)

FOR THE GADO GADO

8 baby potatoes
8 ounces trimmed green beans
salt and black pepper, to taste
1 14-ounce package extra-firm
    tofu
1 tablespoon sunflower or
    peanut oil
4 hard-boiled eggs, halved

Many serve gado gado
with crunchy shrimp
crackers called krupuk
for extra crunch!

TO MAKE THE SAUCE

1. To make the sauce, heat the oil in a wok or large skillet over medium heat. Add the shallots and garlic and cook, stirring occasionally, about 2 minutes. Don't let them brown. Remove from the heat.

2. In a mini food processor or blender, combine the cooked shallot mixture with the peanut butter, sugar, soy sauce, chili-garlic sauce, and 2 tablespoons water, and purée until smooth. Taste and add more chili-garlic sauce if you'd like a spicier sauce! Add a little more water, 1 tablespoon at a time, if you like a thinner consistency. Transfer to a bowl.

TO MAKE THE GADO GADO

3. In a medium pot, cover the potatoes with water and bring to a boil over high heat. Season the water generously with salt. Reduce the heat to medium and simmer the potatoes until tender, 15 to 20 minutes. During the last 3 minutes of boiling, add the green beans. Drain the potatoes and green beans and run them under cold water until cooled.

4. Meanwhile, drain the tofu of any liquid and cut it into eight slabs. Dry it well between layers of paper towels and season with salt and pepper. In the same wok or skillet you used for the shallot mixture, heat the oil over medium-high heat. Add the tofu slabs in a single layer and cook until well browned on the bottom, 3 to 5 minutes. Flip and cook until the other side is brown, 3 to 5 minutes longer. (If your pan is crowded, you can cook the tofu in two batches.) Transfer the cooked tofu to one part of a serving platter.

5. Arrange the potatoes, green beans, and hard-boiled eggs in separate piles on the platter.

6. Drizzle some of the peanut sauce on top and serve.

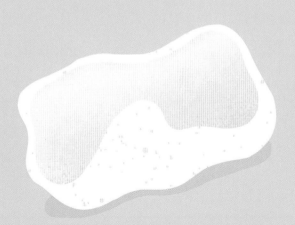

CHILI PEPPERS

AROUND THE WORLD

Columbus sailed across the Atlantic looking for a shortcut to pick up the spice called black pepper. Instead, he ran into Hispaniola and pocketed something spicy he thought might substitute for pepper: chili peppers. Spaniards started growing the hot little fruits and soon bred their own varieties like pimento and padrón. Portuguese ships then brought chilies to West Africa, the Middle East, India, and Southeast Asia, where they became essential and changed global food flavors forever.

CHILIES IN CHINA

Chilies arrived in China port cities in the late sixteenth century. Today, Chinese cuisine is unimaginable without their heat. In China, where red is a good-luck color, many people string up peppers for Lunar New Year, like little firecrackers. Chinese chili-infused oil is a super spicy condiment that can act like a firecracker in your mouth!

JALAPEÑOS AND CHIPOTLES

Fresh, green jalapeño peppers have an alter ego. They can be dried and smoked, emerging as wrinkled, browned chipotles, which are simmered into everything from chili con carne to barbecue sauce.

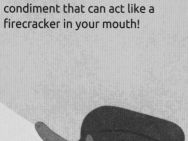

BELL PEPPER

Northern European cuisines don't have much heat. Italians instead bred sweet bell peppers, which range from yellow to dark purple. Bells can be snacked on crisp and raw, and are especially beloved roasted.

AJI AMARILLO

Literally meaning "yellow pepper," aji amarillo is the most important ingredient in Peruvian cuisine. This pepper is hot, but fruity. It adds its sweet heat to everything from papa a la huancaina (potatoes in spicy cheese) to fried yuca to ceviche (citrus-pickled fish).

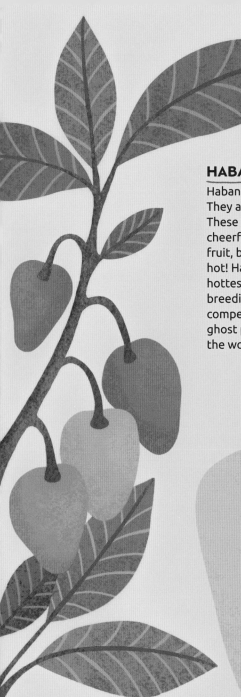

HABANERO PEPPER

Habanero literally means "from Havana." They are essential to Caribbean cuisine. These little, lantern-shaped peppers are a cheerful bright orange and smell like tropical fruit, but don't be fooled—they are very, very hot! Habaneros used to be regarded as the hottest chilies around. Then "chiliheads" made breeding and eating ever-spicier peppers a competitive sport. Today, India's crazy-hot ghost pepper, and the Carolina reaper, are the world's hottest peppers—for now.

HARISSA PASTE

This sweet, smoky paste made of ground chilies spiced with cumin and coriander is the most popular condiment in northern Africa. The iconic flavor is eaten on eggs, whisked into yogurt, and slathered on grilled lamb.

SHISHITO PEPPER

Quickly blistered in a smoking-hot skillet until their green skins blacken, shishitos are sprinkled with salt and served whole as an appetizer or snack from Japan to Spain and beyond. People eat piles of them, seeds, skins, and all, using the stems as handles. About nine out of ten shishitos are mild, but when you eat them by the plateful, you never know which ones will be hot!

WIRI WIRI

Iconic in Guyana, wiri wiri peppers look like little berries—which they are! Bright red, super spicy, and smaller than a marble, wiri wiri are enjoyed morning to night, in everything from eggs to stews, and are essential in Guyana's national dish, pepperpot, a meat soup seasoned with cinnamon and clove.

POBLANO PEPPER

The mild, dark-green, heart-shaped poblano pepper is named for its origins in the valley of Puebla, Mexico. They're often served as chili rellenos (stuffed chilies)—filled with meat and cheese, then fried in a thin batter and simmered in succulent tomato salsa.

PAPRIKA

Hungary's national spice is one of the most popular spices in the world. Bright red—its name is literally Hungarian for "pepper"—this mild pepper powder is used to flavor Hungary's favorite recipes like chicken paprikash and beef goulash, and sprinkled by the pretty pinch over everything from hummus to deviled eggs. Spanish paprika is similar, but smoked.

TABBOULEH

BULGUR WHEAT, HERB, AND TOMATO SALAD

PREPARATION TIME	COOKING TIME	LEVEL OF DIFFICULTY	SERVES
1 hr 30 mins	0 mins	●	4

Whether it's spelled tabbouleh, tabouli, or tabouleh, this traditional summer salad is fragrant, healthful, and refreshing! Common throughout the Middle East, it's made with bulgur—a nutritious, nutty cracked wheat that's been partially cooked and then dried—plus tomatoes, lemon juice, olive oil, and enough fresh parsley to turn the finished dish bright green. The parsley is traditionally chopped by hand, but a food processor will do it in a snap. If you have extra parsley to use up, this is the dish for you.

INGREDIENTS

¼ cup fine bulgur wheat
8 cups curly parsley leaves and tender stems (from about 4 bunches)
1 small bunch fresh mint, leaves picked from the stem and finely chopped
2 scallions, thinly sliced
½ pound tomatoes, finely chopped
2 large lemons, juiced (about ⅓ cup juice)
salt, to taste
¼ cup extra-virgin olive oil

1. In a bowl, soak the bulgur with water to cover by ½ inch and let stand until softened, about 20 minutes. Drain in a fine sieve, shaking well. Transfer to a bowl.

2. In a food processor, pulse the parsley until finely chopped. (You might need to do this in batches.) Add the parsley to the bowl.

3. Add the mint, scallions, and tomatoes to the bowl and toss. Add the lemon juice and a large pinch of salt and toss.

4. Refrigerate the salad for 1 hour, then add the olive oil and toss. Taste and season with more salt and lemon juice, if desired. Serve.

Some people soak the bulgur not in water but in the juice of the chopped tomatoes, with more lemon juice, for extra flavor!

IRAN

Iranian cuisine is full of bright, beautiful ingredients like red pomegranates, golden saffron, sour cherries, pink rose petals, and bunches of fresh green herbs. The ancient Persians used the snowmelt from nearby mountains to create an irrigation system for their large deserts. So, despite the climate—and the landscape—they were able to grow all kinds of fruits and vegetables in glorious gardens. A classic Persian meal consists of fluffy saffron rice, vegetables like cucumbers or beets in spiced yogurt sauce, a meat stew or grilled kabobs, and a platter of flatbread with fresh herbs and salty white cheese. Don't forget the sour pickles, and definitely not the raw onions.

FRUIT LEATHER

Children here love to eat lavashak, a traditional fruit leather. It's made each summer from harvests of ripe fruits like sour cherries, plums, or tiny red berries called barberries, that are puréed, poured out into thin layers, and dried to last all year. No sugar is added; in fact, a little salt is thrown in the pot. It can be deliciously sour.

BEETS TO GO!

Bright-red boiled beets are the most popular street food in Iran. Called laboo, they're sold piping hot all fall and winter by vendors with wheeled carts who display them in tall stacks according to size.

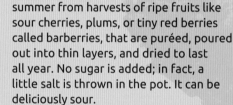

TAHDIG

The most famous treat here is the fried, crunchy layer that forms at the bottom of the rice pot that can be flipped out of the pot whole. It's called tahdig. Iranian cooks make different kinds of tahdig by adding ingredients like noodles, flatbread, potatoes—even a whole fish!—at the bottom of the pot, so that when the tahdig is flipped over, it has a crown of fried food on top.

RHUBARB

According to Persian lore, the very first man and woman sprang from a rhubarb plant in paradise. Today, Iranians use rhubarb in dishes like khoresh riva—a stew made with the sour stalks, plus onions, spices, a meat like lamb, and fresh mint on top.

SWEETENED YEASTED BUNS

The city of Fuman is famous for a sweet treat called koloocheh. These are yeasted buns filled with a sticky mixture of walnuts and dates, seasoned with cinnamon and cardamom, and made in a special press that stamps the buns with a beautiful geometric pattern.

SAFFRON

Saffron is the signature flavor of Iranian food. It's the world's most expensive spice, worth more than gold by weight, but you only need a tiny amount to perfume a dish. Each tiny thread comes from the stigma of a crocus flower and must be carefully picked from the center of each bloom by hand!

POMEGRANATES

Pomegranates with their jewellike seeds have been central to Iranian cuisine for centuries. They are native to Iran, and today you can find fresh pomegranates, dried pomegranate seeds, freshly squeezed pomegranate juice, and all manner of pomegranate pastes that range from sweet to sour. More than half the world's pomegranates are grown here today.

PERSIAN NEW YEAR PICNICS

For the Persian New Year, known as *Nowruz*, just about everyone goes on a picnic. They feast on meat-and-potato patties called kotlet, savor spring foods like herbs and eggs in a kuku sabzi frittata, and dip spring lettuce into a vinegar-honey mixture called sekanjabin.

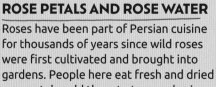

ROSE PETALS AND ROSE WATER

Roses have been part of Persian cuisine for thousands of years since wild roses were first cultivated and brought into gardens. People here eat fresh and dried rose petals, add them to teas and spice mixtures, and use rose water to flavor drinks or desserts, like ferni—a rose water rice pudding.

BORANI CHOGONDAR

YOGURT WITH BEETS AND MINT

PREPARATION TIME	COOKING TIME	LEVEL OF DIFFICULTY	SERVES
1 hr 10 mins	0 mins	●	6

In Iranian cuisine there are many yogurt-vegetable "salads," and they're often served with rice and stew, or grilled kebabs. This one also makes a delicious dip, served with flatbread or even potato chips. Bright-pink beet yogurt is a showstopper and is simple to make. For the best flavor, let it sit in the refrigerator for a day or two before serving.

Note: to roast the beet, preheat the oven to 450°F. Place the beet, unpeeled, in a pan with an ovenproof lid. Add a few tablespoons of water and a dash of salt and close the lid. (Alternatively, you can also cook the beet wrapped in aluminum foil.) Roast the beet until a knife slips in very easily—about an hour. Wait until it's cool enough to touch and then rub off the skin with your fingers.

INGREDIENTS

1 red beet, roasted, cooled, and
   peeled (see Note)
1 clove garlic
2 tablespoons dried mint, plus
   extra for garnish
3 tablespoons extra-virgin olive
   oil
2 cups thick, Greek-style yogurt
salt and black pepper

1. Coarsely chop the beet, then pulse together with the garlic in a food processor to form a smooth purée.

2. Transfer the purée to a bowl and mix in the mint and 2 tablespoons of the olive oil. Stir in the yogurt. Season to taste with salt and pepper.

3. Cover and chill in the refrigerator for at least 1 hour, or up to 48 hours.

4. To serve, spoon the remaining 1 tablespoon olive oil over the yogurt and garnish with a pinch of dried mint.

CONDIMENTS

AROUND THE WORLD

Sometimes a little drizzle or dollop can transform a whole dish—making it sweet, tart, tangy, rich, pungent, spicy, salty—or all of the above! Throughout history and around the world, people have cherished little bottles and jars of sauces with strong flavors, from Ancient Egypt, China, India, and Rome to modern-day Mexico, Malawi, and Malaysia. Eaters add soy sauce, fish sauce, tzatziki, mayo, tahini, ketchup, mustard, relishes, and hot sauces, each with magical abilities to make food sing.

ACHAR

These Indian pickles are made from a variety of vegetables and underripe fruits, packed with spices in oil or brine or both. Nearly always on the table throughout the Indian subcontinent, achar is now also made in parts of South Asia, Africa, and the Caribbean.

WORCESTERSHIRE SAUCE

This sauce was born in the 1830s in Worcester, UK, when a barrel of soy sauce and spiced vinegar was accidentally left in the cellar for years. People have been making it on purpose ever since. Cooks use a drop of the tangy-sweet liquid in marinades, seafood dishes, steaks, stews, soups, sauces, and even cocktails.

KETCHUP

Slathered on American burgers, hot dogs, onions rings, fries, and even breakfast eggs, ketchup is thick, sweet, and tart, thanks to tomatoes, sugar, and vinegar. Although it's an American icon, ketchup is the culinary descendent of an Asian fermented fish sauce called ketsiap that traders brought to Europe centuries ago.

TKEMALI

A sweet-sour sauce made of tiny tart, purple, and green plums. It's used like ketchup in the Caucasus country of Georgia. Locals dab it on cheese-filled breads, roast pork, and sausages.

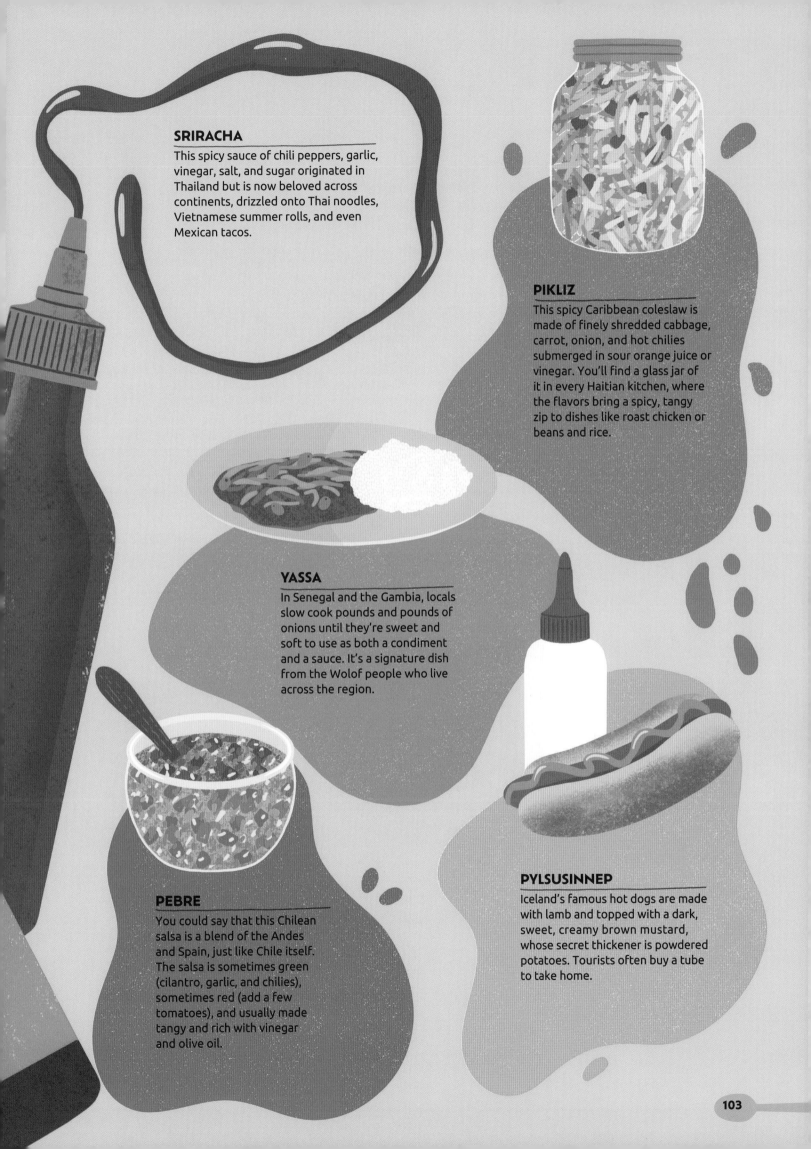

SRIRACHA

This spicy sauce of chili peppers, garlic, vinegar, salt, and sugar originated in Thailand but is now beloved across continents, drizzled onto Thai noodles, Vietnamese summer rolls, and even Mexican tacos.

PIKLIZ

This spicy Caribbean coleslaw is made of finely shredded cabbage, carrot, onion, and hot chilies submerged in sour orange juice or vinegar. You'll find a glass jar of it in every Haitian kitchen, where the flavors bring a spicy, tangy zip to dishes like roast chicken or beans and rice.

YASSA

In Senegal and the Gambia, locals slow cook pounds and pounds of onions until they're sweet and soft to use as both a condiment and a sauce. It's a signature dish from the Wolof people who live across the region.

PEBRE

You could say that this Chilean salsa is a blend of the Andes and Spain, just like Chile itself. The salsa is sometimes green (cilantro, garlic, and chilies), sometimes red (add a few tomatoes), and usually made tangy and rich with vinegar and olive oil.

PYLSUSINNEP

Iceland's famous hot dogs are made with lamb and topped with a dark, sweet, creamy brown mustard, whose secret thickener is powdered potatoes. Tourists often buy a tube to take home.

IRAQ

Iraq is a Middle Eastern country with huge cultural diversity. Most people in Iraq are Muslim, but there are five other recognized religions, reflecting the many ethnic groups that call this country home. Iraq has a varied landscape, from vast deserts to rolling green hills and craggy mountains. Its two main rivers, the Tigris and the Euphrates, create a moon-shaped region of rich soil called the Fertile Crescent that is often referred to as the "cradle of civilization," where people first developed farming and writing—both essential to this book!

ANCIENT CUISINE

Iraq's culinary history dates back at least 10,000 years. Ancient 3,700-year-old tablets, which some people call the world's first cookbooks, include recipes for stews with cumin, coriander, mint, dill, and sheep's tail. A version of this ancient stew is still enjoyed here today.

MASGOUF

Many Iraqis consider masgouf to be their national dish. It's a whole carp, spread open, marinated in olive oil, salt, tamarind, and turmeric, and then impaled on sticks and grilled around a fire. Today, restaurants along the Tigris river serve the freshly grilled fish late into the night.

LAMB LOVERS

Iraqis have loved lamb for millennia. Traditionally, all parts of the animal are used, so nothing goes to waste. A special breed of Iraqi fat-tailed sheep called liyya are prized for their tasty tails! Sheep heads, stomachs, tails, and feet are key ingredients in a traditional broth called pacha.

YOGURT

Milk from sheep and goats is made into rich yogurt, especially in spring when the animals are grazing lush green pastures and giving the best milk of the year. In summer, Iraqis pour thinned, salted yogurt over ice for a refreshing drink called shineena.

SKIP THE POPCORN

Baghdadis enjoy beef tongue, which can be served by the slice with lemon or stuffed into sandwiches with pickled cucumbers. Some Iraqis even bring this snack to the movie theater!

WARM UP OR COOL DOWN

In winter, many Iraqis wake up to cured sausage with eggs, clotted cream, and date syrup. In summer, they might choose cheese sandwiches with refreshing watermelon or cucumber. For an elaborate weekend brunch, families might cook fava beans topped with river mint and hot oil.

TURNIPS FOR THE WIN(TER)

Turnips store well all winter, and some Iraqis believe they help relieve colds. The roots are a key ingredient in a warming white stew of ground almonds, milk, rice, chickpeas, and meatballs. Street vendors even sell turnips with a drizzle of date syrup.

GREAT STUFF(ED)!

Iraqi cooking includes many stuffed dishes. The most famous is kubba, rice and potato balls filled with minced meat. Iraqis also love stuffed vegetables, like squash or leaves of swiss chard, carefully filled with a savory mixture of seasoned rice and ground meat.

FRIED FOODS

Up until the 1950s, most people did not have an oven, and frying was the preferred option for cooking. These days, some Iraqis tweak traditional recipes. For example, pueta chap—deep-fried potato discs stuffed with meat—are often assembled in layers and baked like a casserole instead.

HOLY DATE PALMS

Super sweet date palms are prized here, and even mentioned in religious texts. In ancient Mesopotamia, Ishtar, the goddess of love and fertility, lived in a date palm, earning her the nickname "Lady of the date clusters." Now, dates are eaten on their own, in desserts like stuffed sweet bread, and drunk as date wine!

BABA GANOUSH

EGGPLANT DIP

PREPARATION TIME	**COOKING TIME**	**LEVEL OF DIFFICULTY**	**MAKES**
15 mins	30 mins	●	4 to 6 appetizer servings

This creamy, smoky eggplant dip is a close cousin to hummus—and the two are often served together across the Middle East. Both dips are made with the sesame paste called tahini, and the two recipes are almost interchangeable—to make hummus instead, simply swap out the cooked eggplant for a can of drained chickpeas.

INGREDIENTS

1 large eggplant
juice of 1 lemon
4 tablespoons sesame tahini,
    stirred if separated
2 garlic cloves, peeled and
    smashed
salt, to taste
1 to 2 tablespoons plain yogurt,
    to thin (optional)
extra virgin olive oil, to drizzle

1. Preheat oven to 300°F.

2. Pierce the eggplant a few times with the tip of a knife. Place on a baking sheet and bake until soft, 30 to 40 minutes.

3. Once the eggplant is cool enough to handle, cut it open and scoop the cooked flesh into a blender or food processor, discarding the skin. Add the lemon juice, tahini, garlic, and salt to taste. Blend until smooth, or leave a chunkier texture if you like.

4. If the baba ganoush is thicker than you'd prefer, add 1 to 2 tablespoons of plain yogurt or cold water and purée again, to thin.

5. Serve in a bowl, drizzled with a glug of your best olive oil. Baba ganoush keeps several days in the refrigerator and will thicken as it cools.

The amounts here are just a guide—add as much garlic, lemon juice, tahini, and salt as you like.

Garnish with sesame seeds, parsley,
pine nuts, or pink pomegranate seeds.

JAPAN

Japan is made up of nearly 15,000 islands! Inland, much of the country is covered in steep, mountainous terrain. This is why Japanese people describe their food as "umi no sachi, yama no sachi"—"the delights of the sea and the mountains." With borders that were long closed, today the population is nearly 100% ethnically Japanese, and the traditional cuisine still celebrates indigenous ingredients. While essential seasonings include soy sauce, rice vinegar, dashi broth, and sweet rice wine called mirin, Japanese kitchens use very few spices, instead emphasizing the freshest ingredients and a refined presentation, letting the flavors shine as themselves.

SOYBEANS

These little beans are big in Japan. They're made into shoyu (soy sauce), tofu, and miso—a deliciously complex fermented paste that gives a distinctive, nutty flavor to hundreds of Japanese dishes. Young soybeans, called edamame, are delicious steamed, salted, and eaten as a snack; you pop the beans from their pods into your mouth and pile the empty shells up.

SEAWEED

Japanese people harvest many delicious wild seaweeds! These include nori, dried, greenish-black and paper thin, used for wrapping sushi, and kombu (kelp), which is simmered into the famous soup stock, dashi. Other delicious sea vegetables include wakame and hijiki.

EELS

Eels have been eaten in Japan since ancient times. Traditionally caught wild, today eels are raised in ponds or tanks. The most popular preparation is kabayaki—filets of eel skewered, dipped in a sweet soy sauce, and grilled.

SUSHI

This island nation has such spectacular seafood that many people eat it at every meal. For sushi, raw fish is paired with vinegared rice, often wrapped in paper-thin pieces of nori (dried seaweed). Sashimi—exquisitely fresh raw seafood—is carefully sliced and traditionally served with soy sauce, wasabi (special horseradish), and pickled ginger.

SYMBOLIC SHRIMP

Many foods here have special meanings. Shrimp can convey longevity, as their rounded backs and long whiskers make them look a bit like old men!

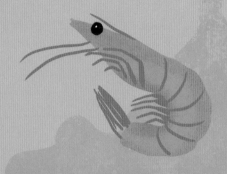

WASABI

One of the most famous flavors in Japanese cuisine, this special horseradish was originally picked wild and is now grown along mountain streams or in flooded mountain terraces. The prized root is peeled and grated into a pale-green paste that brings a hot, spicy, punch to everything from soups to sushi.

OODLES OF NOODLES

Noodles were introduced from China to Japan in the 700s, and today they're an edible art form. The two main types are soba (thin buckwheat noodles) and udon (thick, soft wheat noodles). Both are beloved hot or cold, piled high on plates or in ramen broth.

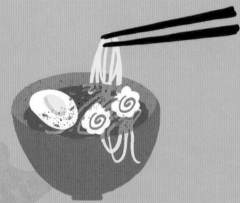

SUMO STEW

Many sumo wrestlers swear by huge bowls of a stew called chanko-nabe. Recipes vary but often include meat, vegetables, fish, soft-boiled mushrooms, and noodles, all cooked together in a rich, flavorful broth. This packed stew helps bodybuilding athletes keep up their impressive weight before a match!

WAGYU BEEF

Literally meaning "Japanese cow," wagyu is a prized Japanese breed of beef whose meat is so supremely tender, marbled, rich, buttery, and luxurious, it's widely considered the finest steak in the world. One animal can go for 30,000 dollars, and a single steak can cost hundreds of dollars!

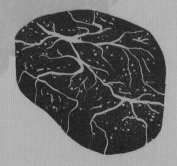

BENTO BOXES

People of all ages love these special lunch boxes. Each bento box includes lots of little compartments, brimming with treats like onigiri (rice balls), boiled eggs, seafood, salads, and pickles. Some people design ingredients elaborately into kyaraben, or "character bento"—shaping them into popular anime or manga characters, or adorable animals.

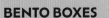

ONIGIRI

RICE BALLS WITH TUNA, MAYONNAISE, AND SEAWEED

PREPARATION TIME
1 hr 15 mins

COOKING TIME
20 mins

LEVEL OF DIFFICULTY
●●●

MAKES
8

These traditional balls of rice are tucked into toasted seaweed and filled with salty salmon, mayo-kissed tuna, pickled plums, cod roe, or even fried chicken! People here have been making onigiri for more than a thousand years. Whether sold in stores or made at home and tucked into bento boxes, they're a beloved snack on the go or on picnics. Most often shaped into triangles, onigiri can be made into rounds, logs, or even into cute animal shapes such as pandas.

INGREDIENTS

1½ cups Japanese short-grain
    white rice (sometimes sold as
    sushi rice)
fine sea salt, for sprinkling
1 5-ounce can tuna in water
2 tablespoons Kewpie
    mayonnaise or other
    mayonnaise
1 teaspoon soy sauce
8 (3 x 1-inch) sheets nori

Don't forget to wash and
drain the rice well before
cooking. This removes
starch, helping create the
perfect texture of rice that
sticks together with grains
that feel separate.

1. Place the rice in a large bowl and add water to cover the rice. Using your hands, stir the rice until the water becomes cloudy, then drain. Cover again with fresh water and repeat the washing process until the water runs almost clear. Pour the cleaned rice through a sieve set over a bowl and let it drain for 30 minutes.

2. In a medium, heavy-bottomed saucepan, cover the rice with 1¾ cups of water and bring to a boil. Cover the pot with a lid, reduce the heat to low, and cook until the rice absorbs all the water, about 10 minutes.

3. While the rice cooks, drain the canned tuna and transfer to a bowl. Add the mayonnaise and soy sauce and use a fork to mix.

4. When the rice is cooked, turn off the heat and let the rice stand, covered, until fluffy, about 5 minutes. Using a rice paddle or flat spoon, stir the rice to fluff and separate the grains.

5. Arrange a sheet of plastic wrap on a work surface. Lightly sprinkle the plastic wrap with salt. Scoop a packed ¼ cup of the rice onto the plastic wrap.

6. Use a spoon to make an indentation in the rice and add about 1 heaped teaspoon of the tuna-mayo mixture into the indentation. Lift up the sides of the plastic wrap to help you press the rice so you can enclose the filling, then fully wrap the rice in the plastic and lightly press it to form a triangle or square shape.

7. Turn on one burner of the stove to medium. Holding a sheet of nori with tongs, wave the seaweed over the hot burner for about 5 seconds until fragrant and pliable. Unwrap the onigiri from the plastic and press the seaweed so it wraps one side of the onigiri.

8. Repeat with the remaining rice, tuna, and seaweed, remembering to sprinkle the wrap with salt each time. (You can reuse the same plastic wrap each time, if it's not too messy.)

RICE

AROUND THE WORLD

Some people call rice the most important ingredient in the world, with billions of people relying on it as a daily staple. People began cultivating this water-loving grass 10,000 years ago, along China's Yangtze River and India's Ganges River. Today, you can try many varieties, from jasmine to basmati, short grain to long. You'll find rice steamed, fried, rolled into sushi, slowly simmered into congee, and transformed into rice noodles, edible rice paper, and even rice wine. Used in cuisines around the globe, there seem to be as many prized rice recipes as there are grains of rice. Favorites include Indian biryani with saffron and cardamom, Iranian tahdig with its crunchy golden crust, and sweet Nordic rice pudding, crowned with plenty of butter.

RICE FESTIVAL FOODS

Chuseok is a Korean harvest festival when people honor their ancestors and express thanks for the rice harvest during a three-day celebration. Families play games, sing traditional songs, and eat special foods made from rice. Rice flour is made into traditional half-moon-shaped songpyeon rice cakes, which are steamed over a layer of pine needles.

RISOTTO

One of the most famous recipes in Italian cuisine features Italian arborio rice. To make risotto, you don't just put a pot of rice on to boil and leave it to cook. Instead, you add flavorful broth or wine, just a little at a time, stirring all the while, for a creamy, luxurious, fragrant dish that may be studded with anything from porcini mushrooms to peas to pumpkin.

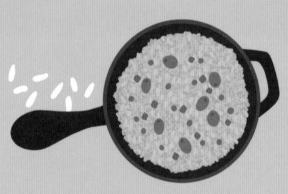

ARROZ CON GANDULES

Every family in Puerto Rico has their own recipe for arroz con gandules. A classic combination of rice and pigeon peas is seasoned with sofrito—a combination of peppers, onions, garlic, and cilantro is the essential base for Puerto Rican cuisine.

SUSHI

When someone says sushi, do you think of fish? Seaweed? Don't forget the rice! Sushi chefs have perfected cooking sticky short-grained sushi rice and seasoning it just so with vinegar. Japanese cuisine also stars rice in everything from kids' adorable onigiri to adults' sake, which is wine made of rice.

BLACK WILD RICE

On the U.S.–Canada border, along the shores of Lake Superior, native Anishinaabe people have been harvesting deliciously nutty-tasting black wild rice for thousands of years. After harvesting the crop by canoe and drying it over a fire, people traditionally jumped up and down on the rice to husk it. Today, people still enjoy wild rice in salads with nuts and berries.

ROPAIN FESTIVAL

This festival in Nepal takes place during the monsoon season to celebrate planting rice. Everyone enjoys special dishes like deep-fried ring-shaped rice-flour roti or beaten rice served with curd. Young people traditionally play in the mud and get covered head to toe!

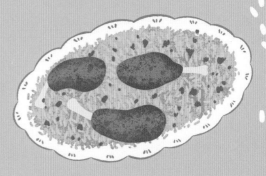

LA BANDERA DOMINICANA

Beans and rice are common around the Caribbean, but one national rice dish is super symbolic. La Bandera Dominicana is the national lunch of the Dominican Republic. That's because the three colors on the plate—rice, beans, and braised meat—remind residents of the colors of the Dominican flag.

MANDI

Have you ever eaten something from an underground oven? Mandi is a saffron-seasoned Yemeni rice dish popular throughout the Arabian Gulf. Rice is placed in a clay pit dug into the ground and meat, like goat, chicken, or even camel, is suspended above. The pit is sealed with more clay, and the smoky oven slow roasts the meat while the rice is infused with the drippings.

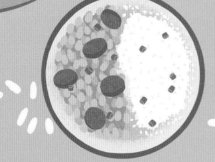

CAROLINA GOLD

Enslaved West Africans brought their rice cultivation expertise and harvesting technologies to North America. One variety they developed, Carolina Gold rice, is now proudly served in expensive restaurants. On New Year's Day, many American southerners still eat Hoppin' John, a dish of cow peas, bacon, and Carolina Gold rice served with cooked greens, for good luck.

CHAMPORADO

What happens when a Spanish ship takes an Aztec corn-and-chocolate breakfast-drink recipe around the world? Filipinos developed a porridge called champorado made with chocolate discs and glutinous rice. Now it's a popular breakfast with sweetened condensed milk, sometimes served with salted fish.

MYANMAR

Myanmar—formerly known as Burma, for the country's largest ethnic group—has suffered invasions and conflict for 150 years, but through the people's resilience and resourcefulness, their culture, community, and culinary heritage have endured. The largest country in mainland Southeast Asia, Myanmar is extremely diverse, with 135 distinct ethnic groups and more than one hundred different languages spoken. Its food is considered some of the most delicious in the world, containing distinct flavor combinations that blend elements of neighboring Chinese, Indian, and Thai cuisine.

TEA SHOPS

You'll find tea shops on nearly every street corner in Myanmar. Each morning, people rush in for a cup before work. By afternoon, tea shops fill up with friends at low tables, chatting, snacking, and sipping teas such as thick, creamy cho seint made with sweetened condensed milk.

LUNCH LOVE

Lunch—the biggest meal of the day—usually includes rice, at least one meat-based curry, and sides like steamed vegetables, clear soup, fresh salads, and spicy chili paste. Lunch comes with condiments, like Kachin salsa (a mix of chilies, tomatoes, shallots, and dried shrimp powder), sour-plum chutney, or tomato chutney. Dessert is usually fresh fruit and a bowl of palm sugar for dipping, and the meal is usually washed down with a pale, clear warm tea.

TEA SALAD

Myanmar is famous for its thoke, or "salads," which may contain a dozen or more ingredients. A salad might include tea leaves, poached fish, roasted seeds or nuts, grapefruit, tofu, banana flowers, or roasted eggplant.

TURMERIC

Brilliant yellow-orange turmeric is a favorite spice in Myanmar. People usually add a pinch of it to their cooking oil as it heats up. This is as much for health as it is for flavor: turmeric is believed to have antibacterial and antiinflammatory properties. It's also an antiflatulent—a polite way of saying it prevents farts!

NOODLES FOR BREAKFAST

Many people here start their day with a big bowl of mohinga—Myanmar's national dish. This flavor-packed breakfast soup features fresh fish, thin noodles, plus rice powder, lemongrass, ginger, turmeric, red onions, lime wedges, cilantro, and hard-boiled eggs.

FESTIVALS AND CELEBRATIONS

Thadingyut is a festival held on the full moon day of the seventh month of the country's traditional calendar to welcome the Buddha's descent from heaven. After a day of fasting, at night, people celebrate by visiting food stalls selling barbecue meat skewers, curries, and fried snacks amid firecrackers, and beautiful paper lanterns.

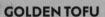

GOLDEN TOFU

Tofu in Myanmar is not made from soybeans—it's made from the flour of ground yellow split peas and chickpeas. The result is wonderfully light and creamy, with a gorgeous golden color from turmeric. It is eaten fresh in salads or deep-fried into fritters.

ELDERS

When enjoying a meal in Myanmar, elders at the table are always served first. Even if no grandparents are present, it's customary for a family to set aside a small bowl of rice in honor of their older relatives.

ALMS

Myanmar is a predominately Buddhist country, and in the morning, you'll see scarlet-robed monks walking barefoot and carrying bowls. This is an ancient ritual called the alms round. People in the community drop offerings of food into the bowls. Before eating, the monks mix everything together so as not to favor any one food over the other. Sometimes this leads to unusual blends, such as cake mixed with curry.

MOHINGA

FISH NOODLE SOUP

PREPARATION TIME
45 mins

COOKING TIME
45 mins

LEVEL OF DIFFICULTY
● ●

SERVES
4 to 6

This wonderfully aromatic fish noodle soup is considered the quintessential dish of Myanmar, where it's most often enjoyed at breakfast. While there are endless variations across the country, whether simmered at home or slurped on the street, you'll almost always find flavorful lemongrass, ginger, and fish sauce perfuming the broth, and gorgeous garnishes of hard-boiled eggs, lime wedges, and fresh cilantro. Catfish is common in Myanmar, and this dish often calls for whole fish, but you can swap in any mild white fish.

INGREDIENTS

FOR THE BROTH
1 stalk fresh lemongrass, cut into
    2-inch pieces
1 small piece ginger, thinly sliced
4 garlic cloves, smashed
½ teaspoon whole black
    peppercorns
1 teaspoon ground turmeric
¾ teaspoon salt
2 to 2½ pound fillets catfish or
    other mild fish, cut into bite-
    sized pieces

FOR THE SOUP
1 stalk lemongrass, papery layers
    and tops removed
8 cloves garlic, roughly chopped
2 large shallots, roughly chopped
2 inches fresh ginger, peeled and
    chopped
salt
¼ cup vegetable oil
1½ teaspoons paprika or cayenne
    pepper (if you like it spicier)
½ teaspoon ground turmeric
¼ cup toasted rice powder (see
    Note)
1 tablespoon fish sauce
12 ounces thin rice noodles
    (sometimes labeled as
    vermicelli)

GARNISHES FOR SERVING
6 hard-boiled eggs, sliced
1 cup cilantro, chopped
2 limes, cut into wedges
thinly sliced red onions

TO MAKE THE BROTH

1. For the broth, combine the lemongrass, ginger, garlic, peppercorns, turmeric, salt, and fish with 4 cups of water in a deep skillet. Bring to a boil, reduce heat and simmer, covered, until the fish is just cooked, about 15 minutes. Transfer the fish to a plate and strain the broth into a saucepan.

TO MAKE THE SOUP

2. For the soup, combine the lemongrass, garlic, shallots, ginger, and pinch of salt in a food processor and grind to a paste. In a wok or large, deep skillet, heat the oil. Add the paprika, turmeric, and shallot paste and cook, stirring, for 2 to 3 minutes. Stir in the cooked fish.

3. Bring the saucepan of broth to a boil, whisk in the rice powder until smooth, and cook until thickened. Add the fish mixture to the broth, then add the fish sauce.

4. Bring a pot of water to a boil, add the noodles, and cook 3 minutes or according to the package directions. Serve the noodles in bowls, ladle the soup into the bowls, and serve with the garnishes.

Note: to make toasted rice powder, toast ½ cup uncooked jasmine rice in a dry skillet over medium-high heat, stirring, until fragrant, about 5 minutes. Transfer to a food processor and grind to a powder. Keep any extra to sprinkle over salads.

PAKISTAN

Pakistan is bordered by India, Afghanistan, Iran, and China, and its diverse geography ranges from the towering Hindu Kush mountains to barren deserts, green, fertile plains, and a coastline along the Arabian Sea. People settled in this region at least 8,500 years ago, and the country's cuisine has been shaped by many influences over the centuries. Middle Eastern scholars brought rose water, saffron, almonds, pistachios, dried fruits, and other delicacies between the twelfth and fifteenth centuries, and the Mughal Empire's influence from the fifteenth to nineteenth centuries introduced cloves, cardamom, nutmeg, mace, and other spices, plus yogurt, cream, and butter.

CURRY FAVOR

There are a seemingly endless variety of curries to choose from in Pakistan, but the one that perhaps reigns supreme is haleem. This stewlike dish features a mix of meat and legumes flavored with lemon, ginger, and coriander, and cooked for several hours at least. Pakistanis call haleem the "king of curry."

MANY INFLUENCES

While Pakistan shares many ingredients and recipes with neighboring India— they were one country until 1947— Pakistani food also reflects many Middle Eastern traditions, such as its use of pomegranate seeds and saffron.

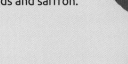

TANDOOR

Pakistan has a long history of using the tandoor, a type of super hot oven now popular throughout the Middle East and South and Central Asia. Tandoors are traditionally made of clay and used over fire (although there are modern, electric versions now too). Shaped like a cylinder that tapers in at the top and then opens up to let heat escape, they're used for cooking Pakistani breads, kebabs, and biryani.

CARDAMOM

A favorite spice in Pakistani cuisine is cardamom, which can take the form of whole, dried seed pods or an aromatic ground blend of several types of cardamom. It's used in many recipes, including thandal, a popular drink made from milk, ground almonds, and rose petals.

NIHARI

This classic, slow-cooked dish features beef, or sometimes lamb, goat, or mutton shanks, simmered for hours overnight in a rich bone broth with cardamom, cumin, cloves, coriander, ginger, and chilies. Originally a filling breakfast for cold mornings, it's now so popular that restaurants across the region serve it all day long.

RAMADAN FEASTING

As an Islamic republic, Pakistan observes Ramadan, a holy month when people fast from dawn until sunset. After sunset, many Pakistanis traditionally break their fast with fresh dates and homemade lemonade, followed by a meal called *iftar*, which may include an array of delicious foods such as samosas, kebabs, and biryani.

CHUTNEY

Pakistani dishes are often served with a side of chutney—or several. These sweet-sour condiments come in all types, from fruit chutneys to versions featuring peanuts or chilies. Chutneys are also popular in neighboring India, but there are special varieties specific to Pakistan. Green chutney, usually made with cilantro, is considered the national chutney of Pakistan because it matches the color of the nation's flag.

FOOD STREET

Pakistan's second-largest city, Lahore, was once at the center of the Mughal Empire and is now Pakistan's most famous food district. *Gawalmandi*, which means "food street," is packed with restaurants serving diverse traditional dishes like fried fish, Pakistani barbecue, and classic nankhatai.

MALALA

Malala Yousafzai is a Pakistani activist who has long advocated for girls' education. She survived being shot and, at just seventeen, became the world's youngest winner of the Nobel Peace Prize. Her work and story have inspired people around the world. Now living in the UK, she has said that her favorite dish is still her mom's rice and chicken curry.

BREAD CULTURE

Bread is almost always served with Pakistani meals—and may be soft, puffy, flat, spongy, crispy, baked, fried, or even sautéed. One favorite is naan, a pillowy, leavened flatbread that sometimes contains fillings like minced meat or a sweet mixture of dried coconut, almonds, and sultanas.

HALWA

RICH, SWEET CARROT PUDDING WITH NUTS AND SPICES

PREPARATION TIME	**COOKING TIME**	**LEVEL OF DIFFICULTY**	**SERVES**
15 mins	1 hr 30 mins	●●	2 to 4

Carrots for dessert? Yes, please! There are many types of halwa, from fruit to beans, usually simmered with sugar, spices, and milk, ghee or coconut milk, and eaten for breakfast or dessert, on special occasions or as an everyday treat. In this famous dish, which is especially popular for Diwali and Eid, carrots are coarsely grated, then slowly cooked until completely soft, sweet, and aromatic.

INGREDIENTS

1 pound carrots, trimmed and
　　peeled
¾ cup whole milk
6 tablespoons sugar
¼ cup ghee or clarified butter
¼ teaspoon ground cardamom
shelled pistachios, slivered
　　almonds, and/or crushed
　　cashews, for garnish

1. Grate the carrots using the large holes on a box grater or the grating blade of a food processor.

2. In a dry, heavy-bottomed pot, warm the grated carrots over medium heat for 2 to 3 minutes until they start to dry out a little bit. Stir in the milk and bring to a simmer, then reduce the heat to low. Cook, stirring the carrots every 5 minutes or so, until the carrots are very soft and all the liquid evaporates; this should take 45 minutes to 1 hour.

3. Stir in the sugar and cook over medium heat, stirring, for 6 to 8 minutes. Add the ghee and cook, stirring, for about 5 minutes. Stir in the cardamom and cook until fragrant, for about 1 minute.

4. Serve warm or at room temperature, garnished with the nuts.

PHILIPPINES

There are more than 7,000 islands in the Philippine archipelago, which is one of the most biodiverse places on the planet. Some of these islands don't have any people at all, while the island of Luzon is home to the capital city of Manila, one of the world's biggest cities. The Philippines' vibrant cuisine celebrates rice, fresh fish, roasted pork, all-day snacks, super sour flavors, and lots of sweets!

VINEGAR

In the Philippines, people love sour flavors! Vinegars here may be made from sugarcane, coconut, palm, or pineapple. They're used as a condiment—sometimes infused with hot peppers and garlic—and as an ingredient in dishes like the world-famous adobo, a deliciously tart vinegar-spiked stew.

BAGOONG

This pink seasoning paste is almost as important as vinegar here, and the two are often used together. Bagoong is a thick condiment made of salted and fermented seafood, sometimes with a little garlic, oil, and tomato added in. Bagoong is salty and a little bit fishy, and it gives Filipino food its own special flavor.

PANDESAL

This big, soft, fluffy roll is topped with toasted breadcrumbs and eaten as a snack, sometimes with jam or ham and cheese. Like many Filipino dishes, it has a Spanish name, because Spain colonized the Philippines for more than 300 years. In Spanish, pan de sal means "bread of salt"—even though this roll is more sweet than salty!

PURPLE YAMS

They really are purple! These sweet tubers are a deliciously colorful part of Filipino cooking. Known as ube in Tagalog, the Filipino language, they keep their color when cooked and are made into purple cake, purple ice cream, purple doughnuts, and even purple pandesal!

STREET NAMES

Grilled meats are sold from street carts all over the Philippines, usually on a stick. And every piece has its own nickname! If you want grilled pig ears, you order a "walkman." If you want chicken feet, order an "adidas." And for chicken tails, ask for the "pope's nose."

LUMPIA

These crisp rolls come in many shapes and sizes. Some are skinny, filled with meat, and deep-fried. Others are big like burritos and filled with crunchy vegetables. You can even find fried sweet lumpia, stuffed with sugar and bananas and served for dessert.

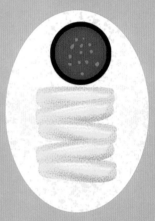

MERYENDA TIME

In the Philippines, snacks between meals have their own name: *meryenda*. These can include a pre breakfast snack, breakfast, a post breakfast snack, lunch, an after-lunch snack, dinner, and then snacks before bed. *Meryenda* may include mooncakes, noodles, dumplings, or sticky-rice pastries.

HALO-HALO

Halo-halo, which means "mix-mix," is a wild dessert of many flavors, colors, and textures. To make halo-halo, fill a tall glass with shaved ice, evaporated milk, ice cream, and a rainbow of treats like coconut strips, jackfruit, purple-yam jam, tapioca pearls, and shredded cheese. Then take a tall spoon and—as the name says—mix it all up!

SINIGANG NA ISDA

Another Filipino dish is the sinigang na isda, which means "sour fish stew." Locals add ingredients, such as tamarind-tree pod pulp, green tomatoes, tiny limes, and unripe pineapple, to make their soup extra sour.

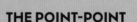

THE POINT-POINT

For lunch, Filipinos often go to what is known as a *turo-turo* spot, meaning "point-point." At a *turo-turo*, the food sits on display. You might find trays of rice, lines of stews, big simmering pots of soup, or piles of fried fish and vegetables. All you have to do is point at what you want!

ADOBO

CHICKEN STEWED IN VINEGAR

PREPARATION TIME
5 mins

COOKING TIME
40 mins

LEVEL OF DIFFICULTY
●●

SERVES
4

This quintessential Philippine chicken stew uses so much vinegar it's famously tart, though this can be adjusted depending on your taste. Filipino people have been stewing food in vinegar for centuries, and when the Spanish arrived and tasted this dish, they called it after a similar Spanish recipe, adoboado, and the name—or a version of it—stuck. Today, people use the traditional acidic bath of vinegar and soy sauce to cook any kind of meat or vegetable, such as beef, pork, squid, catfish, water spinach, or even lizard. This version sticks to chicken.

INGREDIENTS

2 pounds skin-on chicken thighs
    and/or legs
½ teaspoon salt
1 tablespoon oil
5 cloves of garlic, thinly sliced
2 bay leaves (optional)
1 cup soy sauce
1 cup white or rice vinegar
1 teaspoon brown sugar
white rice, to serve
scallions, sliced, to garnish

1. Dry the chicken with paper towels and season with salt.

2. In a large, heavy-bottomed pot, heat the oil and brown the chicken pieces, uncovered, about 5 minutes per side. It's best to do this in batches so the pan is not too crowded. Add more oil if the pan gets dry. Using tongs, transfer the chicken pieces to a plate.

3. Add the garlic to the pot and cook, stirring, for 30 seconds. Add the bay leaves, if using, soy sauce, vinegar, ⅔ cup water, brown sugar, and the browned chicken to the pot. Bring to a boil, then reduce to a simmer and cook, covered, for about 25 minutes, turning the chicken pieces over occasionally for even cooking.

4. Remove the bay leaves.

5. Serve with white rice and scallions, for garnish.

The vinegar nearly pickles the meat, which helped it to last before refrigerators were common.

Turn up the acidity by marinating the meat in the refrigerator for a few hours before cooking.

SOUTH KOREA

South Korea boasts diverse geography—mountains in the north and fertile plains in the south—and a varied climate, with hot and humid summers and very cold winters. Today, the ancient country boasts super modern cities, but the culture's long history is alive in its traditional dishes. Essential elements of Korean meals are rice, kimchi, and soups made with lots of vegetables, soy, meat, and seafood, all seasoned with chilies, onions, ginger, garlic, sesame, and vinegar.

RICE

Boiled, short-grain rice is eaten at almost every meal—unless you're having noodles (which may also be made of rice)! During the Lunar New Year festival, many people enjoy dumpling and rice cake soup, and during the harvest moon festival, foods include rice wine, and crescent-shaped rice cakes stuffed with pumpkin, chestnut paste, sesame seeds, or acorns.

GOCHU

Chili peppers (gochu), first brought to Korea in the fifteenth or sixteenth century by Portuguese or Dutch traders, transformed the country's cuisine. Ground up, they can be mixed with rice and fermented into gochujang, a sweet, savory, spicy condiment essential in Korean cooking.

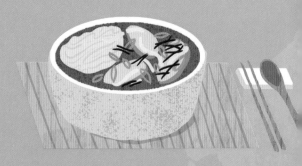

KIMCHI

Long before refrigeration, Korean people developed a way to preserve and ferment vegetables like Napa cabbage, radishes, and cucumbers into magically spicy pickled kimchi. It is served at just about every meal, and many people have special refrigerators just for kimchi!

BIBIMBAP

This beloved dish is often prepared for special events. A mound of rice, topped with vegetables, an egg, seasonings, and gochujang, is served in a dolsot—a hot, heavy bowl of stone or cast iron. The heat from the stone or iron browns the rice at the bottom to form a delicious crust. The name means "mixed rice" because just before eating, you mix the ingredients together.

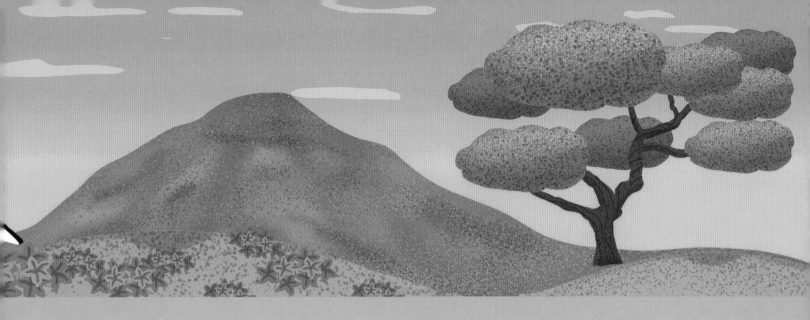

SWEETS

While Korean cuisine is famous for salty and spicy flavors, they're also great at sweet treats! Favorite desserts include hotteok pancakes, honey and sesame cookies called yakgwa, and bingsoo, a centuries-old recipe of shaved ice commonly crowned with sweet toppings like fruit syrup, condensed milk, and sweet red beans.

EAT YOUR INSECTS!

A popular snack in the fall is crickets boiled whole, and seasoned with soy sauce. Another street snack is beondegi (pupa) made with silkworm pupae that are boiled or steamed, and served in little paper cups with toothpick skewers. The snacks look like prawns and are nutty and crunchy on the outside but chewy on the inside!

SEAFOOD

South Korea enjoys a long coastline and spectacularly fresh seafood. All types of fish and shellfish—sea cucumbers, oysters, crabs, cod, cuttlefish, herring, clams, shrimp, and even jellyfish—are marinated, fried, or enjoyed raw. For centuries, specially trained and experienced women divers on South Korea's largest island, Jeju, have plunged more than thirty feet beneath the ocean—without oxygen tanks—to collect sea urchins, abalone, conch, and sea snails.

SOUP ALL DAY

Soup or stew is eaten all day, every day, and there are lots to choose from! This includes seolleongtang, made from simmering ox bone for a white, milky broth, combined with brisket and seasoned at the table, and samgyetang, or chicken ginseng soup, for which a whole young chicken is stuffed with garlic, rice, ginseng, and jujube (a kind of date).

TABLE-SIDE COOKING

Some Korean dishes are made right at the table! Korean barbecue is often prepared on gas or charcoal grills built into dining tables or using portable stoves placed table-side. Thinly sliced beef, pork, or chicken is seasoned or marinated and then quickly grilled to order—by a chef or by diners themselves!

HAEMUL PAJEON

SCALLION AND SEAFOOD PANCAKE

PREPARATION TIME
15 mins

COOKING TIME
15 mins

LEVEL OF DIFFICULTY
●●

SERVES
1 10-inch
pancake for sharing
as an appetizer

This savory Korean pancake has a surprisingly simple batter—just flour,
egg, and water. Pajeon pancakes are usually studded with scallions and
seafood like scallops or squid—but you can customize them endlessly.
Some people add oysters, sliced veggies, leftover rice or meat, or that most
quintessentially Korean ingredient: kimchi. It all cooks in just a few minutes
and is delicious anytime, day or night. If you like a little heat, consider adding
a few threads of pretty, dried Korean peppers at the end of Step 3.
It's even more delicious with the simple dipping sauce included here.

INGREDIENTS

FOR THE DIPPING SAUCE

3 tablespoons soy sauce
1½ tablespoons rice vinegar
¼ teaspoon toasted sesame oil

FOR THE PANCAKE

½ cup all-purpose flour
1 large egg
½ cup cold water
salt
¼ pound peeled shrimp or
    scallops, cut into bite-sized
    pieces
3 tablespoons canola oil or
    vegetable oil
3 scallions, cut into 1-inch lengths

TO MAKE THE DIPPING SAUCE

1. In a small bowl, mix together the soy sauce, rice vinegar, and sesame oil.

TO MAKE THE PANCAKE

2. In a separate bowl, for the pancake, stir together the flour, water, and ½ teaspoon salt until just combined. Stir in the shrimp. In a 10-inch nonstick or cast-iron skillet, heat 2 tablespoons of the oil over medium-high heat. Add the scallions in a single layer, and cook for 1 minute. Pour the batter over the scallions, using a spatula to spread it into a pancake.

3. In the same bowl used for the batter, lightly beat the egg with a fork. Season with a pinch of salt, then pour over the batter.

4. Let the pancake cook until it's set and golden on the bottom and the shrimp are cooked, 3 to 4 minutes.

5. Slide the pancake onto a cutting board or plate, cut it into wedges, and serve hot with the dipping sauce.

NOODLES

AROUND THE WORLD

Pasta and noodles go back millennia to the Shang Dynasty in China (1700–1100 BCE), when rice or wheat flour was made into the very first noodles. Legend has it that explorer Marco Polo first brought pasta from Asia to Italy, but some historians say Greeks were cooking pasta by the first century CE; others say that what we know as pasta was introduced to Sicily by Arabs in the ninth century. Whichever way it arrived in Europe, pasta dishes began to appear in literature during the Renaissance. Dried—and therefore much more portable and long-lasting—noodles also allowed the ingredient to travel in merchant ships, furthering its popularity around the globe!

THAI

Thai people feast on noodles of many shapes, from wide and thick rice noodles (sen yai) to slender glass noodles made from mung-bean flour (woon sen). And don't forget the noodles in the country's national dish, pad thai.

CHINA

In China, skilled chefs make lamian wheat noodles by hand from a single piece of dough that is pulled, stretched, and folded over and over until the noodles are verrrrrrry long and very thin!

ETHIOPIA

The Ethiopian recipe for pasta saltata traces its roots to the Italians' brief occupation of the country in the 1930s. Today, this Ethiopian dish combines penne with potatoes topped with a sauce of garlic, onions, lemon juice, and harissa, plus basil and arugula folded in just before serving.

GERMANY

German spätzle are made from a super simple dough of eggs, flour, water, and salt, pressed through a colander into little squiggly pastas whose name originally meant "little sparrows." Spätzle is often served with butter, cheese, caramelized onions, or gravy alongside rich meat dishes like sauerbraten, goulash, and schnitzel.

HALUSKI

This dish—noodles with buttery fried cabbage, bacon, and onions—is a favorite comfort food in Austria, Poland, Hungary, Slovakia, and Ukraine. Related to a Viennese specialty called krautfleckerl, it includes caramelized cabbage with square noodles known as fleckerl—it's a delicious way to warm up during Austria's cold winters.

CROATIA

In Croatia, dough is shaped into a roll, stuffed with fillings, and cooked to make štrukli—like a dumpling crossed with lasagna! The Slovenians have štruklji, a sheet of pasta filled with apples or cheese, rolled up, poached, and sliced. When arranged on a plate for serving, they look like cinnamon buns.

MEXICO

In Mexico, noodles get a spicy treatment with lots of chilies! For fideos secos (dry noodles), noodles are boiled, fried in oil, mixed with chipotle sauce, and then baked in the oven. Another pasta dish in Mexico is espagueti verde (green spaghetti), pasta topped with spicy green chili poblano.

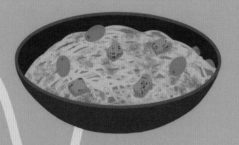

DOMINICAN REPUBLIC

Here, locals top spaghetti with garlic, tomato sauce, olives, and salami, and like to eat it at the beach, with fried plantains, slices of pan sobao (a sweetened bread), or pan de agua (water bread).

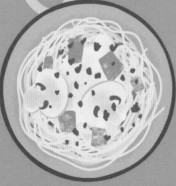

URUGUAY

Many Italians immigrated to South America, bringing with them a rich food heritage. Uruguayans enjoy pasta con salsa caruso, pasta with a rich sauce of cream, nuts, mushrooms, ham, and cheese. Further north, Peruvians enjoy tallarines verdes, spaghetti tossed with a green sauce of basil, cheese, spinach, and onion.

FINLAND

In Finland, people enjoy suomen makaronilaatikko, baked macaroni with ground beef and a creamy egg sauce, topped with cheese. Next door in Sweden, stuvade macaroni, or "milk-stewed macaroni"—is seasoned with nutmeg and served with meatballs. Some Swedes also enjoy a quick meal of pasta topped with ketchup!

THAILAND

Thailand, in Southeast Asia, is known for its royal palaces, tropical beaches, and gorgeous national parks, which cover almost 30% of the country. In Bangkok, the capital city, you can find sleek skyscrapers next to ancient temples and buy delicious meals from street vendors. Thai cuisine is centered on the concept of yam—literally! The Thai word yam means "mix," to get just the right combination of spicy, sour, salty, and sweet. Recipes here call for lots of coconut milk, fresh herbs, and fiery chilies. Favorite dishes vary by region and foods may be tom (boiled), yam (spicy salads), tam (pounded), and gaeng (curries).

CURRY

Curries (gaeng) are essential to Thai cuisine. Versions of Thai red, green, and yellow curry pastes can be found on supermarket shelves worldwide. Each color has a different flavor and green is considered by many to be the spiciest!

NAM PLA

Fish sauce or paste is essential to many Thai recipes. It's made by taking little fish and shellfish that are salted, dried, pounded into a paste, and then fermented in jars for a month or more. Nam pla can be used on seafood, to enhance meat dishes, or as a dip for spring rolls.

ESSENTIAL INGREDIENTS

Thai cuisine features lots of flavorful herbs and spices like turmeric, garlic, galangal, chilies, lemongrass, cilantro, and coriander root, many of which are also prized for medicinal properties. Pastes made from shrimp, fish, and chilies bring big flavors to many sauces and dishes.

JASMINE RICE

Known as hom mali, jasmine rice is the staple food here, made into noodles, flour, special desserts, and even wine. Rice also plays an important role in Thai folklore and culture. Many Thai homes and restaurants have small shrines where special bowls filled with rice are offered to ancestors.

FISH

Thailand has long coastlines and shellfish like lobster, crab, and shrimp, as well as squid and octopus, star in many Thai recipes. Snapper, catfish, and mackerel are among the most popular fish in Thai cuisine. Many rural, inland Thai families raise fish in small ponds, so they can always catch fresh fish for dinner!

KAE SA LUK

This is an ancient art form you can eat! The practice of *kae sa luk* (fruit carving) dates back at least 700 years to the royal court, and is now beloved across the country. Special schools teach the skill, and people also learn from masters how to create amazing displays.

SOM TAM

This sweet-tangy-spicy salad is made from shredded, unripe green papaya, mixed with lime, chilis, fish sauce, and sugar. Some cooks also add dried peanuts, shrimp, freshwater crabs, and asparagus beans. In Bangkok, you can get som tam containing an entire fistful of spicy chilies!

PRESENTATION

In Thai culture, when plating food, every detail is important, from the color combinations to how the food is arranged. But food isn't always served on plates or bowls—it might be wrapped in banana leaves or presented in coconuts, cucumbers, or pineapples!

COCONUTS

Coconuts grow well here and their rich, creamy milk transforms many Thai recipes, from mango sticky rice to spicy curries and seafood stews. Tender young coconuts offer a refreshing drink, while the white flesh of mature coconuts is grated for rich, velvety cream.

PAD THAI

FRIED NOODLES WITH SHRIMP

PREPARATION TIME
25 mins

COOKING TIME
15 mins

LEVEL OF DIFFICULTY
●●

SERVES
4

The national dish of Thailand was actually created in the 1930s by the country's prime minister, who wanted a unique dish to unite the nation. Pad thai—meaning "Thai-style fried noodles"—first became popular as a street food in Bangkok. Today, the irresistible combination of stir-fried rice noodles with eggs and aromatics topped with lime slices, peanuts, sliced cucumbers, and fresh herbs is popular worldwide. Some cooks also add palm sugar, tamarind paste, chili-vinegar sauce, or Thai fish sauce for maximum flavor.

INGREDIENTS

FOR THE SAUCE AND NOODLES

8 ounces flat rice noodles (sometimes sold as pad thai noodles)

4 tablespoons chicken broth or water

3 tablespoons fish sauce (nam pla)

¼ cup palm sugar (or coconut sugar)

1 tablespoon tamarind paste

FOR THE SHRIMP

12 ounces medium shelled and deveined shrimp

salt

2 tablespoons cornstarch

2 tablespoons sunflower or peanut oil

FOR THE PAD THAI

1 tablespoon sunflower or peanut oil

2 medium shallots, thinly sliced

4 cloves garlic, thinly sliced

2 eggs, lightly beaten

1 cup mung bean sprouts, for serving

½ cup roasted peanuts, finely chopped or crushed, for serving

1 lime, cut into wedges

fresh cilantro or basil leaves, for serving (optional)

TO MAKE THE SAUCE AND NOODLES

1. In a medium bowl, soak the noodles in warm water until just bendable, 10 to 20 minutes. Drain them well in a colander and cut them into 8-inch pieces.

2. In a small bowl, stir together the broth, fish sauce, palm sugar, tamarind paste, and noodles.

TO MAKE THE SHRIMP

3. In a bowl, toss the shrimp with ½ teaspoon salt and the cornstarch.

4. In a wok or large nonstick skillet, heat 1 tablespoon of the oil over high heat until shimmering. Add the shrimp and stir-fry until pink on the outside and white throughout, 2 to 3 minutes. Transfer to a clean bowl.

TO MAKE THE PAD THAI

5. In the same wok or skillet, heat another tablespoon of oil. Add the shallots and cook, stirring, until softened, about 2 minutes. Add the garlic and cook until softened, about 2 minutes longer. Add the noodles and your sauce and stir-fry until the sauce is incorporated with the noodles, 1 to 2 minutes. Push the noodles to one side of the pan. Add the lightly beaten eggs and cook, moving them around slightly but keeping them away from the noodles, until set, 1 to 2 minutes.

6. Toss the cooked eggs with the noodles, breaking them up slightly. Return the shrimp to the pan and toss to heat through.

7. Serve the pad thai with mung bean sprouts, crushed peanuts, lime wedges, and cilantro or basil leaves, if using.

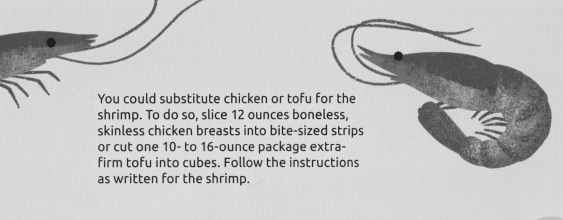

You could substitute chicken or tofu for the shrimp. To do so, slice 12 ounces boneless, skinless chicken breasts into bite-sized strips or cut one 10- to 16-ounce package extra-firm tofu into cubes. Follow the instructions as written for the shrimp.

TURKEY

At the crossroads of Europe, Asia, and the Middle East for thousands of years, Turkey is the meeting place of many cultures—and many cuisines. Its high mountainous terrain and rich farmland have made it the world's leading producer of hazelnuts, raisins, dried figs, dried apricots, dried cherries, and quince. Turkish rituals and recipes blend with those of Central Asia and the Middle East, reaching to the Mediterranean and the Black Sea and all the way back in time to Mesopotamia, when farming first began in this region.

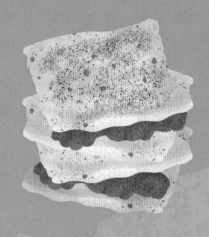

STRONG COFFEE—NO FILTER!

Istanbul's first-known coffeehouse opened in the 1600s, and coffee culture has been central here ever since. According to one Turkish saying, coffee should be "strong as death, sweet as love." This is due not to the type of beans used, but to the method: boil finely ground beans but don't filter them; simply let the solids settle, usually in a copper pot with wooden handles.

POPULAR PASTRIES

Yufka—layered sheets of paper-thin dough—are made in almost every neighborhood here and baked into borek pastries filled with meat, cheese, or spinach. Originally cooked on the *saj* (a flat sheet of iron used by nomadic Turks), these days they may be fried or baked.

TURKISH DELIGHT

Known here as lokum, delicate gummylike jellies cut into cubes and rolled in sugar are popular throughout the Middle East. Favorite flavors include lemon, orange, rose, and orange blossom.

BREAD AND YOGURT

A Turkish-Arabic dictionary from the eleventh century includes names for breads and yufka (see above), and dairy products like yogurt and cheeses. Today, Turkey has a wide range of delicious breads and yogurts that still appear in everything from soups to desserts to drinks.

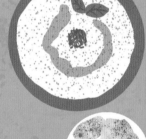

VERSATILE EGGPLANT

Iconic eggplant recipes in Turkey include musakka (sautéed with peppers, onions, and ground meat but, unlike in Greece, not layered), Sultan's delight (puréed with cheese), and the beloved appetizer imam bayildi (meaning "the holy man fainted"—because it tastes so good!).

PICK YOUR PROTEIN

Lamb or mutton is one of Turkey's favorite meats—often roasted, grilled, baked, slow-cooked, or made into kofte (meatballs). People don't waste any part of the animal, enjoying lamb's head, trotters, liver, tripe, brain, and kidneys. Lamb intestines are perfect for making little sausages—which are grilled as a street snack.

SWEET SIPPING

A cold drink enjoyed here for centuries is sherbet: fruit juice sweetened with honey or sugar, sometimes with spices, served over ice or snow. Turkish sherbet is an ancestor of global frozen treats, including Italian sorbetto, French sorbet, and English sherbet. Traditional flavors here include violet juice, rose water, tamarind, or mulberry, each a different beautiful color.

CATCH OF THE DAY

The Black Sea is renowned for fresh anchovies, called hamsi, also sea bass, red mullet, bream, sole, turbot, bonito, swordfish, and sardines. Some of the most consumed seafoods include mussels, squid, octopus, and shrimp.

ANCIENT OVENS

The *tandir* is a traditional oven consisting of a large earthenware pot in the ground. Most Turkish towns continue the tradition of stone-lined, wood-burning communal ovens, called *tas firin*.

BREADS

AROUND THE WORLD

Is there anything better than the smell of fresh-baked bread? People have been perfecting combinations of flour, water, and leavening since the days of ancient Egypt. Today, cultures around the world cherish their daily bread, like South Asian roti flatbread, Middle Eastern pita pockets, Italian focaccia, Ethiopian injera, French baguettes, Colombian pan de bono, and loaves of sliced white bread from the U.S. People start their day with toast and jam, tear off flatbread to sop up curry, and pack sandwiches, pitas, and rolls for lunch, all slathered with toppings from mustard to Marmite™, hummus to herring. You might say that few things unite humanity as much as breaking bread.

JAPANESE MILK BREAD

This moist, fluffy bread, known as shokupan, has a pillowy, featherlight texture and subtly sweet flavor. Each loaf has a tender crumb and a crisp golden crust. A staple for many Japanese families, milk bread may be spread with butter and jam at breakfast, made into bento-box sandwiches for lunch, or served at Japanese tea ceremonies.

PÃO DE QUEIJO

The name literally means "cheese bread," but some say the ancestral recipe didn't contain any dairy. Originally made by enslaved Africans who baked the South African manioc into balls of starchy sustenance, the bread was eventually enriched with cheese and milk. Today, pão de queijo is puffy, soft, gooey, and cheesy. Sold at bakeries and coffee shops across Brazil and northern Argentina, it is often enjoyed with a mug of hot chocolate.

BLACK PUMPERNICKEL

Made from the flour of Russia's famous rye, this dark, dense, chewy, deeply flavorful bread can feature minced onion, caraway and fennel seeds, and molasses. Usually baked overnight, it's delicious topped with smoked herring with fresh dill, caviar, or just butter!

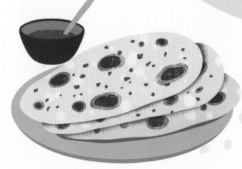

NAAN

This famous flatbread from the Indian subcontinent and the Middle East is made from a yeasted dough moistened with plain yogurt. Traditionally, naan isn't cooked on a stovetop skillet or baked on a tray. Instead, skilled bakers slap the dough against the interior of a clay oven called a tandoor, and it bakes clinging to the hot walls! Once out, the smoke-tinged naans are often brushed with ghee, a golden clarified butter.

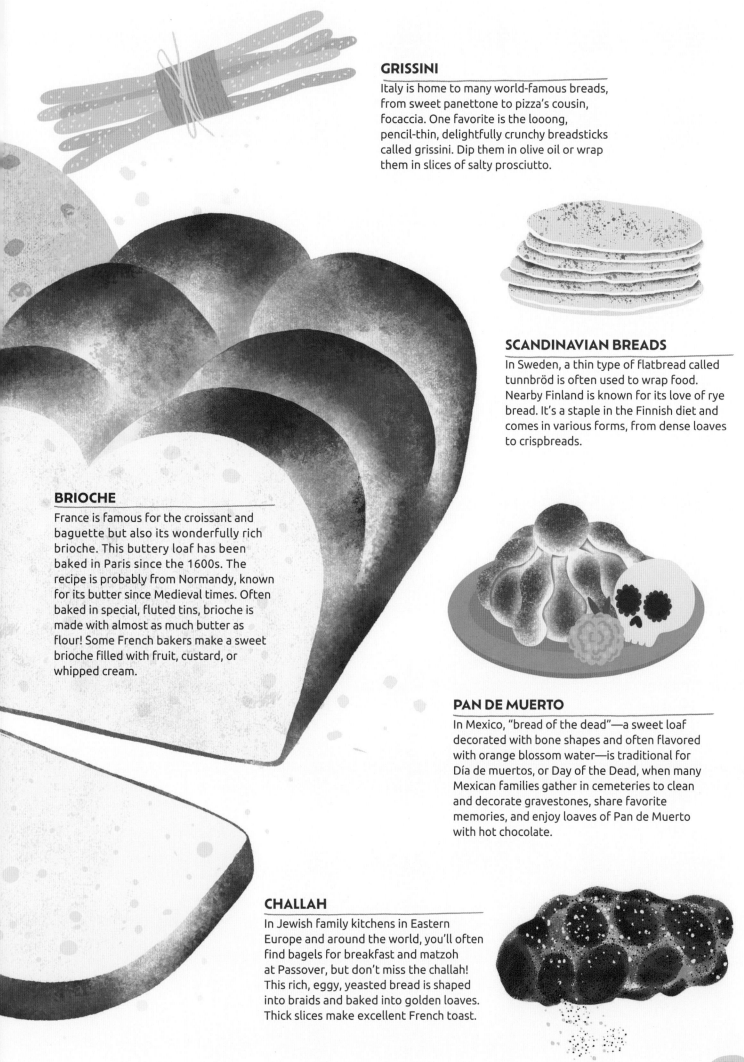

GRISSINI

Italy is home to many world-famous breads, from sweet panettone to pizza's cousin, focaccia. One favorite is the looong, pencil-thin, delightfully crunchy breadsticks called grissini. Dip them in olive oil or wrap them in slices of salty prosciutto.

SCANDINAVIAN BREADS

In Sweden, a thin type of flatbread called tunnbröd is often used to wrap food. Nearby Finland is known for its love of rye bread. It's a staple in the Finnish diet and comes in various forms, from dense loaves to crispbreads.

BRIOCHE

France is famous for the croissant and baguette but also its wonderfully rich brioche. This buttery loaf has been baked in Paris since the 1600s. The recipe is probably from Normandy, known for its butter since Medieval times. Often baked in special, fluted tins, brioche is made with almost as much butter as flour! Some French bakers make a sweet brioche filled with fruit, custard, or whipped cream.

PAN DE MUERTO

In Mexico, "bread of the dead"—a sweet loaf decorated with bone shapes and often flavored with orange blossom water—is traditional for Día de muertos, or Day of the Dead, when many Mexican families gather in cemeteries to clean and decorate gravestones, share favorite memories, and enjoy loaves of Pan de Muerto with hot chocolate.

CHALLAH

In Jewish family kitchens in Eastern Europe and around the world, you'll often find bagels for breakfast and matzoh at Passover, but don't miss the challah! This rich, eggy, yeasted bread is shaped into braids and baked into golden loaves. Thick slices make excellent French toast.

PITA

ROUND FLATBREAD POCKETS

PREPARATION TIME	COOKING TIME	LEVEL OF DIFFICULTY	MAKES
2 hr 30 mins	5 mins	● ●	6 pitas

This little flatbread shaped in a circle has been a staple in the Middle East for a long time—some say for 4,000 years! It's now daily bread in Syria, Iraq, Turkey, Jordan, Lebanon, Egypt, Iran, Greece, Bulgaria, and more, where that little bread pocket is stuffed with delicious fillings like shawarma, kebabs, falafel, baba ganoush, and hummus. The pita's pocket forms as if by magic while baking—so long as you roll the dough verrry thinly and bake it in a super hot oven!

INGREDIENTS

2 teaspoons active dry yeast
1 tablespoon honey or sugar
1 teaspoon salt
1 tablespoon olive oil, plus more
    for the bowl
¼ cup whole-wheat flour
2 cups all-purpose flour

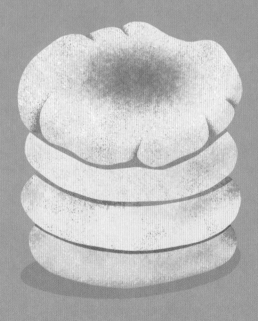

1. In a large mixing bowl, dissolve the yeast in 1 cup warm water with 1 teaspoon of honey or sugar. Leave until bubbles form, about 10 minutes.

2. Add the remaining ingredients and stir with a wooden spoon until a shaggy dough forms. With clean hands, knead the dough in the bowl for 5 to 10 minutes, until it's smooth, soft, and stretchy. Turn the dough onto a floured board and knead for a few more minutes, until smooth and elastic. Cover with a clean tea towel and let the dough rest for 10 minutes, then knead again for 2 more minutes.

3. Rub the mixing bowl with a bit of oil to coat, then return the dough to the bowl, cover with the clean tea towel, and leave it to rise in a warm place until it doubles in size, about 1½ hours.

4. Arrange an oven rack in the lowest rung and heat the oven to 475° F.

5. Meanwhile, gently punch down the dough to deflate it, divide it into six equal pieces, and roll each piece into a ball. Cover with a clean towel and let rest for 15 minutes.

6. Once the oven is fully preheated, roll out the dough: working with one ball at a time, roll to ¼-inch thickness. Place each onto an ungreased cookie sheet. They should not touch—bake in batches if needed.

7. Bake in the bottom of the preheated oven for about 5 minutes. Watch through the oven window—as soon as the pitas puff up, they're done! Take care not to overbake.

8. After baking, wrap the hot pita in a clean tea towel to prevent it from drying out while you wait for it to cool. Some even place the cooling pita in a brown paper bag for 15 minutes, to keep it soft.

Pitas are often served on a meze plate with hummus or baba ganoush, tabbouleh, or falafel.

Whole-wheat flour adds a nice nuttiness, but you can use all white flour if you prefer.

If your pita didn't form a pocket, try topping it with tomato sauce and cheese to make another flatbread: pizza!

VIETNAM

Vietnam is long and narrow—in some places it is only 30 miles wide. In addition to 2,000 miles of coastline, this biodiverse Southeast Asian country also has many rivers, jungles, deltas, mountains, and islands. Vietnamese cuisine reflects its complicated history with ties to China and France, both of which ruled Vietnam in the past. But while some recipes include stir-fries or freshly baked baguettes, Vietnamese chefs always add their own unique spin.

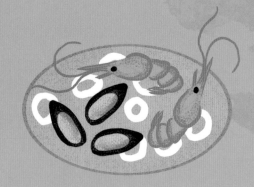

RICE

More than half of Vietnam's arable land is used to grow rice—from fragrant, long-grain jasmine rice to white rice to deep purple glutinous rice, which becomes super sticky once cooked. Rice is also turned into noodles, translucent rice "paper," rice wine, and a sweet, nutty powder made from the toasted grains.

FISH AND SEAFOOD

Catfish, eel, shrimp, crabs, and shellfish are all favorites in Vietnamese cuisine. People buy fish caught the same day, so fresh it's frequently still alive. Seafood is often simply steamed and seasoned with lime juice, salt, and pepper, plus a side of a tangy dip made from fish sauce, lime, sugar, and hot peppers.

BÁNH TRÁNG

Vietnam's famous rice "paper," or bánh tráng, is super thin, circular wrappers. To make them, rice-flour batter is spread over fabric, which is dried in the sun. The result looks like translucent paper! People then dip the brittle, dried rice paper into water for a few seconds, making it instantly soft and ready to be stuffed with fresh fillings.

GỎI CUỐN

These fresh summer rolls are one of the most popular treats made from bánh tráng, stuffed with freshly boiled shrimp, cilantro, cucumbers, pickled carrots and radishes, and rice noodles. Gỏi cuốn are served with a deliciously rich, thick, peanut dipping sauce.

NƯỚC MẮM

Vietnamese flavors get a big boost from nước mắm, a dipping sauce with a 300-year history! Its sweet and tangy taste is the result of a delicious mix of lime juice, garlic, chilies, sugar, and fish sauce, in which tiny fish, shrimp, and crab are preserved in salt and fermented for months.

VEGGIES AND HERBS

Aromatic herbs are essential to Vietnamese cuisine, with cilantro, basil, mint, and leafy lettuce starring in almost every dish. Everything must be fresh, and greens are often served raw or only lightly cooked. Vietnamese soups and stir-fries celebrate bitter melon, long beans, taro stems, and rau muống, or "water spinach"—which grows wild along Vietnam's rivers and canals.

BÁNH MÌ

French colonizers brought the baguette to Vietnam, and locals still enjoy their own lighter, pillowy version of the bread. Baguette sandwiches, here are called bánh mì and are popularly served by street vendors for breakfast and lunch. Breakfast bánh mì usually features fried eggs, while lunch sandwiches include a mouth-watering array of ingredients like pâté, sliced cucumber, pickled radish, and plenty of fresh aromatic herbs.

FRUIT AND FRUIT DRINKS

A popular fruit drink is limeade with bubbly water, sometimes flavored with salty plums. Coconut trees grow everywhere here, and people love to sip nước dừa, the clear, refreshing liquid found inside young coconuts. Another popular drink is the sweet juice of freshly squeezed sugarcane, which is probably as close as you can get to drinking liquid sugar.

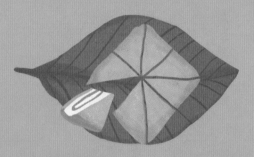

VIETNAM'S FAVORITE HOLIDAY

Celebrations for Tét, the Lunar New Year, in Vietnam last for a week and include much feasting, as well as symbolic foods given as gifts. A favorite holiday dish includes glutinous rice cakes stuffed with mung beans and pork, seasoned with fermented shrimp paste, chili peppers, lemongrass, and black pepper. The cakes are wrapped in banana leaves and boiled, creating sticky, flavor-infused morsels.

PHO

BROTH WITH BEEF AND RICE NOODLES

PREPARATION TIME
10 mins

COOKING TIME
40 mins

LEVEL OF DIFFICULTY
● ●

SERVES
4

Originally a street food and now Vietnam's national dish, pho is a soup of rich, beefy broth with rice noodles, thinly sliced meat, and aromatic herbs. At its heart, great pho is a wonderfully flavorful clear broth, usually made from long-simmered beef bones—the broth is traditionally cooked over low heat for many, many hours or even overnight for a deep, rich, complex flavor. This version saves time by calling for stock, which you quickly infuse with aromatics like ginger, cloves, cinnamon, and star anise, so that it all comes together in less than an hour.

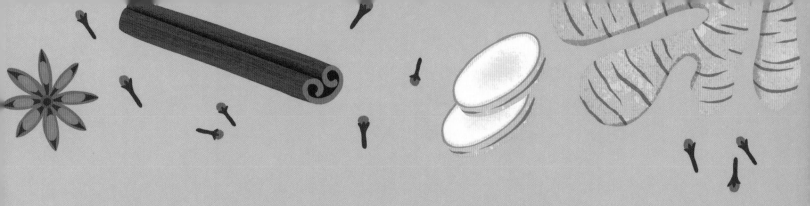

INGREDIENTS

¾ pound boneless top sirloin
1 2-inch piece of ginger, halved
     lengthwise
2 onions, halved
3 cloves
2 star anise pods
1 small cinnamon stick
8 cups good-quality beef or
     chicken stock (or 1 quart
     of each)
10 ounces dried flat rice noodles
     or pho noodles
1 tablespoon fish sauce
1 teaspoon brown sugar
salt

GARNISHES, FOR SERVING:

1 cup mung bean sprouts
4 scallions, thinly sliced
2 limes, quartered into wedges
2 cups of mixed herbs: mint,
     cilantro, and Thai basil
1 jalapeño, thinly sliced into
     rounds
hoisin sauce
sriracha

1. Place the meat in the freezer for 30 minutes to make it easy to slice.

2. In a large pot, toast the ginger, onions, cloves, star anise, and cinnamon over medium-high heat, stirring frequently, until fragrant, 2 to 3 minutes. Add the stock and 2 cups of water and bring to a boil, then reduce the heat to medium-low and cook for 30 minutes, allowing the aromatics to infuse the broth.

3. While the broth simmers, soak the noodles in a bowl of hot water until they bend and look bright white, then drain in a heatproof strainer.

4. Remove the beef from the freezer and slice it very, very thinly.

5. Using a slotted spoon, remove the solids from the broth and discard them. Add the fish sauce and sugar, then taste and season with salt and more fish sauce and sugar, if you like. Keep on a low simmer.

6. When you're nearly ready to eat, dunk the noodles in the broth to warm, then transfer them to 4 bowls.

7. Increase the heat of the broth to medium and add the thinly sliced beef. Cook for 2 minutes for medium-rare meat, or longer if you prefer.

8. Ladle the cooked beef and hot broth over the noodles, dividing the beef evenly.

9. Serve the pho with garnishes of bean sprouts, scallions, lime wedges, herbs, jalapeño slices, hoisin sauce, and sriracha.

In this recipe, the beef is sliced so thin, it cooks almost instantly in the hot broth. If you prefer, you can replace the beef with cubed tofu or cooked, shredded chicken.

AUSTRALASIA
AND OCEANIA

This island-rich region spans a vast expanse of the Southern Hemisphere, including Australia, New Zealand, New Guinea, and thousands of islands, from Indonesia and Guam to Fiji and Tahiti.

While Australasia is home to lush rainforests, arid deserts, towering mountain ranges, and even glaciers and volcanoes, this part of the globe is dominated by water. Here people swim, surf, and sail the Indian Ocean, the Pacific Ocean, and the world's third-largest ocean—the Southern Ocean. Even young children in Australasia are often expert swimmers and fishers. Locals feast on the freshest catch, like tuna, barramundi, sea urchins, octopus, squid, and prawns, and meet many more sea creatures while snorkeling in the Great Barrier Reef, the world's largest coral reef system. No wonder this watery part of the world is also known as Oceania!

If fish don't float your boat, fear not. Coconut palm trees line many island shores here, and people drink coconut water, bake coconut bread, add coconut cream to curries, and sweeten desserts with coconut sugar. Taro root, a centuries-old starchy staple, can be boiled, steamed, fried, or baked, but is beloved as poi, a thick, sticky dish popular across Polynesia.

FROZEN DESSERTS

AROUND THE WORLD

Whether eaten from a cup on the street or from a bowl after dinner, people around the world enjoy frozen sweets—especially delightful on a hot summer afternoon. Most evidence indicates that the first true ice cream originated in the seventeenth century in Italy. From there, it spread to France, England, India, and beyond, becoming an internationally beloved sweet treat on hot days.

FROZEN FRUIT

At least 2,500 years ago, ancient Mesopotamians liked to add crushed ice to bowls of dates or honey. In modern Iraq, specialized parlors sell ice cream flavored with pistachio and qamar'l deen, or "apricot fruit leather"—apricots boiled in sugar and then set out in the sun to dry.

GELATO

In summer, Italians line up for scoops of luscious ice cream that goes by the name gelato. It contains 4 to 9% fat compared to American ice cream's 14 to 25% fat, giving it a less creamy but more intense taste.

SORBETEROS

The Philippines are home to amazingly diverse ice cream flavors. Vendors called sorbeteros push brightly colored carts and tout scoops with flavors like avocado, corn, and purple yam. There's even a salty-sweet cheddar-cheese-flavored ice cream, sometimes studded with corn kernels for extra crunch.

MOCHI

Mochi is a traditional sweet snack in Japan made by shaping pounded sticky rice into small cakes filled with sweet bean or yam paste. In California in the 1990s, the recipe was tweaked to include a filling of ice cream, a delicious version that quickly spread around the globe.

I-TIM-PAD

Also known as rolled ice cream or stir-fried ice cream, this is a unique innovation pioneered by Thai street vendors. It's made by pouring then swishing sweet, flavored milk onto a freezing-cold steel surface until it hardens, then rolling the frozen cream into tight cylinders.

IRANIAN DESSERTS

After dinner in Iran, people often eat faloodeh, a frozen sorbetlike dessert made primarily from thin, starchy noodles—similar to vermicelli—covered in a semi frozen syrup flavored with saffron, rose water, or pistachio. Iranians also enjoy a thick ice cream called bastani sonnati—flavored with rose water, saffron, vanilla, and pistachios, sometimes with pure chunks of frozen clotted cream.

HAWAIIAN ICES

Also known as snowballs in the Southern U.S., Hawaiian ices are made by grinding off shavings from a huge block of ice and dousing them with brightly colored sweet syrups. First introduced to Hawaii in the early twentieth century by Japanese immigrants, kakigōri, as the chilly desserts were known in Japan, were invented centuries before as a special extravagance for wealthy people.

KULFI

This ice cream, enjoyed in Bangladesh, Pakistan, Myanmar, Nepal, India, and Sri Lanka, is made from reduced milk, giving it a custardlike consistency. It is often shaped like a cone and served on a stick like a Popsicle™. Some accounts indicate kulfi originated in the sixteenth century, as a favorite treat of Indian royalty. If true, India is the inventor of ice cream.

FAGYLALT

Hungarians love fagylalt—several scoops are served in a small cone. In summer, one can also buy hókristály (snow crystal)—ground or crushed ice with a shot of brightly colored fruit syrup.

AUSTRALIA

Australia is a country, a continent, *and* the largest island on Earth! It's also home to tropical rainforests, dry deserts, snowcapped mountains, palm-fringed coasts, and beautiful beaches. Aboriginal people have lived here for 50,000 years. But in the 1700s, the British arrived, turning parts of Australia into a prison colony. Today, of Australia's 21 million citizens, approximately 3% are indigenous, descended from ancestors who lived here and on nearby islands before the British arrived—but they cherish their cultural and culinary heritage and maintain vibrant food traditions, which now blend with the food cultures of Australia's many citizens of European ancestry.

KANGAROO FOR DINNER

Wild game meat includes kangaroo, wallabies, emus, echidna (porcupine), turtles, and tiny little marsupials called bandicoots. Today, you can find kangaroo meat in grocery stores— people cook it over coals or in a stew.

WILD FOODS

Aboriginal Australians developed knowledge of over a thousand wild plants, from the desert to the rainforest. This expertise was largely ignored by white settlers, but today people are rediscovering bush tucker (as wild foods are called) like watercress oil, wild mountain pepper, wattleseed (which has a coffee-hazelnut flavor), and bunya nuts, collected from the giant cones of bunya pine trees.

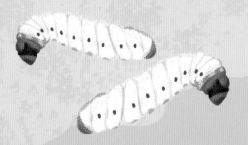

WITCHETTY GRUBS

These plump, white moth larvae look like little mushy marshmallows. A traditional wild food, some Australians still enjoy these grubs roasted over the barbie's coals.

THE BARBIE

Avid outdoors people, many Australians love cooking and eating outside too. They gather around the barbecue—the *barbie*—to grill steak and sausages. Goanna lizard is also often grilled, and "carpetbag steak"—a thick steak split open and stuffed with oysters—is popular, served with anchovy sauce.

VEGEMITE™

Just about every Australian kitchen has a jar of this thick, salty dark brown, yeast paste. It's very high in vitamin B and people here love to spread it on toast.

FRUITS

Fruit salad is popular at the barbie! The Australian climate grows amazing fruits, including passionfruit, pineapples, pawpaws, figs, guava, chokos, tamarillos, cumquats, lychees, kiwi, custard apples, and plums.

ANZAC COOKIES

Anzac Day (April 25) honors people who died in wars for Australia and New Zealand. People commemorate them by baking and eating Anzac biscuits, big oat cookies that were traditionally sent to soldiers.

MEAT PIES

Australia and neighboring New Zealand are home to so many shepherds, they are two of the world's leading producers of lamb. Australians love lamb prepared many ways, including baked into little pies with a pastry crust. Some Australians serve meat pies floating in split pea soup!

GLOBAL FLAVORS

The British brought their favorite foods like tea, biscuits, and corned beef. Australia is also home to many immigrants from nearby Indonesia, Vietnam, Malaysia, India, and the Philippines, making satay and stir-fries with noodles or rice daily favorites.

DAMPER

This Aboriginal Australian flatbread is made by grinding seeds into flour, making dough, and then cooking it over fire. It is still popular today, but is now often made with self-raising flour and baked in an oven.

PAVLOVA

MERINGUE WITH WHIPPED CREAM, STRAWBERRIES, AND KIWI

PREPARATION TIME
1 hr

COOKING TIME
1 hr 15 mins

LEVEL OF DIFFICULTY
● ●

MAKES
1 8-inch
pavlova

This meringue cake with a marshmallow-soft center is as light as air. The national dessert of Australia, it is also beloved in nearby New Zealand. Some say the recipe was created for the ballerina Anna Pavlova, who danced her way through both countries in 1926. After all, pavlova floats on your tongue like a ballerina sailing through the air, and the sides of it look a bit like a tutu.

But while being a ballerina is hard work, making this dessert is not. If you haven't made meringue before, you'll be surprised how easy it is to whip up! Just be sure to start with a perfectly clean, dry bowl, and don't allow even a smidge of yolks in. If you try to beat the whites by hand, you'll get a ballerina-level workout—but use the whisk attachment of a hand mixer or stand mixer and you'll have magically fluffy meringue in just a few minutes!

This version is topped with kiwi, the fuzzy-skinned, green-fleshed fruit that was first commercially grown in New Zealand—but you can crown pavlova with berries, peaches, passionfruit, or any favorite fruit in peak season.

INGREDIENTS

FOR THE PAVLOVA

4 large egg whites
pinch of salt
1 cup super fine sugar
1 teaspoon apple cider or
    distilled white vinegar
1½ teaspoons cornstarch
1 teaspoon pure vanilla extract

FOR THE TOPPING

1 cup heavy cream
2 tablespoons super fine sugar
1 cup strawberries, sliced about
    ¼ inch thick
2 kiwi, peeled and sliced about ¼
    inch thick

TO MAKE THE PAVLOVA

1. Preheat the oven to 350°F. Line a baking sheet with parchment paper.

2. In a large bowl, combine the egg whites and salt. Using an electric mixer (or a stand mixer fitted with a whisk attachment), beat the egg whites at medium-high speed until they form soft peaks, about 5 minutes. (When you flip over one of the beaters, the peak of the whipped egg white will flop over into soft peaks, like a Santa hat.) With the mixer running, add the sugar, 1 tablespoon at a time, until you have a stiff, shiny meringue. Gently fold in the vinegar, cornstarch, and vanilla.

3. Spread the meringue on the parchment paper in a circle-blob about 8 inches across. Use the spatula to create fun, artful swoops if you like. These will set as the pavlova bakes.

4. Place the meringue in the oven, lower the temperature to 300°F, and bake for 1 hour and 15 minutes or until crisp on the edges. Let cool completely. Don't worry if the surface is cracked—you'll soon slather it in whipped cream!

TO MAKE THE TOPPING

5. In a small bowl, whip the heavy cream and sugar until stiff peaks form.

6. When ready to serve, spoon whipped cream over the cooled pavlova, then top with the sliced fruit. Serve sliced into wedges.

REFRESHING DRINKS

AROUND THE WORLD

When you're heated up, nothing cools you down like a nice, cold drink. While minty herbs and citrus slices are popular in glasses worldwide, regional beverages are also made with locally beloved ingredients like ginger, kola nuts, black tea, boba, sugar syrups, corn, rice, and even bread. The refreshing results may be sweet or salty, light or thick, flat or bubbly, and topped with anything from cinnamon sticks to pineapple chunks.

SIMA
In Finland, they make a bubbly lemonade with lemon, honey, raisins, and a little bit of yeast. The resulting fermentation creates fizzy bubbles!

NIMBU PANI
This thirst-quenching Indian drink is made with a yellow-green citrus called the nimbu, finished with Himalayan salt, and sold from street carts all summer.

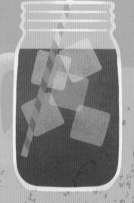

LIMONANA
This lemonade is green! That's because it's made with mint leaves, which get blended with sugar, lemon juice, and water. It's so good it's the national drink in Israel, but it's made all over the Middle East.

PAPELÓN CON LIMÓN
In Venezuela, the secret lemonade ingredient is a special brown sugar. It's called papelón, and it comes in a big brick! A bit gets dissolved in hot water for sweetness, then mixed with sour lemon or lime juice and chilled with lots of ice.

ARNOLD PALMER

In the United States, an Arnold Palmer is half lemonade and half iced tea. It's named for a famous golfer who always cooled down with this refreshing combination.

SALTY LEMONADE

In Vietnam, lemons and limes are preserved in salt so they will keep throughout the year. Put half of one in a glass with a little sugar and water—ta-da! You've got salty lemonade.

GINGER BEER

This nonalcoholic fizzy drink has a sweet flavor, a spicy kick, and a global history. First brewed in eighteenth-century England using spices from Asia and sugar from the Caribbean, it's now sipped around the world.

SLAVIC KVASS

Drink your bread! This traditional Slavic drink is made from black or rye bread mixed with water, sugar, and yeast, then left to ferment until fizzy. Sweet and sour, sometimes kvass is flavored with fruits like raspberry, cherry, or lemon.

HORCHATA

In Mexico, this thick, white drink is made from cooked, puréed rice, seasoned with cinnamon and vanilla, and often served over ice. It's like a rice pudding that you sip through a straw!

CHICHA MORADA

People in Peru make this sweet drink from an ancient type of purple corn still grown in the Andes. It's often seasoned with cinnamon and cloves, and studded with chunks of pineapple.

LAMB CHOPS

LAMB CHOPS IN A ROSEMARY MARINADE

PREPARATION TIME
2 hrs 30 mins

COOKING TIME
10 mins

LEVEL OF DIFFICULTY
● ●

SERVES
4

In New Zealand, sheep outnumber people and its lamb is famous around the world. Locals, too, love it many ways, from slow-roasted leg of lamb to spicy little lamb sausages. One of the quickest, most delicious preparations is lamb chops, which cook up juicy and tender in just a few minutes. Many people like their lamb medium rare with a dark sear and rosy-pink interior. If you have an instant-read thermometer, these chops are done when they reach 135°F. You can cook them slightly longer if you prefer medium, but the meat can quickly go from tender and juicy to tough and dry, so take care not to overcook it.

INGREDIENTS

1 tablespoon of fresh, minced
    rosemary or ½ teaspoon dried
2 tablespoons olive oil
3 cloves garlic, peeled and
    minced
salt and black pepper
4 loin lamb chops

1. In a small bowl, combine the dried or fresh rosemary with the olive oil and garlic to make a paste marinade. Season well with salt and pepper.

2. Place the chops on a large plate, pat them dry with paper towels, then rub them on all sides with the marinade. Seal the chops in a ziplock bag and marinate in the refrigerator for 2 hours.

3. Let the marinated chops sit for about 20 to 30 minutes, to reach room temperature. Meanwhile, preheat the oven to 400°F.

4. Heat a large, heavy skillet or cast-iron pan over high heat. Once it's hot, add the chops and let them sear on one side for 2 to 3 minutes. Using tongs, carefully turn each chop over, then transfer the pan to the hot oven and cook for an additional 6 minutes. Test for desired doneness (you can slice into one to be sure the inside is done to your preference); allow chops to rest for 5 minutes before serving.

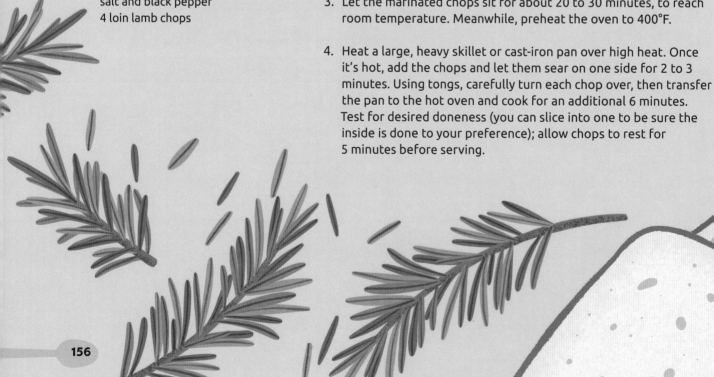

Serve with a fresh salad, steamed asparagus, sautéed spinach, glazed parsnips, or buttered peas, plus roasted potatoes or fresh bread.

EUROPE

Europe is one of the smallest continents—and one of the most densely populated. Ancient Greek and Roman civilizations from thousands of years ago still influence government, philosophy, and architecture today. Many food traditions—like harvesting mushrooms, olives, root vegetables, and berries; turning milk into butter, yogurt, and cheeses; growing grain for breads, pasta, and pastries; and fermenting grapes into wine and apples into hard cider—go back thousands of years.

Europe is now home to over 700 million people, some in rural villages, others inhabiting big cities like London, Paris, Rome, Madrid, Istanbul, and Berlin. The continent also draws immigrants from around the world—including from the many global countries once colonized by European powers, from Barbados and Brazil to Botswana and Bangladesh.

FRANCE

As the largest country in western Europe, France enjoys coastlines on both the Atlantic Ocean and Mediterranean Sea, and also enjoys the towering French Alps, beautiful beaches, bustling cities, and famously fertile farmland. People here have been growing wheat, grapes, and olives—and making them into bread, wine, and olive oil—for thousands of years. France is so celebrated for great cooks and food culture that people worldwide have adopted the French words "chef" and "cuisine."

FAVORITE VEGETABLES

The French love in-season and perfectly fresh vegetables. Favorites include artichokes, asparagus, little beans called haricots verts, and young fresh peas called petite pois, shimmering in buttery glaze or a French salad dressing, known as vinaigrette.

BOULANGERIES AND BAGUETTES

French families seldom bake their own bread because every neighborhood has great *boulangeries*! Here, they bake perhaps France's best-known daily bread: the baguette. These long loaves have a crisp crust and soft center, and the French eat up to 30 million each day. Fresh baguettes are on the table for almost every meal, but *s'il vous plaît*, don't ask for butter— baguettes are only buttered at breakfast!

CROISSANTS

Made from yeasted dough, rolled to incorporate lots and lots of butter, and baked to flaky perfection, the crescent-shaped croissant is sometimes filled with ham and cheese, almond paste, or chocolate, though many consider them perfect just as they are.

CREAM IN EVERYTHING

Milk and cream go into everything from café au lait to cheesy gratins. Many French sauces are golden with eggs, too, like mayonnaise, hollandaise, and bearnaise. One pastry favorite, choux a la crème, is filled with plenty of whipped cream!

CHEESE

Charles de Gaulle, France's former prime minister, once asked, "How can anyone govern a nation that has 246 different kinds of cheese?" Today, there are over 400! From creamy Brie and Camembert to blue Roquefort, a cheese course appears on the menu of just about every restaurant in France.

BOUCHERIES AND CHARCUTERIES

The French eat lots of meat. *Boucheries* (butchers) sell goose, rabbit, duck, quail, beef, lamb, goat, pork, and horsemeat, including cuts like veal, brain, tongue, kidneys, and the famously fattened livers called foie gras. The French have made an art of charcuterie, and special shops sell these cured, smoked, and pickled meats, as well as pâté, the classic spread made of liver cooked in butter and wine.

DIJON

France's world-famous mustard is named for a town in Burgundy, where people have been making the smooth, creamy, strong-flavored spread since the Middle Ages. Made with mustard seeds and white wine, it's stirred into vinaigrette, slathered on sausages, or smoothed into a jambon beurre (ham with butter) sandwich.

OYSTERS

In Brittany and Normandy on France's northeast coast, oysters reign supreme. Over the centuries, the French have refined raising and harvesting oysters along the shore, but their preparation remains sublimely simple: a spritz of lemon or a dab of a vinegar–shallot dressing. Or simply shuck, slurp, and swallow.

GLOBAL FLAVORS

Global trade brought France beans and potatoes from the Americas, coffee and chocolate from Africa, tea from Asia, and sugar from the Caribbean. Today, it is Europe's most ethnically diverse nation. These days, you'll find everything here from Egyptian falafel to Vietnamese bánh mì!

CRÊPES

People here have been eating crêpes—France's beloved, super thin pancakes—since the thirteenth century. During the twentieth century, crêperies opened all over but especially in the Paris neighborhood of Montparnasse. Enjoyed in cafés or at home, crêpes may be savory or sweet, filled with ham and cheese, mushrooms, strawberry jam, or hazelnut chocolate spread, or simply enjoyed with butter.

TRUFFETTES

CHOCOLATE TRUFFLES

PREPARATION TIME	COOKING TIME	LEVEL OF DIFFICULTY	MAKES
3 hrs	10 mins	●	About 35 truffettes

You may have heard of wild truffles, which are underground fungus that people hunt with specially trained sniffing dogs. French farmers forage nearly a third of the world's truffles, which are so intensely flavored that people pay lots of money to have even a tiny bit shaved over their dinner.

Chocolate truffles, however, have no relation to the wild kind—other than being as round, brown, beloved, luxurious, and intensely flavored as the little dug-up orbs for which they're named. And while they're famously luscious, chocolate truffles are surprisingly simple to make. Just chop up some chocolate, melt it with butter, whisk in some cream, and roll spoonfuls into little balls of rich ganache. Once cooled, toss them in cocoa powder. That's it!

INGREDIENTS

2 cups bittersweet or semisweet chocolate, chopped
3 tablespoons cold unsalted butter
pinch of salt
1 cup heavy cream
½ cup unsweetened cocoa powder or ¼ cup cocoa powder mixed with ¼ cup confectioner's sugar

1. In a mixing bowl, combine the chopped chocolate with the butter and salt.

2. In a small saucepan, bring the cream just to a simmer. Pour the hot cream over the chocolate. Let stand until the chocolate and butter are melted, about 5 minutes. Whisk until the mixture, called a ganache, is smooth and shiny. (If you're going to add any extracts to flavor, do so now.)

3. Cover and refrigerate the ganache until firm, 1 to 2 hours.

4. Line a baking sheet with parchment paper. For each truffle, scoop out about 1 tablespoon of the ganache, roll it into a ball, and set it on the baking sheet. Refrigerate until firm, about 1 hour.

5. Put the cocoa powder in a large bowl and line another baking sheet with parchment paper. Roll the ganache in the cocoa powder until well coated. That's it!

6. Pack the truffles in a resealable container and refrigerate for up to 5 days.

You can have fun flavoring your truffles. Try stirring in a dash of almond extract, grating some lemon or orange zest over them, or adding a pinch of sea salt.

Serve truffles with coffee or after dessert, or give them as a gift. Your friends will say, "Ooh la la!"

GERMANY

In 100 CE, a Roman described German food as simple and hearty: breads, grains, fruits and berries, milk and cheese, and wild game roasted on huge spits. These days, few Germans roast meat on huge spits, but in other ways, that description holds true! Modern Germans still savor traditional foods that date back centuries: satisfying stews, squiggly little pasta called spätzle, rich lard known as schmaltz, rye bread spiked with caraway seeds, and plenty of pork and sauerkraut.

PASS THE PORK

Until the 1800s, most Germans were peasants who raised their own pigs. Today, most Germans live in cities, but pork still reigns supreme. Every part of the pig is used: tongues, brains, ears, tails, trotters— even the blood, in beloved blood sausage.

DAILY BREAD

Bread is served with just about every German meal. You'll see dark, whole-grain loaves, chewy rye called pumpernickel, and an incredible array of soft and crisp, plain or seeded, yeasted or sourdough loaves, made from wheat, oats, spelt, buckwheat, linseed, or millet, in every shape and size.

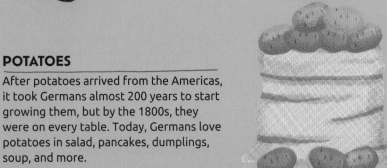

POTATOES

After potatoes arrived from the Americas, it took Germans almost 200 years to start growing them, but by the 1800s, they were on every table. Today, Germans love potatoes in salad, pancakes, dumplings, soup, and more.

SPEAKING OF SAUSAGE . . .

Dinner here is the wurst! That's the German word for sausage, and there are more than a thousand varieties. Bratwurst are sausages to boil or grill; weisswurst means "white sausage," traditionally made of veal; while liverwurst is a spreadable pâté.

ASPARAGUS

Prized white asparagus is an annual spring obsession in Germany. Families cook it at home, chefs create special menus highlighting it, and it is savored in all sizes and styles. In fact, April, May, and June are known as the *Spargelzeit*, or "asparagus time."

BLACK FOREST CAKE

Germany's most famous cake is this chocolate sponge cake filled with sweetened cream, decorated with cherries, and brushed with kirschwasser—a cherry liqueur. Some say the cake looks like the traditional white blouse, black dress, and hat with red pom-poms worn by women in the Black Forest region!

KAFFEE UND KUCHEN

Many gather to catch up over coffee and cakes, a *zwischenmahlzeiten,* or "in-between meal," also enjoyed in neighboring Austria and Luxembourg.

BEER HERE

Traditionally, beer here was made in winter and stored in underground cellars. In summer, brewers would set up tables at the cellar entrance to give buyers a shady spot. This *biergarten* or "beer garden," dates back to the seventeenth century. Beer is often served in a large, heavy glass called a stein, especially during the annual *Oktoberfest*—beer festival.

HAMBURG(ERS)!

The German city of Hamburg is the ancestral home of the hamburger, the ground beef sandwich on a bun now popular all over the world. Its sausage friend the frankfurter (rechristened in New York as the hot dog) takes its name from the German city of Frankfurt.

BREZEL

Brezels, called pretzels in English, get their crunchy exterior and brown color from being dipped in lye (an alkaline liquid). In Bavaria, a popular midmorning snack is a soft pretzel with weisswurst.

CABBAGE AND BRATWURST

SWEET-AND-SOUR BRAISED CABBAGE WITH PORK SAUSAGES

PREPARATION TIME	COOKING TIME	LEVEL OF DIFFICULTY	SERVES
20 mins	1 hr	●●	4

Germans love both cabbages and sausages—and they're even better together! This sweet-and-sour braised cabbage gets extra flavor from a tart apple and the zing of apple cider vinegar, plus juniper berries or caraway seeds, if you like. You can use red or green cabbage, but the purply red gives the dish a pretty color. Cabbage stores well all winter and traditionally kept peasants fed months after harvest. Today, this dish will warm you from the inside out on a cold, dark night. In this recipe, the pork sausages cook on the stovetop, but it's also easy to pop them into the oven to bake while the cabbage cooks.

Consider serving this with a pile of mashed potatoes, a slice of hearty German bread, and some strong mustard!

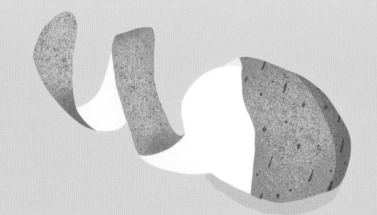

INGREDIENTS

3 tablespoons oil
1 medium yellow onion, diced
½ head cabbage, thinly sliced
1 medium-sized tart apple, diced
½ cup chicken or vegetable
  stock, or apple cider or water
1 tablespoon sugar, plus more to
  taste
1 bay leaf
3 whole cloves
3 juniper berries or ½ teaspoon
  caraway seeds (optional)
½ teaspoon salt, plus more to
  taste
4 bratwurst sausages
2 tablespoons apple cider
  vinegar, plus more to taste

1. In a heavy pot or Dutch oven, heat 2 tablespoons of the oil. Add the diced onion and cook until it begins to brown, about 8 minutes.

2. Add the cabbage and cook, stirring, until wilted, about 5 minutes. Add the apple, broth, vinegar, sugar, bay leaf, cloves, juniper berries or caraway seeds, and salt. Bring the liquid to a boil, reduce the heat to medium-low, cover and simmer, stirring occasionally, until the cabbage is tender and infused with all of the flavors, 20 to 30 minutes. Add more liquid if the pan starts to dry out.

3. While the cabbage cooks, heat 1 tablespoon of oil in a large skillet over medium-high heat. Add the sausages in a single layer and cook until browned on the bottom, about 4 minutes. Turn the sausages and cook until browned on the other side, about 3 minutes longer. Add 1 cup of water to the skillet and simmer until the sausages are cooked through, about 10 minutes.

4. Taste the cabbage and season with more salt, sugar, and vinegar, to taste. Serve with the sausages.

ITALY

For millennia, the Italian peninsula's location—jutting into the Mediterranean Sea—made its ports busy places for exchanging ideas—and ingredients! In the Middle Ages, Venice was part of the spice route connecting Europe to Asia. Soon, sailors like the Italian-born Christopher Columbus brought ingredients from the Americas, like tomatoes, beans, and chocolate, which would become essential to Italian cuisine. Thousands of years ago, ancient Romans were already making breads, salads, olive oil, spiced sausages, wine, cheeses, and cakes! Variations on cuisines from ancient Rome are all still enjoyed here today.

PASTA

Some historians say Marco Polo introduced noodles from China to Italy in the 1200s. Whatever the lineage, there are now over 600 shapes of pasta here, many with names that describe how they look. Orecchiette resemble ears, linguine are like long tongues, and rotelle are like wagon wheels, while radiatori resemble a car's radiator.

PORK

Italians eat lots of pork and also wild boar, which they make into sausages like salami and mortadella. Some pork legs are salted, hung to dry for months, and cured into prosciutto, which is served as a thinly shaved delicacy.

BREAD

Thousands of specialty bakeries across the country bake breads, including grissini, ciabatta, panini, crostini, bruschetta, and focaccia for every occasion. Archaeologists excavating the ancient city of Pompeii discovered a bakery with an oven that still contained round loaves of sourdough bread!

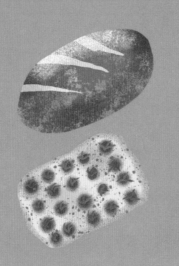

VEGETABLES

Italian gardens are lush with eggplants, artichokes, beans, spinach, fennel, chicory, broccoli rabe, and aromatic herbs like oregano, basil, and rosemary. Global exploration brought tomatoes, which Italians called the pomo d'oro (golden apple). Today, tomatoes are essential to Italian cuisine.

SEAFOOD

Italian cuisine has always boasted amazing fresh seafood. Recipes call for octopus, clams, mussels, eel, shrimp, prawns, squid, and more. It may be grilled, fried, simmered in stews, served in cold salads, or tossed with pasta.

NUTELLA®

The Italian confection called gianduja—a paste of chocolate, sugar and hazelnuts—can be used as a candy filler, in ice cream, or as thick frosting. In 1951, Pietro Ferrero developed his own recipe of spreadable gianduja. In 1964, a variation of this spread became Nutella®. Today, children and adults around the world slather it on toast.

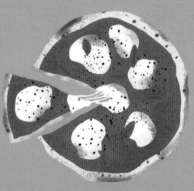

PIZZA

Italians have been covering flatbreads with toppings since long before tomatoes arrived, and many variations have stories behind them. In 1889, after Italy's unification, Queen Margherita of Savoy visited Naples and asked its most celebrated *pizzaiolo* (pizza maker) to make her something new. Her favorite was a new, simple combination: tomato, mozzarella, and basil, in the colors of the Italian flag. Today, it is called pizza Margherita.

CHEESES

Italians make hundreds of cheeses from the milk of cows, sheep, goats, and even water buffalo. Favorites include nutty, aged parmesan, mild asiago, quick-melting fontina, fresh mozzarella, and blue-veined gorgonzola. Parmesan was mentioned in 1398 in one of Italy's most famous books, Boccaccio's *Decameron* and ricotta gets a mention in Homer's 800 BCE epic poem *The Odyssey*!

PESTO

In Italian, pesto means "smashed" or "made into a paste," which you can do with a diverse combination of fresh greens, types of nuts, and a fat like olive oil. Look for the tomato-based pesto rosso (red pesto), as well as parsley pesto, kale pesto, fava bean pesto, avocado pesto, and pesto trentino (from the city of Trento), which includes egg yolks.

FOCACCIA

OVEN-BAKED FLATBREAD

PREPARATION TIME	COOKING TIME	LEVEL OF DIFFICULTY	MAKES
2 hr 50 mins	20 mins	●●	1 9-x-13-inch flatbread

This traditional Italian recipe was known as panis focacius in ancient Rome, and today focaccia remains as popular as ever. A close cousin to pizza, this yeasted flatbread is rich and golden with generous use of Italy's famous olive oil. Topping combinations are endless—experiment by adding fresh rosemary, sliced onions, whole olives, garlic cloves, cherry tomatoes, and parmesan cheese—or just savor the simple perfection of flaky salt. Serve with more olive oil, of course!

INGREDIENTS

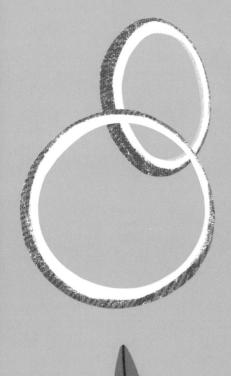

1 envelope (¼ ounce) active dry
    yeast
1½ cups warm water
2 teaspoons honey
3½ cups all-purpose or bread
    flour
1¼ teaspoons fine salt
6 tablespoons olive oil, plus more
    for drizzling
flaky salt, for sprinkling

1. In a large bowl, whisk the yeast with the warm water and honey and let stand until foamy, about 5 minutes. (If it doesn't foam, discard the mixture and start with a fresh packet of yeast.)

2. Stir in the flour, fine salt, and 3 tablespoons of the olive oil, and vigorously mix with a wooden spoon until a dough forms, about 2 minutes.

3. Lightly flour a work surface and turn out the dough onto it. Knead the dough until smooth and elastic, 10 to 15 minutes. (If you have a stand mixer, you can mix and knead the dough with the dough hook attachment.) Form the dough into a smooth ball and transfer to an oiled bowl.

4. Cover the dough with plastic wrap and let rise at room temperature until doubled in size, 60 to 90 minutes.

5. Pour 3 tablespoons olive oil into a 9-x-13-inch pan and use a brush to coat the sides of the pan, allowing the rest to pool at the bottom.

6. Deflate the dough by softly punching it down and turning it out into the prepared pan. Gently stretch the dough to help it fill the pan. Cover again and let rise until puffy, about 30 minutes.

7. While the dough is rising, preheat the oven to 425°F.

8. Using your fingers, poke the dough all over to create focaccia's famous dimples.

9. Drizzle the dough with a few more tablespoons of olive oil and use a brush to spread it around. Sprinkle with a few pinches of flaky salt or other toppings, as you wish.

10. Bake until golden brown, about 20 minutes.

11. Let cool for 5 minutes, then place upside down onto the rack, releasing it from the pan. Now carefully flip it so it's right side up. Serve warm or at room temperature.

POLAND

Poland is a large country in Eastern Europe that shares borders with Germany and Ukraine—and the Baltic sea. It has beautiful beaches, fertile farmland, and thousands of lakes, mountains, and rivers. Poland became a unified state in the tenth century, expanded its borders, and endured tumultuous times. Throughout it all, Polish cuisine has been a hearty celebration of potatoes, cabbage, and beets, with beloved dishes of rustic breads, tangy sauerkraut, pillowy pierogi dumplings, mouthwatering kielbasa sausages and roast pork, and sweet, jam-filled doughnuts.

BAGELS

In the late Middle Ages, Poland became a haven for European Jews, who shared their baking traditions that led to the development of bagels. In the first written account describing bagels, the city of Krakow required that they be fed to women after giving birth.

HUNTER'S STEW

Bigos, or "hunter's stew," is a national dish that often features wild game, kielbasa sausage, foraged mushrooms, sweet plums, and spicy juniper berries, all cooked with cabbage or sauerkraut. It's often served with rye bread or mashed potatoes.

FOUR MEALS A DAY

Most people in Poland eat four meals a day, which goes back to farming times. Early breakfast is *śniadanie*, and it's usually bread with jam, cheese, or cold meats. Second breakfast, *drugie śniadanie*, is often fruit and yogurt. Then comes a hearty dinner or *obiad*, in late afternoon, when famished farmers come in from the field. The fourth meal, or *kolacja*, is when Poles often enjoy cold meats, toast, cheese, or tomatoes before bed.

DUMPLINGS

Some dumplings are hearty like kartacze, which is made of mashed potatoes, some are doughnut-shaped kluski śląskie served with meat sauce, and then there are tiny uszka—"little ears"—served in beet soup on Christmas Eve. The most popular, pierogi, can be stuffed with mushrooms, meat, potatoes, or onions, or with sweet cheese for a berry-topped dessert.

DOUGHNUTS

Pączki are soft, rich doughnuts often filled with plum jam or wild rose jam, with a pinch of orange zest. Polish Catholics enjoy them on Fat Tuesday, the seventh week before Easter.

PUCKER UP FOR PICKLES

Polish winters are cold, so people here long ago learned to preserve their fresh vegetables. They pickle cabbage, often as sauerkraut, but they also pickle cucumbers, beets, cauliflower—as well as fish and mushrooms. Poles love pickles so much they even make pickle soup!

MILK AND DAIRY

Poles savor the sour flavors of fermented dairy, like buttermilk, kefir, and yogurt. There's even a Polish cheese soup called polewka z serwatki. It's hard to think of food that wouldn't receive a kiss of sour cream here, where it is a common garnish for meats, salads, cakes, kasha, and soups.

HERBS AND SPICE CABINET

You'll find dill in every Polish kitchen, alongside parsley and caraway seeds. Marjoram and juniper berries often flavor meat dishes. Polish farm fields grow lots of pretty poppy flowers, an essential ingredient in Polish cakes, buns, and rolls!

CHEESECAKE

Poles love cheese, including in cheesecake! First, a fresh, firm, creamy cheese, known as twaróg or ser biały ("white cheese")—which also appears in breakfast spreads and pierogi—is stirred into a rich batter with eggs and sugar, for a popular Christmas and Easter dessert.

STUFFED CABBAGE

Stuffed cabbage, or gołąbki, is a favorite Polish dish. Meats, rice, onion, and herbs are cooked in butter, then stuffed into a rolled-up cabbage leaf and baked. People say this hearty meal gave Polish troops the strength to beat Teutonic knights in the fifteenth century.

ZUPA OGÓRKOWA

PICKLE SOUP

PREPARATION TIME	COOKING TIME	LEVEL OF DIFFICULTY	SERVES
20 mins	30 mins	●●	5

Eastern European cuisine includes lots of pickles—including this traditional pickle soup! Like many Polish and Ukrainian recipes, this dish also features rich, tart sour cream. Tangy, hearty, creamy, and bright with just a little dill-pickle flavor, this simple soup will warm you up on a cold winter's day. Serve with slices of crusty bread.

INGREDIENTS

2 tablespoons butter
1 medium onion, diced
2 carrots, diced
1 celery stalk, minced
2 garlic cloves, minced
6 cups vegetable or chicken stock
4 new potatoes, diced
6 dill pickles, roughly chopped
    and grated, plus more for
    garnish
½ cup sour cream, plus more for
    garnish
1 tablespoon flour
⅔ cup pickle brine

1. In a large pot, melt the butter over medium-high heat, add the onion and carrot, and sauté until soft, about 5 minutes. Add the celery and garlic, and cook, stirring occasionally, until the vegetables soften and begin to brown, about 8 more minutes. Add the stock, cover, and raise the heat to high.

2. Once the stock comes to a boil, add the potatoes and pickles, reduce the heat to medium-low, and simmer, covered, until the potatoes are cooked through and a fork slips in easily, about 25 to 30 minutes. Remove from heat.

3. Ladle a cup of warm broth into a bowl, add the sour cream and flour, and whisk until smooth. Then stir the mixture into the soup.

4. Use a potato masher to partially mash the cooked vegetables, leaving some of them chunky if you like.

5. Add the pickle brine and stir to combine. Ladle into bowls and serve warm, garnished with sour cream and extra pickle slices, if you prefer!

Want even more dill flavor? Garnish each bowl with a pinch of minced fresh dill.

SPICES
AROUND THE WORLD

Since ancient times, people have used the intense tastes of herbs and spices to preserve foods and boost flavors. Egyptians were using fennel seeds, coriander seeds, juniper berries, cumin, garlic, and thyme in cooking as far back as 3500 BCE. Today, people around the world use countless varieties of spice blends, and just a pinch can provide essential, iconic flavors that have come to define regional cuisines.

FIVE-SPICE POWDER

Five-spice powder combines five core elements prized in Chinese cuisine: sweet, bitter, sour, salty, and spicy. The powder almost always includes ground star anise, cloves, cinnamon, Sichuan pepper, and fennel seeds, but despite its name, sometimes it can include many more. Chinese recipes use it to flavor rich meats like roasted duck or pork, while in Vietnam, the blend more often seasons roast chicken.

MASALA

Masala means "mixture of spices," and there are dozens of types of masala in India. While each version varies with the region and maker, in north India, a classic garam masala likely includes coriander, cumin, cloves, nutmeg, and chilies—all roasted and ground together.

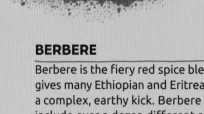

ZA'ATAR

This spice mix, which usually includes dried thyme, oregano, salt, sesame seeds, and sumac, has been used throughout the Middle East for thousands of years. Traces of what seems to be za'atar were discovered in the tomb of the Egyptian pharaoh Tutankhamun! In Lebanon, a classic breakfast is manaqish flatbread topped with za'atar, drizzled with olive oil, and eaten with olives, cucumbers, tomatoes, fresh mint, and a creamy dairy spread called labneh.

BERBERE

Berbere is the fiery red spice blend that gives many Ethiopian and Eritrean dishes a complex, earthy kick. Berbere can include over a dozen different spices, most notably red chili peppers, fenugreek, ginger, coriander, cardamom, cumin, allspice, peppercorns, cloves, and cinnamon. Essential in slow-cooked stews, it can also be made into a dipping sauce for injera, Ethiopia's iconic flatbread.

JERK SPICE

Jamaica's famous jerk spice combines allspice, thyme, nutmeg, onion, garlic, and Scotch bonnet peppers. Jerk spice is believed to have been invented by the Maroons, Jamaican descendants of Africans who freed themselves from slavery. The Maroons used jerk spice primarily as a preservative for meat, which they cooked in holes they dug and covered up to prevent smoke from escaping and giving away their location.

TOGARASHI

Togarashi is the Japanese word for a number of chili-pepper-based spice blends made in Japan since about the seventeenth century. Shichimi is probably the most famous, and includes red chili pepper, sesame seeds, dried seaweed, orange peel, and a Japanese pepper. Today, it's often set out as a condiment at ramen and udon restaurants.

HARISSA

Prepared as a paste or powder, this is a favorite way for North Africans to turn up the heat. Harissa's name derives from the Arabic verb for "to pound" or "to break into pieces" because the blend is made by pounding together roasted peppers, garlic, caraway seeds, coriander seeds, and cumin.

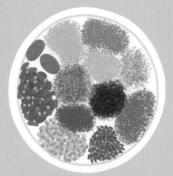

RAS EL HANOUT

Beloved in Tunisia, Morocco, and Algeria, there are infinite varieties, but most include cinnamon, cumin, coriander, allspice, black pepper, ginger, and salt, toasted and ground together in a mortar. Ras el hanout is a key ingredient in b'stilla, a savory Moroccan pie traditionally made with pigeon.

HERBS DE PROVENCE

Provence, in southeastern France, is known for picturesque villages, lavender fields, and sunshine. Traditionally, home cooks would gather their herbs from the countryside—especially rosemary, thyme, oregano, savory, and even lavender—and create their own blends. Today, you can buy jars of dried, mixed herbs de Provence around the world.

PUMPKIN PIE SPICE

The origins of this spice blend predate the founding of the United States, to the seventeenth century, when Dutch spice traders visited Indonesia and made a blend of cinnamon, ginger, nutmeg, and allspice. By 1796, a similar blend of mace, nutmeg, and ginger turned up in a recipe for "pumpkin" pie in the U.S.. In 1934, McCormick, the world's largest spice seller, started selling the mix as "pumpkin pie spice."

RUSSIA

The world's largest country spans eleven time zones and is home to more than 240 million people! The landscape is diverse with mountains, treeless plains called steppes, coastline, marshes, Arctic tundra, and forests. Today, Moscow has one of the highest concentrations of billionaires in the world and is a center of great chefs and culinary innovation. However Russians still savor traditional hearty fare of black bread, sour yogurt, cabbage and potatoes, handmade dumplings, and big communal soups—seasoned with the bright, sharp flavors of garlic, dill, peppercorns, salty brine, and lots of horseradish.

PICKLES

Russians enjoy lots of pickled vegetables year-round, including tart and tangy pickled garlic, cucumbers, and peppers. Many families buy abundant fresh produce in summer to pickle and preserve to enjoy all winter.

CABBAGE

Cabbage soup is an iconic national dish. And no Russian can go long without eating kvashenaya kapusta—fermented cabbage similar to sauerkraut. Russians use it in salads, stuffings, sides, and stews—in fact, soup made with fresh, rather than fermented, cabbage is called "lazy soup."

POTATOES

Peeled, boiled potatoes are often topped with butter, dill, and sour cream. Russians also enjoy potatoes mashed, in salads, stuffed into dumplings, fried with bacon and mushrooms, or fermented to make vodka.

BREAD

The average Russian eats two pounds of bread each day. Tables here may offer white bread, dark rye bread, Russia's famous black bread—or all three! Bread is the foundation of the Russian diet and is so important that the Russian term for hospitality, *khlebosol'stvo*, means "bread and salt."

FISH

In Russia, fish is often smoked or salt cured. Little salted Baltic herring are enjoyed with onions or in a cold salad. A mixed platter of smoked fish here may include eel, mackerel sturgeon, whitefish, shad, and salmon. Large, bright-orange Siberian salmon caviar and black caviar from sturgeon fish are famous worldwide.

WILD MUSHROOMS

Nearly a thousand years ago, in the 1100s and 1200s, starving people survived on foraged wild foods, including mushrooms. Many wonderful mushrooms still grow in Russian woods, and hunting for them is a national obsession.

KASHA

Boiled buckwheat groats called *kasha* are a Russian superfood that has nourished people here for more than 1,000 years. Kasha can be sweet or savory, boiled with milk or water, and served as breakfast or a side dish. Almost anything might be mixed in—including fruit, cheese, eggs, pork, liver, onions, or mushrooms.

MEAT MANIA

Russians are the world's leading eaters of meat, and some say the manual meat grinder is the most important tool in a Russian kitchen! Beloved dishes include meat pies, pelmeni dumplings, and meat rolled in cabbage.

RUSSIAN SALAD

Russian salad is neither green nor raw! Potatoes, carrots, beets, or turnips are boiled, chilled, and dressed in sour cream or mayonnaise.

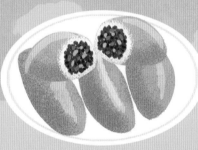

PIES

Handmade pies are the glory of the Russian kitchen. A savory slice is served alongside almost every soup, whether it's a little handpie called pieroski, an open-faced pie filled with farmers' cheese, or a grand pie stuffed with fish.

BLINI

TINY BUCKWHEAT PANCAKES

PREPARATION TIME	**COOKING TIME**	**LEVEL OF DIFFICULTY**	**MAKES**
20 mins	15 mins	● ●	20 to 25

These tiny pancakes are beloved throughout Russia and Eastern Europe, where they're traditionally made with buckwheat flour that cooks into a soft, spongy treat. An iconic appetizer, you can enjoy blini with sweet or savory toppings— sometimes butter, jam, or honey but often with rich sour cream and salty caviar. Buckwheat is actually a plant from the rhubarb family, and its tiny, triangular fruit seeds are used to make rich, hearty, gluten-free flour. While some blini recipes call for yeasted batter that needs time to rise, this version comes together quickly with just a bit of baking powder.

Old Slavic folklore celebrates the Sun's return in late winter, symbolized by the round blini. The Russian Orthodox Church incorporated the tradition of eating blini into "Butter Week," or *maslenitsa*. Russians make as many buttery blini as they can eat all week long, as part of a Russian Carnival celebration before fasting for Lent.

You can also enjoy blinis with sweet toppings such as butter, honey, or jam.

INGREDIENTS

½ cup plain flour
½ cup buckwheat flour
½ teaspoon salt
½ teaspoon baking powder
1 large egg, separated
1 cup milk
1 tablespoon melted, unsalted
    butter, plus more melted
    butter for cooking
sour cream and smoked salmon
    and/or caviar, for serving

1. In a bowl, whisk together the plain flour with the buckwheat flour, salt, and baking powder. Push the flour mixture to the sides of the bowl to form a well in the middle. Add the egg yolk, milk, and 1 tablespoon of melted butter to the well and whisk until the wet ingredients are well mixed, and then stir it together with the flour mixture.

2. In another bowl, using a handheld mixer, beat the egg white until it becomes cloudlike. It's ready when you lift a beater out of the egg white and its peaks turn over like a Santa hat (soft peaks).

3. Using a flexible spatula, gently stir the egg white into the batter until no streaks remain.

4. Brush a large nonstick skillet with melted butter and set over medium heat. Add 1 tablespoon of batter to the skillet for each little pancake and cook until you see bubbles form at the edge and the bottom turns golden, about 2 minutes. Flip and cook the blini until golden on the other slide, about 1 minute longer. Transfer to a plate.

5. Cook the remaining blini, brushing the skillet with more butter as needed.

6. Serve with a small dollop of sour cream and a small piece of smoked salmon or a ½ teaspoon of caviar.

SPAIN

With fertile plains, snowcapped mountains, the Mediterranean Sea, and the Atlantic Ocean, Spain is a food-lover's delight, offering deliciously fresh seafood, abundant olives, almonds, and pimenton (paprika), a spice made from smoked peppers. People here have long feasted on everything from octopus to wild boar, with food influences from around the world. North African Muslims, known as Moors, introduced chickpeas, rice, citrus, saffron, and couscous, while Spanish conquistadors returned from the Americas with potatoes, beans, tomatoes, peppers, and chocolate.

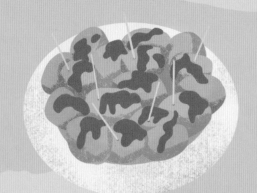

GAZPACHO

This red, refreshingly chilled soup originated in southern Spain's sunny Andalucía and is almost like a salad you can slurp with a spoon. Best at the peak of the summer tomato season, gazpacho is a purée of raw tomatoes, cucumbers, onion, sweet peppers, garlic, olive oil, salt, and vinegar.

PATATAS BRAVAS

Today, Spanish cuisine is unimaginable without potatoes, tomatoes, and peppers—all brought to Spain from Mesoamerica—which star together in this beloved recipe of fried potatoes slathered in a sauce of olive oil or mayonnaise with pimenton.

TAPAS

These little bites with big flavors, widely served at bars, might include steamed mussels, tiny fried fish, chorizo slices, olives, shaved jamón, triangles of manchego cheese, or pan con tomate, tasty grilled bread rubbed with tomato, garlic, salt, and olive oil.

JAMÓN IBÉRICO

Spaniards have been curing ham for generations. First, black Iberian pigs eat a rich diet of acorns, which gives their meat a wonderfully nutty flavor. After butchering, the legs are salted and hung up, sometimes for years. This cures, or preserves, the ham, until it is shaved into thin slices. One leg can cost 4,000 dollars!

PAELLA

This iconic Spanish dish includes rice, saffron, vegetables, and seafood or meat, all cooked in a wide paella pan. Every family has their own recipe, but Valencians, who likely invented the dish, say a real paella must include rabbit, chicken, and white broad beans.

CHURROS CON CHOCOLATE

This may sound like a dessert, but in Spain, it is breakfast. A sweet dough is squeezed through a star-shaped nozzle called a *churrera*. The ridged cylinders that emerge—some over a foot long—are deep-fried until crisp. Eat while hot, dipped into a cup of thick hot chocolate.

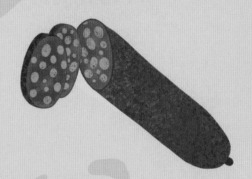

WORLD-FAMOUS

Ferran Adrià never went to culinary school but his restaurant, El Bulli (the bulldog), was named the best in the world. Chef Adrià used chemistry to invent new ways of cooking, making edible paper, food in tubes, and airy foams and sprays.

CHORIZO

Spanish chorizo is ready to eat, unlike Mexican chorizo, which needs to be cooked. Butchers stuff ground pork, garlic, and lots of paprika into a sausage casing, then cure it. Different regions add sweeter or spicier paprika, and some smoke the sausage. Slices of spicy chorizo are enjoyed as a snack or lend their deep flavor to stews and paella.

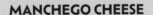

MANCHEGO CHEESE

Spaniards on the central plains have long herded sheep and made their milk into fine cheeses, of which manchego is the most famous. Wheels of the rich, slightly salty cheese have a zigzag pattern from the special basket molds they're aged in, which are traditionally made of braided grass.

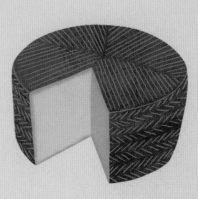

TORTILLA DE PATATAS

POTATO FRITTATA

PREPARATION TIME
20 mins

COOKING TIME
40 mins

LEVEL OF DIFFICULTY
● ● ●

MAKES
1 10-inch tortilla

Unlike the Mexican flatbread of the same name, a Spanish tortilla is a thick, savory potato and egg omelette, deliciously rich thanks to lots of Spanish olive oil. One of the most popular dishes in Spain, tortillas are tucked into lunchboxes and eaten as a snack or meal, anytime, day or night! They're quite easy to make—sometimes made with yesterday's potatoes or even leftover French fries—though flipping the tortilla in the pan without spilling takes a bit of practice.

INGREDIENTS

½ cup plus 1 tablespoon olive oil
1½ pounds potatoes, peeled and
     thinly sliced
1 small onion, finely chopped
5 eggs
salt and pepper

1. In an 8- or 10-inch nonstick skillet, heat ½ cup of the oil over medium heat, until shimmering. Add the potatoes, onions, and a generous pinch of salt and cook, stirring occasionally. They'll seem crowded but will shrink as they cook.

2. Meanwhile, beat the eggs well in a bowl, and season with 1 teaspoon salt and a few grinds of pepper.

3. When the potatoes are tender, after about 25 minutes, reduce the heat to medium-low and add the eggs to the pan, moving the potatoes around to allow them to settle.

4. After the edge of the tortilla looks firm, cook for 5 more minutes, then peek under the edge. When the bottom of the tortilla is set and browned and the top is somewhat set but still soft and maybe a little runny, carefully flip the tortilla. To do so: place a plate over the top, then quickly flip the skillet and plate over so the tortilla is cooked side up on the plate. Return the pan to the heat. Add 1 tablespoon olive oil and swirl it around. Slide the tortilla back into the skillet, cooked side up, to finish cooking the bottom, until done, about 5 more minutes.

5. Transfer the tortilla onto a plate or cutting board and let cool slightly. Slice into wedges and serve.

Bored of your lunchtime sandwich?
Pack this in your lunchbox instead!

You can skip the flip and instead finish
cooking the tortilla in a 375° F oven,
until the eggs are just done. This will
create a bit of a different texture and
shape, but it's still delicious!

UKRAINE

Ukraine's capital city, Kyiv, has been a center of Slavic culture since the Middle Ages. Ukraine's cuisine has some dishes and ingredients in common with many of its bordering countries, but Ukrainian recipes retain their own distinctive national identity. With its temperate climate and vast fertile steppe lands, Ukraine is one of the largest producers of grains in the world and is often referred to as the "breadbasket of Europe." Ukraine's four meals a day are often served family style, with platters arranged on tables decorated with hand-embroidered cloths.

PREPARATION

Typical Ukrainian dishes involve many ingredients and complex steps, and traditional methods for preserving foods in winter are still employed today. These include storing vegetables like beets and potatoes in wooden chests buried in the ground, and drying, brining, or smoking meat and fish so they are still tasty months later!

ESSENTIALS

Ukrainian food is not spicy, but it is very flavorful. Tart, sour, and sweet-and-sour flavors shine in popular drinks such as kvass (a fermented cereal-based drink), or in the pickles served with many meals; juice from pickles and sauerkraut are added to soups for flavor. Spices like dill and caraway are beloved in Ukrainian kitchens, as are onion and garlic.

BREAD

There are estimated to be almost 780 varieties of breads baked here! Breads are often braided or formed into gorgeous, elaborate shapes for special occasions. Grains of rye are even scattered across coffins.

PORK

Pork is stuffed into dumplings (varenyky), made into sausages like kyshka and sardelky, and even seasoned into salt-cured pork. Bacon ends and rendered salt pork add a smoky kiss to many favorite dishes, and cured pork fat (salo) is essential to many Ukrainian recipes—a favorite dessert is doughnuts fried in salo.

FRUITS AND VEGETABLES

Both farmed and foraged fruits appear as preserves, relishes, or jams, stewed with sugar into compotes, or stuffed into dumplings. Vegetables are often stuffed, tucked into dumplings, or pickled and brined into condiments like beet relish and sauerkraut.

FISH

Herring, perch, pike, sturgeon, and carp are among the favorite finned foods, which may be poached, jellied, fried, marinated, pickled, or baked. Fish meatballs (kotlety) are popular, as is battered-and-fried fish served with mushrooms and cheese. Pickled herring is a favorite appetizer for Jewish Ukrainians.

SWEETS

Ukraine is home to many beekeepers and beehives, and honey is commonly used in baked goods, drinks, and dishes made with grains. Favorite desserts are kutia (poppy seeds, wheat, nuts, and honey), served at Christmas; syrniki (fried cheese fritters served with smetana, honey, or jam); and beautiful jellied fruits called zhele.

DRINKS

Ukrainians love kompot (a sweet beverage made from dried or fresh fruits boiled in water) and baked milk (pryazhene moloko), which has a caramel flavor and is made by simmering milk for at least eight hours. For an extra treat, try ryazhanka, a baked, fermented milk drink!

SUNFLOWERS

Ukrainian farmers grow fields of sunflowers. The seeds are popular as a snack, and feature in many recipes. Sunflower oil is a common cooking oil in every kitchen cabinet.

BORSHCH

BEET SOUP

PREPARATION TIME	**COOKING TIME**	**LEVEL OF DIFFICULTY**	**SERVES**
30 mins	35 mins	● ●	6 to 8

This vibrant ruby-red soup is a staple from Latvia and Poland to Russia, but this root soup originated in Ukraine and it remains the country's national dish. Borshch is best known for its beets—the most beloved vegetable in Ukraine. This hardy, hearty root gives the soup its earthy flavor and gorgeous garnet hue. Some people like meat in their borshch, such as fresh pork shoulder, beef shin, ham hock, bacon, or sausage, but this version is deliciously vegetarian.

INGREDIENTS

3 pounds beets
2 onions
2 carrots or parsnips
1 small red cabbage, or half
    a large red cabbage
2 tablespoons oil
5 cups of water or broth
1 tablespoon of lemon juice
salt, to taste
sour cream, fresh dill, and
    caraway seeds, to garnish

1. Peel the beets. Using a knife, a large box grater, or the shredding attachment of a food processor, thinly slice or shred the vegetables. Take care not to grate your fingers too!

2. Heat the oil over medium-high heat in a large pot, then add all the vegetables and cook, stirring occasionally, for 5 minutes. Add the water or broth, bring to a boil, and reduce to a simmer. Cook for about 25 minutes, until the vegetables are tender. If they are still crunchy, simmer a few minutes longer and try again.

3. When the vegetables are soft, season the soup with the lemon juice and salt to taste.

4. To serve, ladle hot into bowls and garnish with sour cream, a pinch of fresh dill, and a sprinkle of caraway seeds.

There are over 30 main types of borshch in Ukraine alone, including variations made from turnips and celery root.

Some cooks add a little sugar at the end, for more sweet-sour contrast.

Serve warm in winter with some crusty bread or serve refreshingly cold on a hot summer's day.

DAIRY

AROUND THE WORLD

Humans have been drinking milk for thousands of years, from ruminants like cows, goats, camels, horses, water buffalo, yak, sheep, and reindeer. But milk goes bad quickly, so people developed cultured creamy foods that could last. Cheese has been called milk's leap toward immortality. Today, refrigeration keeps milk fresh for weeks or more, but humanity has come to love cheese. It's here to stay.

LABNEH

A bit like a cross between yogurt and cream cheese, labneh is made by adding salt to full-fat yogurt, then straining the liquid out of the yogurt with a cheesecloth and letting the remainder sit out to dry for half a day or so. The longer the labneh sits, the thicker it becomes. People like to eat it as a spread, dip, or simply on its own in yummy spoonfuls.

BUTTERMILK

This looks like milk except it's thicker, tangier, and sometimes has a few yummy lumps. That's because it has been fermented, typically by adding bacteria that produce lactic acid. In North America, buttermilk is a key ingredient for making fluffy pancakes or biscuits, or as the base of a creamy salad dressing. However, in places like India, Pakistan, Nepal, and the Arabian Peninsula, buttermilk is enjoyed as a deliciously refreshing beverage on its own or as a base for smoothies.

YAK-BUTTER TEA

In Tibet and the Himalayan regions of India, Nepal, Bhutan, and Pakistan, there's no better way to warm up and fuel up than with a cup of steaming yak-butter tea. This savory beverage is usually made with black tea that is brewed with salt, with a dollop of yak butter thrown in.

BULGARIAN-STYLE YOGURT

People in Bulgaria like to claim they are the original inventors of yogurt. Whether that's true is up for debate, but we do know that yogurt-making in this part of the world dates back thousands of years, to when the Thracians—the region's ancient inhabitants—carried sheep's milk in animal skin bags around their waists. The heat from their bodies and the bacteria in the bags would slowly ferment the milk into yogurt.

CRÈME FRAÎCHE

This thick, soured cream is made with a bacterial culture. Slightly different versions of the same dairy product exist in most countries in northern Europe and in Central America. In Romania, for example, it's called smântâna, and in Mexico, it's called crema fresca.

AARUUL

These dried curds are pungently sour, extremely hard blocks of dried cheese and a favorite snack for nomadic people in Mongolia. Aaruul is made by first boiling milk from cows, yaks, horses, or camels to thicken it up, then putting it into a cloth bag that's left out in the sun to solidify.

FONDUE

The earliest known fondue recipe, which was published in 1699 in Zürich, Switzerland, called for cut-up cheese to be melted with wine and served with dipping bread. Fondue is now considered one of Switzerland's national dishes, a perfect meal for warming up after a cold day on the ski slopes.

CONDENSED MILK

Condensed milk refers to cow milk from which 60% of the water has been removed. Usually, sugar is added too. The thickened final product is typically sold canned and serves as a popular dessert topping or ingredient around the world, including for snowballs in the Southern U.S., for a type of flan in Brazil, and—when boiled to become even thicker—as cake icing in Russia (essentially, this is dulce de leche). In Vietnam and Cambodia, condensed milk is also a favorite sweetener for strong cups of coffee.

AMERICAN CHEESE

Some people say that American cheese—the thin, rubbery, bright-orange squares individually wrapped in plastic—is not actually cheese. Indeed, depending on the other ingredients, legally, these products must be referred to as "pasteurized process American cheese food" or "pasteurized prepared cheese product" rather than simply "cheese."

UNITED KINGDOM

In England, Scotland, Wales, and Northern Ireland—which together make up the United Kingdom—traditional foods include roast pheasant, blood sausage, spiced cakes, and candied fruits. For centuries the United Kingdom colonized much of the globe, and while the English exported many customs, the cuisines of many former colonies also came to influence British flavors. Today, the United Kingdom has a population of over 60 million, including about 5 million people of Asian, Caribbean, African, and other non-British origin, who have contributed to the diverse cuisine now available. Over the centuries, the UK's diet of wheat, meat, potatoes, vegetables, and dairy has greatly expanded to include tastes from around the world.

PUBS

Short for public house, pubs are centers of social life, hosting everything from quizzes to live music. Going to the local pub for a roast dinner of meat, potatoes, Yorkshire pudding, and vegetables like cabbage and cauliflower is a traditional and much-loved Sunday activity.

TEA

For many in the United Kingdom, drinking tea is an essential daily tradition going back to the 1600s when England's East India Company sailed the world and brought boatloads of tea back to England. Today, the Scots, Irish, Welsh, and English together brew more than half the world's tea!

CHEESES

Farmers here have tended herds of cows and sheep for centuries, and milk from these dairies is made into many fine cheeses. Cheddar, the most famous hard cheese in the world, is named after a village in Somerset. The strongly flavored stilton blue cheese also enjoys international fame—it's the only British cheese to have legal protection!

FULL ENGLISH BREAKFAST

In England, this traditional way to start the day includes bacon, eggs, sausages, black pudding (blood sausage), mushroom, tomatoes, baked beans, and toast, plus tea, of course! A full Irish breakfast may also include white pudding; a full Scottish breakfast often includes haggis; and in Wales you may get laverbread as part of your full Welsh breakfast.

BOUNTIFUL BAKING

British bakers are famous for their breads, pies, cakes, tea cakes, scones, and biscuits. Crumpets are a flat griddled bread with wonderful bubbles, served buttered for breakfast. Desserts are called puddings, and traditional favorites include apple crumble, Eton mess, and trifle (a layered, wine-soaked sponge cake with fruit preserves, custard, and cream).

FISH AND CHIPS

Battered-and-fried cod has been a favorite street food here since the 1800s. Brits still love fish and chips—chips being thick-cut fried potatoes, sold hot, salted, and drenched with malt vinegar before eating.

CLOTTED CREAM

Traditionally from southwest England, thick, rich spreads called Cornish cream and Devonshire cream are slathered on scones with jam at afternoon tea. But which to put on first? The Cornish say jam goes first, but in Devon they argue cream should go on first.

MORE THAN TWO VEG

Readers of Beatrix Potter know that English gardens—like Mister McGregor's, which Peter Rabbit raided—grow gorgeous vegetables! Favorites include cabbages, brussels sprouts, beans, peas, asparagus, cucumbers, radishes, and watercress, plus carrots, turnips, and parsnips in winter.

TASTES OF EMPIRE

In towns and cities across the UK, you can eat your way around the world. Indian tikka masala has been called England's favorite dish, while flavors of many past colonies can be found here in Jamaican jerk chicken, Malaysian laksa, Nigerian jollof rice, South African bobotie, Sri Lankan rotti, Ghanaian fufu and banku, and Barbadian fish cakes.

SCONES

SWEET LITTLE CAKES WITH SULTANAS

PREPARATION TIME
2 hrs

COOKING TIME
15 mins

LEVEL OF DIFFICULTY
●●

MAKES
12 to 14 scones

Light, flaky baked scones are a classic teatime snack in the UK. They're just barely sweet—until you slather them with jam and clotted cream! For that wonderfully flaky texture, use cold butter and chill your dough in the refrigerator after you roll it out—and again before baking. While some use a pastry cutter or stand mixer, you could also crumble the butter into the flour mixture using your fingers. For a golden finish, paint your scones with a little egg mixture before popping them in the oven.

Sweet scones are often studded with dried fruit, like currants, raisins, or cherries. Bakers making savory scones may add cheese or herbs. In Scotland and Northern Ireland, some people add mashed potatoes for potato scones.

INGREDIENTS

⅔ cup golden raisins (optional)

3½ cups all-purpose flour, plus more for dusting

2 tablespoons plus 1 teaspoon baking powder

½ cup sugar

8 tablespoons (1 stick) cold, unsalted butter, cut into small pieces

2 eggs, lightly beaten for the scones, plus 1 egg for the egg wash

¾ cup buttermilk

butter, jam, and clotted cream, for serving

1. If you're using the raisins, place them in a small bowl, cover with hot water, and let stand until plump, about 30 minutes.

2. In a large bowl, whisk together the flour, baking powder, and sugar. Add the butter pieces and, using your fingers, mix the butter into the dry mixture until it is crumbly and the pieces are the size of small peas. (You can also do this in a food processor.)

3. In a medium bowl, whisk the eggs and the buttermilk together. Add the liquid and the raisins to the crumb mixture and stir the dry mixture until only just mixed in. Gently knead a few times until the dough just holds together.

4. Arrange a piece of plastic wrap on the counter. Turn out the dough onto the plastic, then dust the top of the dough with flour.

5. Gently press or roll out the dough until it's 1 inch thick. Wrap the dough in the plastic and refrigerate for 30 minutes to 1 hour.

6. Using a 2-inch round biscuit cutter, stamp out as many rounds as you can and transfer them to plates. Gently press together the dough scraps and stamp out more rounds, putting them onto plates. Cover these plates and refrigerate again for 20 minutes.

7. Meanwhile, preheat the oven to 400°F and line two baking sheets with parchment paper.

8. Place the rounds on the prepared baking sheets, leaving at least an inch between each round. In a small bowl, beat the remaining egg with 1 tablespoon of water and brush this mixture over the rounds.

9. Bake until lightly golden, 12 to 15 minutes. Let cool on the baking sheets. Serve with butter or jam and clotted cream.

There is a hot debate about how to pronounce scone. Some say it rhymes with "bone," while others insist it rhymes with "bon" or "con."

NORTH AMERICA

This vast continent spans from the jungle tropics to the icy Arctic, and from the Atlantic to the Pacific, encompassing mountains, deserts, forests, and more. It includes the nations of Central America like Guatemala and Panama, Caribbean islands like Cuba, and three of the globe's most populous countries—Canada, Mexico, and the United States.

The Rocky Mountains—home to game like wild elk, bighorn sheep, and river trout—extend north from New Mexico to British Columbia. Vast grasslands also span the continent once grazed by bison and now by millions of cattle. These Great Plains also grow great grains, yielding harvests baked into flour tortillas, loaves of bread, pie crusts, and more. Down south, Mexico's highlands yield abundant corn, beans, and squash, plus harvests of avocados, tomatoes, and chili peppers, all at the heart of the culture's traditional cuisine.

While Native peoples still inhabit many parts of these ancient lands, North American cultures and cuisines have been greatly reshaped by immigrants, especially from Europe. Today, nearly everyone here speaks English, French, or Spanish, the languages of the people who colonized this continent centuries ago.

CANADA

Running across the top of the North American continent, Canada is one of the largest countries in the world by size—but it still has fewer people than tiny Japan! This vast land is known for its natural resources, from the snow-speckled mountain forests in the north and the central plains filled with wheat and cows to the sparkling cold waters of the east and west coasts. Toronto—Canada's biggest city—was named the most diverse city in the world by the United Nations. You can enjoy the cuisines of Korea, Vietnam, Greece, the Caribbean, and more, all without leaving town.

THE DEP

In Canada, you can call a small grocery store a dep, short for the French-Canadian word dépanneur. The word came from the eastern Canadian province of Quebec, once a French colony. Dépanneur originally meant "someone who fixes things."

MAPLE SYRUP

For thousands of years, the First Nations people here have collected the late-winter sap of sugar maple trees and boiled it down into sweet, thick (and nutritious!) syrup. Canadians are so proud of their world-famous maple trees, they put its leaf on their flag.

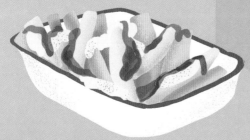

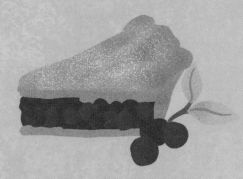

POUTINE

After a long winter's day, nothing will warm you up—and fill you up—like poutine: French fries smothered with gravy and crowned with melted cheese curds. First invented in the province of Quebec, poutine is now one of Canada's most famous foods. Restaurants that specialize in making it are called poutineries!

WILD FOODS

Half of Canada is forest, so it is no surprise wild and foraged foods are still a big part of Canadian cooking. You can hunt for moose and caribou, then make a pie with wild Saskatoon berries, which taste like blueberries mixed with almonds. If you prefer seafood, you can roast Chinook salmon from Canada's Pacific coast.

NANAIMO BARS

Nanaimo bars, named after a city in western Canada, are extra-sweet cookie bars with three delicious layers: a coconut and graham cracker base, a custard-frosting blend in the middle, and a thick and creamy chocolate top.

COWTOWN

The western city of Calgary is called Cowtown, thanks to the cows still raised in the nearby open plains. It's also home to the annual Calgary Stampede, a giant rodeo famous for foods like pancake breakfasts, mini-doughnuts, and beefsteaks, of course!

VICTORIA DAY

This holiday began in honor of a British queen named Victoria, at a time when most of Canada was still a British territory. (They didn't officially become independent until 1982!) Today, this holiday is mainly treated as the unofficial beginning of summer, celebrated with picnics, barbecues, fireworks, and the annual planting of backyard gardens.

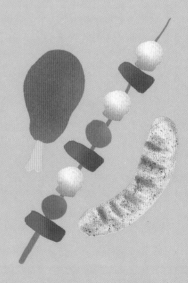

CORNBREAD AND GRAVY

Across Canada, many First Nations people make a boiled bread of ground white corn. In Kahnawake Mohawk Territory just south of the city of Montreal, everyone eats it with steak and brown gravy on Sundays!

KETCHUP CHIPS

From coast to coast, Canadians love ketchup-flavored potato chips, a kind rarely found in other countries. They're sweet and sour and turn your fingers bright red.

BREAKFAST
AROUND THE WORLD

Every hour, the sun rises somewhere and people break their overnight fast, with breakfast! Some start with spicy fish stew, soybean soup, or salted cod cakes. Eggs are popular: with refried beans and pico de gallo in Mexican huevos rancheros, with bacon and black pudding in a full English breakfast, or with peppers and tomatoes in North African shakshuka. Or have a sugar-showered fritter, like Spanish churros, Filipino cascarons, or Ugandan mandazi doughnuts.

MEZE

In the eastern Mediterranean and Middle East, breakfast is often a meze mix of lots of little plates. You might see labneh, fresh tomatoes, cucumbers, feta, olives, ful, and hummus, all served with fresh-baked pita. Another beloved breakfast in the Middle East is shakshuka: eggs poached in a warming tomato-pepper stew.

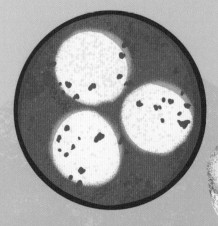

INDIAN BREADS AND SNACKS

In southern Indian regions, people often start their day with appam, a bowl-shaped pancake made with rice flour and coconut milk. You'll also see idli, puffy savory cakes, and dosa, thin crepes, both made with a fermented rice and lentil batter. In northern India, people wake up to paratha, buttery, flaky wheat-based flatbreads, or fried savory pastries, like samosas, poori, and kachori.

RICE PORRIDGE

Throughout Asian cuisines, many people cook white rice for hours until the grains become a silky porridge, often called congee, although the name varies by country. At breakfast, this mild porridge is often topped with lots of delicious strong flavors like salted fish, braised meats, salted duck eggs, seaweed, and spicy vegetables.

MANGÚ

In the Dominican Republic, just about everyone loves to start their day with a plate of boiled green plantains called mangú. They're mashed with oil or butter, and topped with fried eggs, pretty, pink pickled onions, rounds of fried salami, and a slice of salty queso frito (fried cheese).

MUESLI

A Swiss physician in the late 1800s is credited with creating muesli. His original recipe called for raw grated apple, nuts, and oats mixed with water, lemon juice, and condensed milk, and honey. The word muesli comes from the Swiss-German word for "mush," and when combined with milk or yogurt, after a few minutes, that's a good description!

NIHARI

For centuries, people in Pakistan have loved to wake up to nihari—a shank of beef, mutton, or goat, cooked overnight with ginger, fried onions, green chilies, and aromatic spices, served with fresh cilantro. Named for an Arabic word that means "morning," today it's so popular in Pakistan that people enjoy it all day long.

MISO SOUP

A traditional Japanese breakfast balances many types of flavors, textures, and nutrients, including white rice, miso soup, pickled vegetables, cooked fish, and natto—fermented soybeans that have a strong flavor and sticky texture.

PASTELILLOS DE GUAYABA

GUAVA CHEESE PASTRIES

PREPARATION TIME	COOKING TIME	LEVEL OF DIFFICULTY	MAKES
30 mins	25 mins	●	8 pastelillos

The Caribbean is home to many wonderful tropical fruits, like pineapple, mango, papaya, passionfruit, and guava, which are enjoyed in everything from fresh fruit salads to shaved-ice drinks drizzled with sweet syrup. For this recipe, you don't need fresh guava—just pop open a package of thick, sweet guava paste and stack slices with salty cheese to bake into pastelillos (little pastries). These are delicious for breakfast or as a sweet snack anytime of day.

INGREDIENTS

1 17.3-ounce package puff pastry, thawed but still cold

7 ounces guava paste (half a 14-ounce package), cut into 8 even slices

6 ounces queso fresco en hoja, farmer cheese, or well-chilled cream cheese, cut into 8 even slices

1 egg, lightly beaten with a pinch of salt

2 to 3 tablespoons turbinado sugar or powdered sugar

1. Preheat the oven to 400°F. Line a large baking sheet with parchment paper.

2. Spread out one layer of puff pastry on the baking sheet. Arrange the guava-paste slices on the pastry so there are two across and four down, and at least an inch apart. Top each piece of guava paste with a slice of cheese.

3. Arrange the second layer of puff pastry on top. Using a knife, slice the puff pastry between the filling into 8 pastries.

4. Use a fork to crimp the edges and seal in the filling, then arrange each piece evenly on the baking sheet, leaving spaces between. Lightly brush the tops and edges with the beaten egg and sprinkle with turbinado sugar, if using. Using a knife, make two slits on the top of each pastry. Refrigerate for 15 minutes before baking.

5. Bake for 20 to 25 minutes or until pastelillos are golden brown. Let cool for at least 10 to 15 minutes, then enjoy warm or at room temperature.

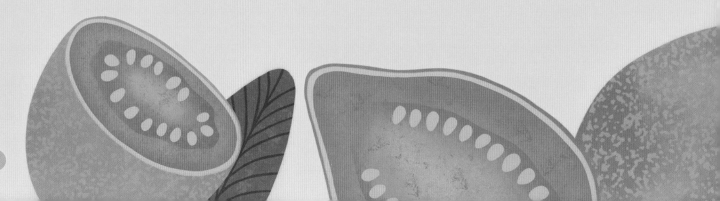

Instead of sprinkling crunchy turbinado sugar before baking, you could dust with powdered sugar after they cool.

Don't worry about making the pastries look perfect—handmade individuality is part of their charm. It's also OK if the filling oozes out of the edges. It caramelizes and tastes delicious.

MEXICO

Mexico's diverse geography varies from warm coasts to inland mountains, from deserts to jungles, from rivers to fertile plains. It is also known for whale-watching, and as the destination of one of the world's largest butterfly populations—monarch butterflies spend the winter in the Michoacán forests. Visitors from around the world also flock here, not just to vacation on the beautiful beaches but to feast on Mexico's world-famous cuisine! Morning and night, markets and public squares fill with taco carts, tamale stands, trays of churros, and spectacular hot chilies, fresh fish, and tropical fruits.

MOLE

There are over forty varieties within this iconic family of special sauces, which are often served over turkey or beans. To be called a mole, a sauce must contain nuts, chilies, and spices. Two of the most beloved are Puebla's mole poblano, complex with chocolate and chilies, and Oaxaca's velvety mole negro, made from chilies cooked until they're as black as coals.

SPANISH FLAVORS

In 1519, Spaniards landed on Mexico's eastern shores. In the following years, Spaniards brought cows, pigs, chickens, sheep, goats, dairy, wheat, citrus, and cilantro. Today, Mexican cuisine combines these foods with traditional foods, including corn, chili peppers, avocado, chocolate, turkey, duck, insects, and beans.

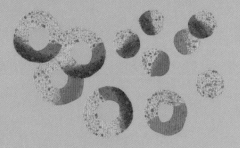

CACAO AND CHOCOLATE

Ancient Mesoamericans valued cacao so much that cacao beans were currency. Today, most drinking chocolate is hot and sweet—but back then, people drank it cold and spicy—spiked with powdered chili! The Spanish adapted the mixture by swapping the cold water for milk and the chili pepper for cinnamon.

SPICY CANDY

Stroll down the candy aisle in a Mexican store, and you'll find hard candy with chili, chewing gum with chili, soft mango and tamarind chews with chili—sometimes with a hint of lime. People say that once you get used to this sweet-spicy combo, the more you eat, the more heat you'll crave!

FISH TACOS

Created in Baja, these tacos feature fresh fish filets cooked in a flour and egg batter. Some say Japanese immigrants adapted the tempura tradition to local catches. Whatever the original source, today fish tacos are topped with shredded lettuce, radish, cilantro, onion, tomato, a squeeze of lime, and spicy salsa.

WHEAT AND MEAT UP NORTH

Iconic corn tortillas are the daily bread in central and southern Mexico, but in the northern states farmers grow beautiful fields of wheat—and make their tortillas of wheat flour instead. This region is also famous for the country's best grilled meats—sometimes tucked into those flour tortillas.

 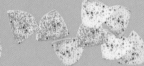 

VITAMIN T

A frequent expression among Mexicans, Vitamin T is the nickname for treats that begin with the letter T. Chief among them is tacos, but vitamin T can also refer just to tortillas, tlacoyos (oblong corn patties filled with cheese or beans), tlayudas (large flat tortillas, typical of Oaxaca), tamales, totopos (tortilla chips), and tostadas (fried tortillas with toppings).

ALEGRÍAS

Alegrías (joys) are one of the most common sweet snacks sold by street vendors in Mexico. Made of popped amaranth seeds mixed with dark sugar syrup, the bars are sold at fairs and outside movie theaters and museums, and beloved for their filling protein and light, sweet flavor!

SWEET TAMALES

You may have heard of bean, chicken, and beef tamales, but did you know there are sweet tamales too? Often eaten in the late afternoon or evening, sweet tamales can be recognized by their pink color, which is added to distinguish them from the pale-yellow savory kind.

QUESADILLAS

In most of Mexico, a quesadilla is a folded tortilla filled with queso (cheese). But in Mexico City, it is a folded, stuffed tortilla cooked in a griddle. That means that when you order a quesadilla in Mexico City, you have to specify whether you want it filled with beans, mushrooms, or . . . cheese!

SALSA VERDE CRUDA

GREEN TOMATILLO SAUCE

PREPARATION TIME	COOKING TIME	LEVEL OF DIFFICULTY	MAKES
20 mins	0 mins	●	About 1½ cups

The word salsa simply means "sauce," and salsa verde means "green sauce." In Mexico, it's often made with tomatillos, which are a cousin of tomatoes and peppers. Tomatillos are not spicy; instead, they can taste wonderfully tart, especially when they're firm and bright green. They get a little sweeter and softer as they ripen, when their skins can take on a pretty purple tinge. Tomatillos come in little papery jackets. When you're ready to cook, slip those off and give the fruits a quick rinse—they can sometimes be slightly sticky under the husks.

In some versions of salsa verde, people cook the tomatillos, onion, chili, and garlic before blending it into a salsa. This is the raw (cruda) version. Enjoy it over just about anything, from tacos and quesadillas to huevos rancheros. Or just eat it straight up with corn tortilla chips!

INGREDIENTS

12 ounces tomatillos (about
    6 small- to medium-sized),
    husks removed
1 jalapeño chili
¼ cup chopped white onion
1 small garlic clove, peeled
¼ cup cilantro leaves
salt

1. Wash and roughly chop the tomatillos and transfer to a food processor or blender.

2. Cut off the stem of the jalapeño and cut it in half lengthwise. To make a salsa that's not spicy, you can remove the seeds from the chili. (Wear gloves so the seeds don't burn your skin). Slice the chili halves and transfer to the processor with or without the seeds.

3. Add the onion, garlic, and cilantro to the processor and purée until you have a chunky salsa. Taste and season with salt.

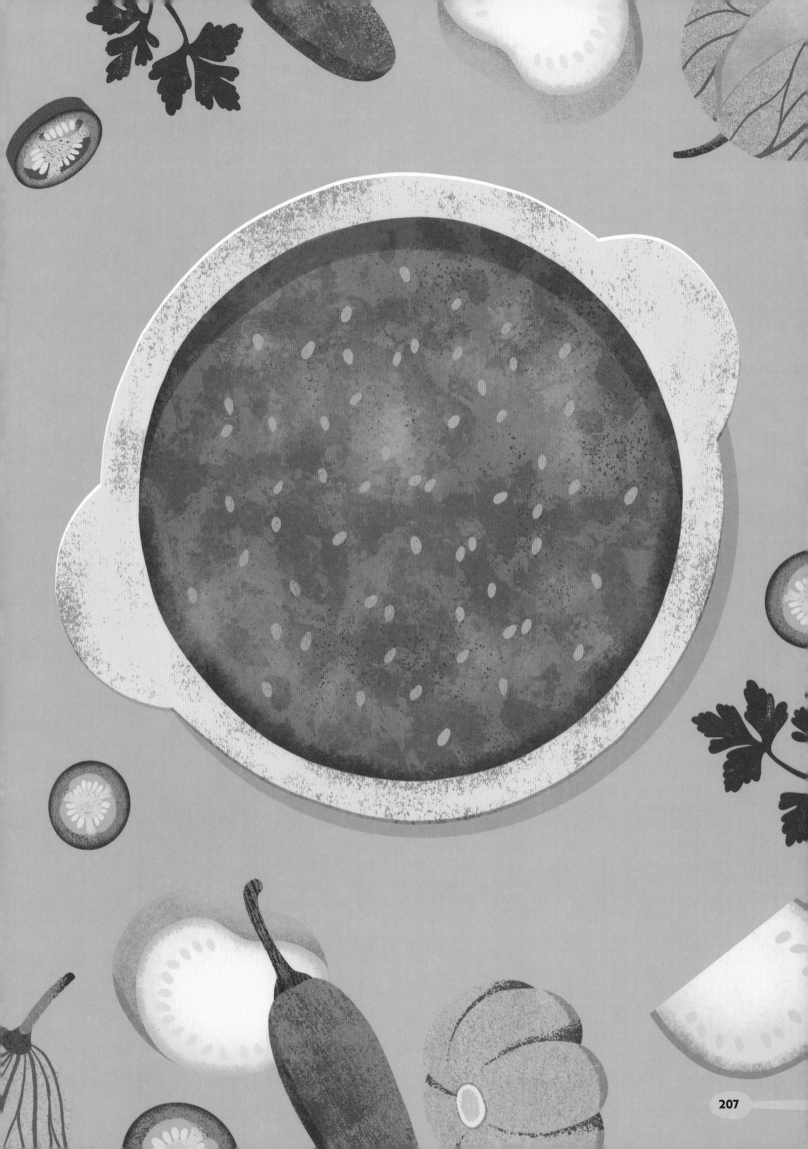

UNITED STATES OF AMERICA

The U.S. is a big, diverse country, with a menu to match! Feast on ancient, indigenous foods—like blueberries, bison, tomatoes, salmon, and corn—served alongside steak and fries, gumbo and jambalaya, tacos and empanadas, fried rice and chop suey, fried chicken and mac and cheese. Regional specialties range from Alaskan king crab to Wisconsin butter on bread made from Kansas's "amber waves of grain." The U.S. is bigger than the fifty states. Its territories include Guam, the U.S. Virgin Islands, American Samoa, and Puerto Rico. Favorite Puerto Rican recipes include pork pernil, rice with peas, and fried plantains.

BELOVED BARBECUE

The roots of barbecue go back to Native American traditions of smoking and slow-roasting meats over an open fire. Enslaved Africans and their descendants also developed barbecue techniques across the American South. Today, regional variations include vinegary Carolina pulled pork, sweet and tangy ribs in Kansas City, and smoked beef brisket in Texas.

THANKSGIVING

This annual American holiday celebrates the fall harvest. First established by President Lincoln after the Civil War to promote unity, many Americans travel home to their families each November. They give thanks over roast turkey, mashed potatoes, cranberry sauce, and pumpkin pie, all of which are made from native ingredients.

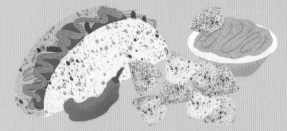

TACOS AND NACHOS

Much of the American Southwest was once a part of Mexico. Today, in states like Arizona, Texas, New Mexico, Colorado, and California, you can still eat Mexican foods, like carne asada, salsa verde, nachos, quesadillas, burritos, and green chilies.

THREE SISTERS

Many Indigenous people here traditionally grew corn, beans, and squash together, in companion planting known as the three sisters. Today, they are pillars in the American daily diet, and around the world.

STATE-FAIR TREATS

At state fairs across the U.S., you can see award-winning farming, from hogs and goats to tractor shows, jam-making contests, and blue-ribbon watermelons. You can also eat all kinds of treats, like corn dogs in Oklahoma, cheese curds in Wisconsin, deep-fried sticks of butter in Iowa, and cotton-candy tacos in Texas.

MELTING POT

The U.S. is often called a nation of immigrants—and many iconic American recipes were brought here from around the world. Immigrants brought burgers and franks from Germany, pizza from Italy, and made "American" apple pie out of fruit native to Afghanistan. Today, people still move here from around the world, mixing foods to create amazing new recipes—like kimchi tacos!

PEANUT PROS

Enslaved Africans brought peanuts to American soils in the 1700s. About 200 years later, an African American man born into slavery named George Washington Carver grew up to be an agricultural scientist who focused on improving the lives of poor Southern farmers. He developed over 300 uses for the peanut, including peanut butter, which is still popular in sandwiches.

BEEF AND BURGERS

Americans raise a lot of beef cattle and are famous for their love of burgers. Burger toppings can vary from state to state—and include Vermont cheddar, Jersey tomatoes, sweet Vidalia™ onions from Georgia, Southwest smoked poblanos, and California avocados.

FROM SEA TO SHINING SEA

The U.S. is bounded by the Atlantic, the Pacific, and the Gulf of Mexico, borders the inland Great Lakes, and hosts huge rivers like the mighty Mississippi. All that water means great fishing! People here love Maine lobster, Maryland crabs, New England clam chowder, Rocky Mountain trout, Alaskan salmon, and Hawaiian ahi tuna.

CHILI CON CARNE

CHILI WITH BEEF AND BEANS

PREPARATION TIME	COOKING TIME	LEVEL OF DIFFICULTY	SERVES
15 mins	45 mins	●	4

While its roots go back to Mexico, writers first described chili con carne in the 1880s, when "chili queens" in San Antonio, Texas, sold cauldrons of it from carts at dusk. Today, chili is eaten daily across the American Southwest, with far too many variations to count. People take chili very seriously, with chili cook-offs where opinions run as hot as a habanero pepper. Some people use dried chili peppers, others add chili powder; some slow-simmer dried beans for hours, others cook beef, turkey, or lamb, and declare that "real chili has no beans!"

INGREDIENTS

2 tablespoons oil
1 medium onion, chopped
2 garlic cloves, thinly sliced
1 pound ground beef
1 tablespoon chili powder
1 14.5-ounce can crushed or diced fire-roasted tomatoes
2 x 15-ounce cans pinto beans, rinsed and drained
2 cups low-sodium chicken stock or water
tortilla chips, for serving

1. In a large pot, heat the oil over medium heat. Add the onion and garlic, season generously with salt, and cook, stirring occasionally, until the onion is translucent, about 10 minutes.

2. Add the ground beef and increase the heat to medium-high. Cook, breaking it up with a spoon, until it is opaque and browned in spots, about 6 minutes. Add the chili powder and continue stirring, until fragrant, about 1 minute.

3. Add the can of tomatoes and use a spoon to break them up into smaller chunks if they are large. Add the beans and chicken broth and bring to a boil over high heat. Reduce the heat to medium-low and simmer until the chili is thick and flavorful, about 20 minutes.

4. Season with salt to taste and serve the chili hot with any—or all!—of the toppings and tortilla chips.

Top with any combination of sour cream, chopped fresh cilantro, chopped white onion, shredded Monterey jack cheese, pickled jalapeños, or diced avocado. Or have them all!

BEANS

AROUND THE WORLD

We've been eating beans throughout human history. There are unique and favorite varieties hailing from cultures across continents. And you may eat even more beans than you realize. Many peas botanically belong to the bean family, and peanuts are technically beans too! Around the world, beans are nutritious, affordable, filling, and delicious. No wonder they're eaten at breakfast, lunch, dinner, and dessert.

HUMMUS

People have been growing chickpeas (also known as garbanzo beans) for thousands of years in the Middle East. And for thousands of years, they've been simmering the beans, and puréeing them with sesame paste to make this delicious dip.

AKARA

This crunchy bean fritter is beloved in West Africa. It's made from black-eyed peas or Nigerian local beans that are peeled, ground into a paste, mixed with onions and spices, and fried into crunchy fritters that are soft on the inside. Enslaved West Africans brought the recipe to Brazil and the Caribbean, where you'll still find akara today.

MUNG BEANS

These little bitty beans are green on the outside, yellow on the inside, and common in many southern, eastern, and southeastern Asian cuisines. In India they're made into a fermented paste that people cook into dosa, a thin pancake. In China, mung beans are used for sweet preparations, like in a tong sui, a type of Cantonese dessert. And fresh, crunchy white mung beans sprouts are tossed into salads and top dishes from pad thai to Vietnamese pho.

SOYBEANS

These beans are essential in many Asian cuisines, where they're made into soy sauce, soy milk, tofu, miso, and more. In Japan, young soybeans—edamame—are eaten straight as a snack. The fuzzy green pods are boiled or steamed, salted, served in bowls, and eaten by hand. Each little green bean is popped from the pod right into your mouth.

BOSTON BAKED BEANS

People have been growing and eating beans in the United States since long before it was the United States. In the area that would become Massachusetts, Native American people traditionally cooked navy or yellow-eye beans with fish, venison, or bear fat, with a little maple syrup. European colonists learned the recipe, and today savory-sweet maple-kissed beans are still so popular that some people call Boston "Beantown."

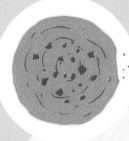

MEXICAN FRIJOLES AND REFRIED BEANS

Frijoles is the Spanish word for the most common bean native to Central and South America. There are over thirty varieties, including yellow eye, black, kidney, and vaquero, which has black and white markings like a Holstein cow. Beans are a daily staple in Mexican cuisine, where a favorite recipe is frijoles refritos, also known as refried beans.

ADZUKI BEANS

These little reddish-brown beans from Asia are often made into a sweet, sticky paste. In China, red-bean paste is added to steamed buns (baozi and zongzi), as well as to mooncakes for the fall festival. In Japan, sweet adzuki paste may be used atop ice cream and is a favorite filling inside mochi.

BEANS ON TOAST

One favorite breakfast in the UK features canned white beans simmered with spices and tomato sauce, served with a thick slice of buttered toast. Introduced to the UK from the United States in the 1910s, baked beans became a filling, affordable staple during World War II.

LIMAS

A native bean from the Andes in South America, limas are a white, broad bean named after Peru's capital city. Like other beans, limas sailed to Europe in the sixteenth century. One variety of limas became the gigante or butter beans still favored in many European cuisines; in Greece, they star in gigantes plaki, cooked in a delicate tomato sauce.

SOUTH AMERICA

Where can you find a rainforest, a pink lagoon (with matching pink flamingos), a desert, the world's largest salt flats, as well as six different types of big felines, a cold-water dolphin, llamas, and penguins? In South America. Measuring 4,722.421 miles from the northernmost point in Punta Gallinas, Colombia, to the southernmost tip of Cape Horn, Chile, South America is a region of contrasts and rich natural beauty. Running along the western side of the continent, and crossing seven countries, is the largest mountain range in the world, the Andes. If this were not enough, South America also boasts the largest rainforest in the world: the Amazon. Incidentally, in the largest rainforest is where you can find the smallest monkeys on the planet, the pygmy marmoset, which are so small, one would fit in the palm of a hand.

ARGENTINA

Argentina is a land that dazzles, from beaches and flatlands to snowcapped mountains. Its wide, grassy, flat pampas are a famously perfect place for raising beef, tended by gauchos—Argentinian "cowboys." With a long history of colonialism and immigration, Argentina is second only to the U.S. in the number of immigrants it has taken in, including from Spain, Italy, and Germany, and with a diverse culinary culture that reflects these influences on indigenous traditions. Now mostly urban, the country is also home to the Andes Mountains, rich farmland, rolling grasslands, famous vineyards, and rugged terrain.

SUBMARINO

The submarino is an indulgently rich, sweet drink sipped here and in neighboring Uruguay. It's made by melting an entire bar of chocolate into a glass of hot milk. Delicious!

SERIOUS BEEF

Since Spaniards arrived, cattle have thrived on the pampas. Beef is the most important staple in the country's cuisine—in fact, Argentina leads the world (per capita) in both raising and eating beef!

ASADO

Argentinians aren't just famous for raising beef—they've perfected cooking it too! Barbecuing is an art here. *Gauchos* are credited with inventing the Argentinian asado, for which meat is cooked over hot coals on a traditional grill called a *parrilla*.

DULCE DE LECHE

Argentina's iconic confection is made by slowly simmering milk and sugar into this sweet, rich, luscious caramellike spread. Whether slathered on bread, stuffed in pastries, or sandwiched between alfajores—chocolate or sugar-glazed cookies rolled in coconut flakes—it is beloved by Argentinians of all ages.

ARGENTINIAN DAIRY

All those cattle aren't just for meat. Their milk is also made into artisanal Argentinian cheese. Among the most popular are queso criollo, a semihard cheese with a mild and creamy flavor, popular in sandwiches and empanadas, and aged queso de campo with a more robust taste.

EMPANADAS

Each region has their own favorite, but these quintessential, half-moon-shaped pastries are usually stuffed with beef, chicken, or lamb, mixed with onions, olives, and spices, though sometimes they're bursting with veggie options like corn, cheese, or spinach. Empanada-making can be a communal activity, with grandparents teaching children to prettily pinch the dough into a frilly edge.

PALITO DE LA SELVA (JUNGLE STICKS)

This classic Argentinian candy, also known as a jungle stick, has been a beloved treat since its introduction in the 1960s. The chewy, gummy, stick-shaped sweets come in vibrant tropical flavors like pineapple and strawberry. Inside the wrapper, you can read about different jungle animals, hence the name.

LOCRO

This traditional, hearty stew with white corn and beans is believed to have its recipe roots in Indigenous Andean cultures. Associated with the May Revolution of 1810, which led to the country's independence from Spain, locro is often served on May 25, celebrated as the National Day of Argentina.

ARTISANAL GELATO

Introduced by Italian immigrants, dense, smooth, creamy, slow-churned frozen gelato is now on offer everywhere here. Gelato shops, known as *heladerías*, can be found in every corner of Argentine cities and towns, offering a wide variety of flavors, including a rainbow of fruits, plus flavors like dulce de leche and even yerba mate.

HONEY

Argentina is one of the world's leading honey producers. Bees in the country's lush forests, Andean valleys, and vast Pampas region each visit their area's unique flowers, yielding honey with special character and quality.

CHIMICHURRI

CHILI AND PARSLEY SAUCE

PREPARATION TIME
25 mins

COOKING TIME
0 mins

LEVEL OF DIFFICULTY
●

MAKES
About 1 cup

This sauce has a name that's fun to say, but it's even more fun to eat! Argentina and Uruguay are world famous for their grass-fed beef—and for their delicious grilled steaks. Cowboys and chefs here know how to cook beef to perfection using only fire and salt, but this famously tangy green parsley sauce makes it all even better. It's a simple purée of parsley, aromatics, oil, and vinegar—some people add oregano or cilantro—that only takes a few minutes to prepare, but the flavor rewards are huge.

INGREDIENTS

1 small chili pepper (optional)
2 to 3 cloves garlic, minced
4 tablespoons red wine vinegar
1 small bunch of parsley
½ cup olive oil
½ teaspoon salt, plus more to
   taste

1. Combine the chili, garlic, and vinegar in a small bowl. Let sit 10 minutes.

2. Meanwhile, finely chop the parsley, including the tender stems. Add the parsley, oil, and salt to the bowl and stir to combine. Let the mixture rest for 10 minutes, for the flavors to combine.

3. Taste and adjust seasonings as desired.

Spoon it over the top of a perfectly charred steak—or use it as a marinade, basting the steak as it cooks.

No steak? No problem. This zingy sauce is also delicious on everything from beans and eggs to roasted veggies.

SALT

AROUND THE WORLD

Salt is the only rock we eat. It's in every cell of our bodies, helping our muscles and nervous systems work. It also makes food taste even more delicious! Chefs say salt makes food taste more like itself. Salt has been a literal lifesaver throughout history for its magical ability to stop bacteria and preserve perishables. Foods that are salted and dried—like salt cod and beef jerky—can be kept for months or even years. Today, we have new ways to preserve food, but traditional salt-making techniques are still practiced and prized. People expertly extract salt from saline springs and evaporate seawater into delicious sea salt.

HIMALAYAN PINK SALT

Pink, coarse crystals of Himalayan pink salt are mined from the Himalayan mountains. Believed to be 250 million years old, this ancient mineral has a sweet floral taste. Cooks all over the globe love the rosy, salty sparkle it adds to a dish.

FLEUR DE SEL

This specialty salt is skimmed off the top of shallow evaporation ponds along France's Brittany coast. You might see it sprinkled on caramels and chocolates for a distinct crystalline burst of salty crunch.

MALDON SALT

Flaky pyramids of British Maldon salt are harvested from a briny tidal river and then gently boiled in big vessels. You can crumble the giant flakes between your fingers—they don't taste bitter—in fact, some people think they taste sweet.

CHARCOAL SALT

On the Mediterranean island of Cyprus, flakes of salt are combined with charcoal from local trees to create a black salt. Its soft, fluffy texture adds a light-tasting but dramatic look to salads!

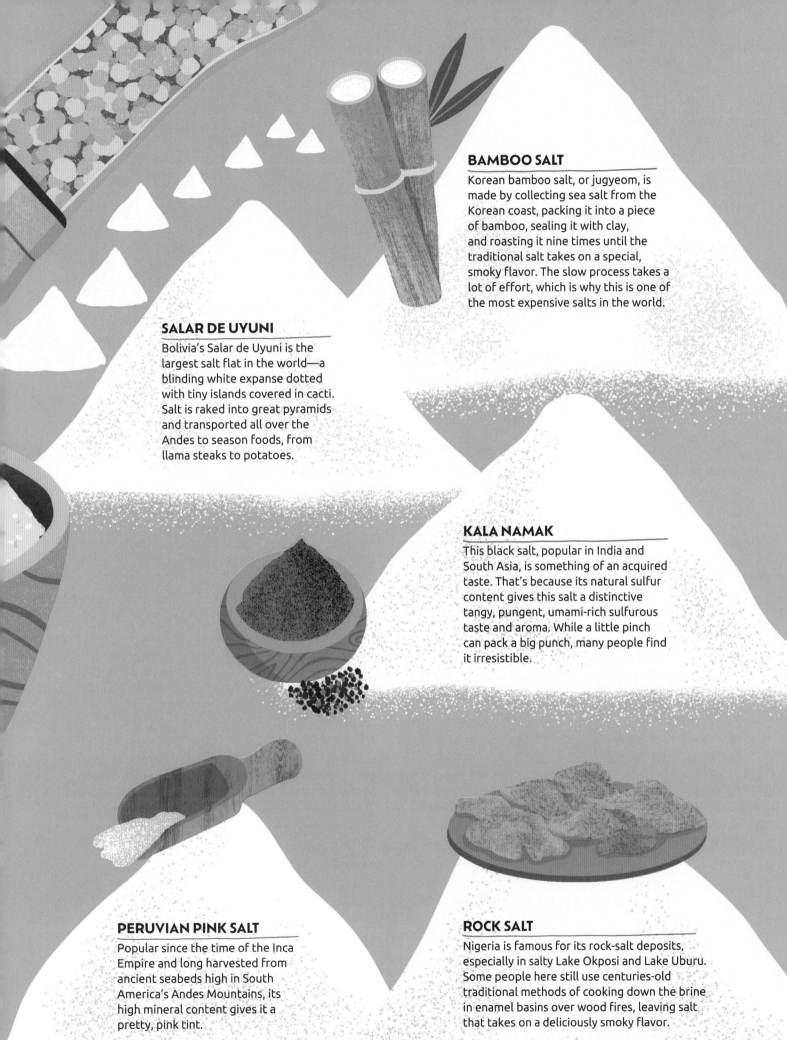

BAMBOO SALT

Korean bamboo salt, or jugyeom, is made by collecting sea salt from the Korean coast, packing it into a piece of bamboo, sealing it with clay, and roasting it nine times until the traditional salt takes on a special, smoky flavor. The slow process takes a lot of effort, which is why this is one of the most expensive salts in the world.

SALAR DE UYUNI

Bolivia's Salar de Uyuni is the largest salt flat in the world—a blinding white expanse dotted with tiny islands covered in cacti. Salt is raked into great pyramids and transported all over the Andes to season foods, from llama steaks to potatoes.

KALA NAMAK

This black salt, popular in India and South Asia, is something of an acquired taste. That's because its natural sulfur content gives this salt a distinctive tangy, pungent, umami-rich sulfurous taste and aroma. While a little pinch can pack a big punch, many people find it irresistible.

PERUVIAN PINK SALT

Popular since the time of the Inca Empire and long harvested from ancient seabeds high in South America's Andes Mountains, its high mineral content gives it a pretty, pink tint.

ROCK SALT

Nigeria is famous for its rock-salt deposits, especially in salty Lake Okposi and Lake Uburu. Some people here still use centuries-old traditional methods of cooking down the brine in enamel basins over wood fires, leaving salt that takes on a deliciously smoky flavor.

BRAZIL

The largest country in South America, Brazil is home to most of the Amazon River basin and its tropical rainforest. There are more species of animals and plants living here than almost anywhere else in the world. Brazilian food and culture is diverse too, as people and customs from the Americas, the Caribbean, Africa, and Europe have blended here for hundreds of years. Brazil exports most of the world's oranges and melons, along with all kinds of tropical fruits like pineapple, guava, papaya, mango, avocado, coconut, and maracuja.

COFFEE BEANS

Some of the most prized coffee beans come from Brazilian farms that grow coffee plants among the tall trees in the rainforest. It takes a lot longer to grow coffee beans in shade rather than in sunny fields, but they taste even better—and are better for the environment too!

ALL-YOU-CAN-EAT MEAT

At Brazilian all-you-can-eat steakhouses, waiters bring grilled meats on huge skewers to your table, then use a giant knife to cut the meat right onto your plate. Everybody gets a card where one side is green, meaning bring more meat, and the other side red, meaning you are full!

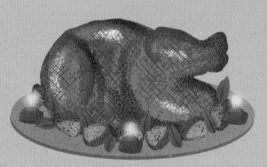

BRIGADEIROS

These soft confections are made by cooking condensed milk with butter and cocoa powder, forming the fudge bonbons into little rounds, and rolling the whole thing in chocolate sprinkles. Some say they were named after a brigadier to serve at his rallies.

THE CHRISTMAS CHESTER

For many Brazilians, it's not Christmas without a Chester on the table! What's a Chester? It's a special breed of giant chicken raised for its extra breast and thigh meat.

SUGARCANE

Portuguese colonists started growing the tall grass called sugarcane in Brazil more than 500 years ago, and today the country grows more than anywhere else in the world. You can crush sugarcane stalks to get a sweet mild juice or boil the juice down into the sugar we use every day. It can also be turned into fuel—in Brazil, many cars now run on sugarcane!

ACARAJÉ AND CARURU

The cooking in the coastal state of Bahia is often called Afro-Brazilian, and a famous dish here is acarajé, or black-eyed pea fritters, served with a chunky condiment called caruru made from okra, onions, shrimp, and toasted nuts.

COXINHA

One of the most popular snacks in Brazil is the coxinha, a golden-fried dumpling shaped like a teardrop or a pyramid. They are filled with creamy cheese and chicken, wrapped in dough, and covered with breading for a very crunchy crust.

AÇAÍ

Many tropical fruits grow in Brazil, but one of the most unique is the small, round super healthy fruit of the açaí palm tree. Now sold worldwide, açaí has been a valuable food for centuries, for those who have lived along the Amazon River.

LUCKY BAY LEAF

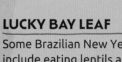

Some Brazilian New Year's Eve traditions include eating lentils and pomegranates for good luck. You can also put a bay leaf in your wallet and keep it there next to a piece of paper money. Next New Year's Eve, donate the money and throw the bay leaf into a river or stream.

CARNAVAL

The roots of this holiday are religious, but today this weeklong spring celebration is one of the world's biggest parties, with music, dancing, and lots of street food. You can try pastel (a savory, stuffed, fried pastry), aipim frito (French fries made from the tuber called yuca), and espetinhos, also known as meat on a stick!

FEIJOADA

SLOW-COOKED BLACK BEAN AND PORK SOUP

PREPARATION TIME
15 mins, plus overnight
soaking time for beans

COOKING TIME
2 hrs and 20 mins

LEVEL OF DIFFICULTY
● ● ●

SERVES
4

Feijoada, a slow-cooked, earthy black bean soup with wonderful pork flavor, is the national dish of Brazil. It is always made with a smoked and salted meat and can be served with rice, collard greens, and farofa, a condiment made from toasted cassava-root flour. It is a mix of influences from Europeans, Native People, and Africans—just like Brazil itself!

INGREDIENTS

12 ounces dried black beans
½ pound bacon, diced
2 yellow onions, diced
1 bunch scallions, roughly
    chopped
2 cloves garlic, minced
1 pound cubed pork or 1 pound
    smoked pork sausage, sliced
1 smoked ham hock
1 bay leaf
cooked white rice, for serving
1 small bunch cilantro
fresh orange slices, for garnish

1. Place the dried beans in a large bowl, cover with plenty of water, and leave to soak at room temperature overnight or for at least 8 hours.

2. In a large pot, cook the diced bacon over medium heat, about 8 minutes or until crisp.

3. Add the onions, scallions, and garlic and cook, stirring, until the onions begin to turn translucent, about 5 minutes.

4. Add the pork or sausage and cook, stirring occasionally, until the meat looks brown, about 5 minutes.

5. Drain and rinse the soaked beans and add them to the large pot, along with the smoked ham hock and the bay leaf and add water until it is an inch above the beans.

6. Simmer, covered, for 2 hours, adding more water if the level goes below the beans. Test beans to be sure they are soft.

7. Serve over rice, garnished with fresh cilantro and orange slices.

Starting with dried beans gives you the best flavor and texture, but if you're in a hurry, you can use canned beans instead. Just skip Step 1 and omit the water in Step 5.

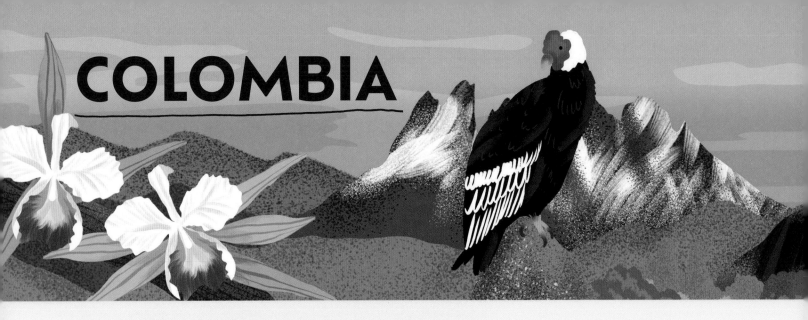

COLOMBIA

Bordering Central America in the north and nestled between the Caribbean and Pacific Ocean, Colombia is one of the most ecologically diverse countries in the world. Covering an area that's almost twice as big as Texas, Colombia's Amazon rainforest, grassland plains, and Andes Mountains hold 10% of the world's biodiversity! In the capital city of Bogotá, restaurants in the Zona G (short for Gourmet) showcase international cuisine, and in the Mercado de la Perseverancia, you can enjoy traditional Colombian flavors.

COFFEE

Brought to Colombia by the Jesuits, a religious order of clerics, in the eighteenth century, coffee plants thrived in the low Andean region, where mild temperatures and frequent rain offered ideal conditions. Today, coffee is Colombia's most popular product, and you can not only drink it but also enjoy it in candy, desserts, and even body scrubs!

HORMIGAS CULONAS

When the rainy season starts in April, the people of the north-central state of Santander know it is time for the hormigas culonas, also known as big-butt ants, to appear. Prized as a delicacy, these ants are harvested, toasted, and eaten as a high-energy snack that tastes like salty peanuts.

FRUVER

Walking around Colombia's cities and towns, you may see several stores with the name *fruver*. It's not a chain store, though. *Fruver* is a combination of the first three letters of *frutas* and *verduras* (fruits and vegetables).

ARROZ CON COCO (COCONUT RICE)

When eating traditional Colombian Caribbean fare, it's likely your order will come with a side of coconut rice. This staple of northern Colombian cuisine is made by cooking rice in caramelized coconut milk. It can be tricky to cook since it can stick to the bottom of the pot! But if you're patient and cook it over a low flame, you will be rewarded.

AREPAS

Round and flat, cooked over a griddle, and usually made of ground corn flour, arepas can be plain or stuffed with cheese, egg, or beef. Or you might find rice, yucca, or plantain arepas. No matter the flavors or filling, it's Colombia's best-known food.

PURPLE PASSIONFRUIT

Colombia's greatest treasures include several types of passionfruit, including the super sweet purple variety called gulupa.

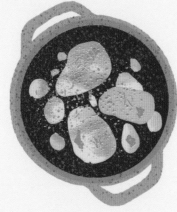
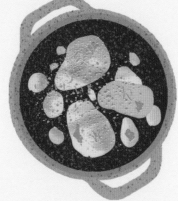

"SWEATY" FOOD

Many dishes in Colombia are called sudado (sweaty). While this may make you think that the main ingredient just went for a jog, its name references the little droplets of water that appear on the food as it's cooking, looking like it just finished a workout.

OBLEAS CON AREQUIPE

Sweetened, caramelized milk, known as arequipe, is sandwiched between two thin, giant, foot-wide wafers and eaten as an after-school snack. If you order one, get extra napkins. It's common for the caramel milk to ooze out and stick to your fingers (yum!).

PERRO CALIENTE COLOMBIANO

Colombians have really mastered the art of the loaded hot dog. A common snack after a sports game, movie, or at a fair, regular toppings include pineapple, guacamole, raw onions, potato chips, and bacon.

CHOCOLATE CON QUESO

For breakfast or a midmorning snack, many Colombians reach for a mug of hot chocolate in which they dunk a slice of cheese. This combination yields a two-punch of flavor and texture: the chocolate's heat melts the cheese, making it stringy and easy to slurp, and the cheese's saltiness makes the chocolate flavor pop!

SEAFOOD
AROUND THE WORLD

Seafood encompasses a breathtaking variety of edible species, from shellfish and crustaceans like scallops, lobsters, and crabs to cephalopods like octopus and squid—not to mention countless kinds of fish! Today, seafood is the world's largest traded food commodity and provides sustenance to billions of people. Unfortunately, you might say we've come to love fish too much—in modern times, we've overharvested some marine species. But there are many sustainable wild choices, including lots of little fishes with big, delicious flavors!

BACALAO

Bacalao is Spanish for dried, salted cod (bacalhau in Portuguese); before freezers, this was the traditional way of preserving the cod catch to eat all year long! When you're ready to cook bacalao, you soak the hard, dried fillets—for hours, or even days—to soften them and remove the salt, changing the water often.

CAVIAR

These yummy, squishy, salty fish eggs are primarily harvested from various species of sturgeon. A luxury food in Europe since at least the fifteenth century, today most caviar comes from the Caspian Sea and the Black Sea, and is produced in Russia and Iran. Caviar is traditionally served with tiny spoons on crackers or on little Russian pancakes called blini, accompanied with lemon wedges, sour cream, and chopped chives or dill.

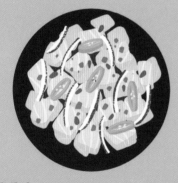

KINILAW

Ceviche is a seafood specialty of Central and South America, made with raw fish, shrimp, squid, or octopus! Bite-sized chunks of fresh seafood are marinated in lime or lemon juice, and the citric acid "cooks" and pickles it. A similar dish in the Philippines is called kinilaw.

HÁKARL

One of Iceland's national dishes, hákarl consists of chunks of Greenland shark that have been cured, traditionally by burying the meat in a shallow, sandy hole for six to twelve weeks, then digging it up and hanging it up to dry for months. The results are an acquired taste, with a cheesy texture and a pungent, ammonialike aroma.

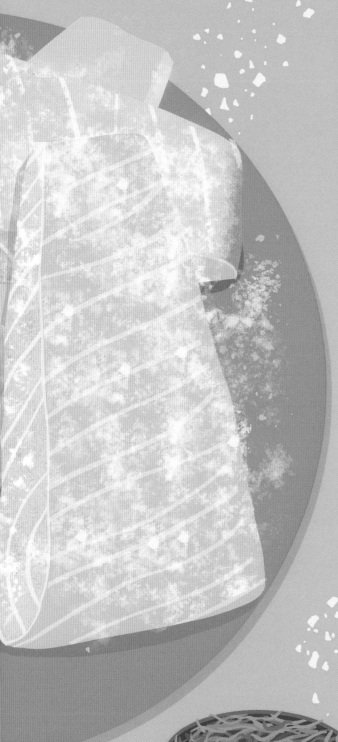

FISH SAUCE

This essential Southeast Asian ingredient is made by fermenting whole little fish (often anchovies) in barrels for up to a year; the resulting liquid brings wonderfully deep, savory flavors to everything from soups to salads. People call it an "umami bomb" and often combine it with lime juice, sugar, chilies, and cilantro in dishes like Vietnamese pho and Thailand's pad thai.

EEL

At least nineteen species of eel are eaten around the world. Freshwater eels are beloved in Japan, where they are called unagi and often served smoked and glazed with a dark, salty-sweet sauce and paired with rice. Other popular eel dishes include smoked eel in the Netherlands and eel soup in Hamburg, Germany.

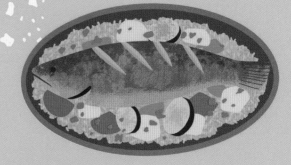

SEAWEED

Today, diverse, delicious, nutritious seaweeds are enjoyed around the world. Nori is essential in Japan for wrapping sushi; dulse, a reddish seaweed, is used to make soda bread in Ireland and serves as a crispy bar snack in Canada; sweet, silky wakame is often added to miso soup and kombu is essential in ramen broth. Indigenous people in Chile have been eating cochayuyo, or bull kelp, for at least 14,000 years.

THIEBOUDIENNE

Thieboudienne is a stewlike mix of fish (usually white grouper) cooked with rice, vegetables, and tomato sauce. It's both the national dish of Senegal and a symbol of Senegalese hospitality, or *terranga*. Traditionally, it's served in a large communal pot that family, friends, and guests gather around and eat from together.

CEVICHE

CITRUS-PICKLED FRESH FISH WITH JALAPEÑO AND CILANTRO

PREPARATION TIME
1 hr

COOKING TIME
0 mins

LEVEL OF DIFFICULTY
●

SERVES
4

In this traditional fish dish from Central and South America—especially Peru, Ecuador, and Mexico—sparklingly fresh seafood is "cooked" not with heat, but with the acidity of fresh citrus juice. It could hardly be easier or more delicious. Start with the freshest seafood you can find, or catch! Then marinate it in lots of fresh citrus juice and let the acid transform the raw seafood into . . . ceviche! For added flavor and color, add fresh diced tomato, avocado, or mango to the finished dish.

INGREDIENTS

1½ pounds fresh, firm-fleshed
   saltwater white fish fillets
   (such as grouper, mahi mahi,
   or sea bass) or scallops
salt
¾ cup fresh lime juice (from
   about 6 limes)
¼ cup fresh orange juice
1 small red onion, halved
   lengthways and very thinly
   sliced
1 jalapeño chili, thinly sliced
¼ cup cilantro, finely chopped

1. Cut the fish or scallops into bite-sized pieces. Place in a bowl and cover with cold water and 1 tablespoon salt. Refrigerate for at least 15 minutes.

2. Meanwhile, in another bowl, toss together the lime juice, orange juice, onion, chili, and cilantro to create the citrus dressing.

3. Drain the fish, rinse with cold water, and pat dry. Add it to the citrus dressing and toss. Cover and refrigerate for 30 minutes, then taste and season with salt and pepper, if desired. Serve chilled.

Some people only let their ceviche take a short bath in lime juice; others prefer a more pickled flavor that results from an hour or more in that tangy citrus.

INDEX OF RECIPES

EASIER THAN AVERAGE

AVERAGE DIFFICULTY

HARDER THAN AVERAGE

INDEX

RECIPE NOTES

Here are a few good rules of thumb to keep in mind when shopping and cooking.
Unless a recipe says otherwise, we use:

- Unsalted butter
- Coarse salt and freshly ground pepper
- Fresh herbs, including flat-leaf (not curly) parsley
- Medium-sized eggs
- Whole milk
- Large garlic cloves (use two if yours are small)

MEASUREMENT NOTES

- All spoon and cup measurements are level.
- 1 teaspoon = 5 ml; 1 tablespoon = 15 ml.
- Cooking and preparation times are for guidance, but individual ovens may vary, so check for doneness. If using a convection (fan), follow manufacturer's instructions.
- When a recipe doesn't specify an exact amount — like when drizzling oil, seasoning with salt and pepper, garnishing with fresh herbs, or sprinkling with powdered sugar to finish a dish — the quantities are flexible. Use the illustration — and your taste — as guides.

NOTE ON SAFETY

This book and the recipes presented in this book are designed for children but assume adult supervision at all times. Although we take care to identify any hazards, we do not take any responsibility for your children during the preparation and cooking of these dishes, or for any adverse reactions to ingredients or finished dishes. It is up to parents and caregivers to choose appropriate recipes and ingredients and to ensure the safety of the children under their supervision.